RAY OF HEART

(Ray Series #5)

E. L. TODD

6-20-17

KMA

Fallen Publishing
Ray of Heart
Editing Services provided by Final-Edits.com

Chapter One

Rae

"You take him." I handed the leash to Zeke, sick of trying to make Safari behave himself. He was a full-grown, heavy German shepherd. Even though I was strong, he pulled me around like a rag doll. "He listens to other people far better than he listens to me..."

Zeke took the leash and chuckled. "You just have to keep a tight grip. Like this." When Safari tried to run after a squirrel, Zeke yanked on the harness and kept him back. The leash was hooked around his chest—not his neck—so Safari was never hurt. "See?"

"Not a very peaceful walk, if you ask me."

Zeke smiled and continued to walk beside me through the park. It was a sunny day in Seattle since the rain had finally passed. Our fight the other night seemed to be forgotten, and now we were spending all of our time being happy.

Sometimes, I thought about Ryker. And when I did, I felt terrible, but I knew I had made the right decision. Zeke was the man I was supposed to be with. He would be a great husband, father, and dog walker.

"How was work?" Zeke asked as we passed another couple on their power walk.

I told him about the new bacteria I was working with and how I intended to promote a landfill program that could diminish waste naturally. The nice thing about dating a doctor was he understood science just as well as I did. And he seemed genuinely interested.

"That's cool."

"Yeah. Jenny has helped me a lot. It's nice having her around."

"Could you imagine working in a lab alone all day?" He pulled Safari's leash again when he tried to sniff a passing jogger. "With just the radio…you'd go crazy. I know I would. I like working with people. Makes the day a lot more interesting."

"Yeah, definitely."

"I'm thinking about taking on a partner," he said. "Someone to share the office with."

"Why?"

He shrugged. "Now that I'm getting older, I don't want to work as much."

I rolled my eyes. "Zeke, you're thirty, not fifty."

He chuckled. "My dad was always around as often as my mom. I had two parents all the time, not one. That's how I want to be. I want to be around as a husband and a father."

I smiled because it was nice hearing his honesty. For the past three months, we never talked about the future, but it was something I thought about. Now that our feelings were out in the open, we could talk about our lives down the road. "Well, I'm never gonna be a housewife, so I could use the help."

"I figured," he said with a laugh. "You aren't the housewife type, which is perfectly fine."

"Maybe Rex can be a nanny," I joked.

"God, no," Zeke said quickly. "They'll be addicted to candy and porn."

"Good point," I said. "But hopefully, Kayden would make sure that didn't happen."

"Rex would sneak everything. I know him."

We finished our walk through the park then jumped in Zeke's Jeep. Safari sat in the backseat and stuck his head between us so he could see the open road. His tongue hung out and licked my cheek a few times.

After we got home, we showered, and I grabbed my bag. "I should get going. I haven't done laundry at my apartment for a while."

Zeke snatched the bag out of my hand and tossed it on the couch. "Stay with me." His hands circled my waist, and he pressed his forehead to mine, smothering me with enough affection to manipulate me into doing whatever he wanted.

I melted at his touch, turning into a puddle on the ground. "Okay." There wasn't any fight within me because I was powerless when those strong arms wrapped around me. "I guess I could turn my underwear inside out..."

"Better yet, you could wear mine." He kissed the corner of my mouth, taking a deep breath as he caressed my lips with his. "Or wear none at all..."

"I guess I could wear your briefs. But no way am I going commando in jeans all day at work."

"Perfect." He kissed me again and directed me to the couch. When the back of my knees hit the cushion, he guided me to my back and pulled off my running shorts, leaving my sneakers on. My panties were gone in a flash, and he was on top of me, his powerful chest pinning me down.

I pulled off his shorts, removing the boxers at the same time. His long cock popped out, hard and ready for me.

He shoved himself inside me quickly, wanting to be inside as soon as possible. With our shoes and shirts still on, we made love on the couch, rocking slowly together with our hands gripping one another. He looked into my eyes the entire time, the love and devotion written all over his face. "I love you."

My fingers moved through his hair until I cupped the back of his neck. "I love you too..."

***

On Friday night, we went out to our favorite part of downtown Seattle. I got there first with the girls, finding a good table in the corner so we wouldn't have to stand all night in our pumps.

5

"So Ryker finally came clean?" Jessie asked with a drink in her hand.

"Yeah," I said. "And it was one of the saddest moments of my life."

"That's some heavy stuff," Kayden said, her hair pulled back into a cute updo. "I wonder why he waited so long to tell you the truth."

"I'm not sure," I answered. "But when you're emotionally disturbed, you do stupid things." I understood Ryker because I went through a hard time after my mom committed suicide. I had done a lot of stupid stuff that I wished I could take back. Even though the behavior was destructive, I couldn't stop myself. If only Ryker had opened up to me sooner, I could have helped him.

"I actually feel bad for him," Jessie said. "I mean, I really hated the guy for a long time, but I can't keep hating him."

"Yeah," Kayden said. "I feel the same way. When I saw him with that skank, I wanted to scratch his eyes out. I hated him so much for hurting you like that. And now, I just want him to feel better... Strange."

"I think we've all had enough time to forgive Ryker for what he did." It took three months for me to finally let go of the heartbreak he'd caused, but when I finally did, my mind and body felt better. "And we should forgive him. Holding grudges doesn't help anyone."

"Yeah," Jessie said in agreement. "True."

"So, Zeke was really pissed?" Kayden asked. "Rex made it sound like World War III had begun."

"Yeah, I've never seen him so mad," I explained. "As soon as he walked in the door, he started behaving like a huge asshole. But we talked it over, and he finally calmed down. Honestly, I understand where he's coming from. He's had to deal with Ryker a lot during this relationship. He's entitled to be frustrated."

"Yeah," Kayden said. "I would be really jealous if Rex was still talking to an ex."

"At least things are good with you guys now," Jessie said. "And Ryker missed his chance for good. I guess that's punishment enough for him." She sipped her drink until it was empty, and then she glanced at the bar. "Hey, there're those two dipshits."

I spotted Zeke and Rex at the bar, talking while they waited for their drinks. "I'll go say hi." I hadn't seen Zeke since I left for work that morning. I walked across the room in my short silver dress and matching heels, excited to see the expression on his face when he looked at me.

Rex spoke in an angry voice, his shoulders tense as he stared down Zeke. "Don't do it. I'm serious."

"I've made up my mind, alright?" Zeke argued. "Frankly, this is my relationship not yours."

"You're so fucking stupid, you know that?" Rex snapped back.

What did I just walk into? "Everything alright?"

Zeke turned around, and his eyes immediately went to my cleavage.

Rex smiled, but it was obviously forced. "I was just telling Zeke not to be an annoying piece of shit. You know, the usual."

I knew that was a lie, but judging by how jumpy they both were, whatever they were talking about was none of my business. "I saw that tight ass in those jeans, and I had to come over here." I moved into Zeke's chest and kissed him hard on the mouth.

He smiled as he kissed me back, moving his palm to my ass before he gave it a squeeze. "You were staring at my ass, baby?"

"A lot more than just your ass."

"Excuse me," Rex said before he walked away. "I need to puke." He disappeared with his drinks, retreating to the table where Jessie and Kayden were waiting.

"It's so easy to get rid of Rex," I said. "Works every time."

"It's bulletproof." Zeke grabbed his beer and the drink he got for me. "Vodka cranberry?"

"You never forget." I grabbed it by the stem and took a drink.

Zeke's eyes went to my chest again, not bothering to be discreet about it. His eyes slowly roamed down my body, taking in the sight of the short dress and ridiculously tall heels. "Are you trying to torture me?"

"How am I torturing you?"

"Don't play dumb with me." He drank his beer, his eyes moving to my face. "You're too smart for that."

"No, torture wasn't what I had in mind. There's a bathroom, you know."

"As much as I'd like to fuck you, I'm not doing it in a stall. Maybe in an alleyway. Maybe in the back of my Jeep. But not in a place where other guys can hear you come."

The idea of him making me come made me want to ditch everyone and go home. I crossed my ankles automatically.

Zeke glanced down when he noticed. "Looks like I'm torturing you now."

"Just a smidge." I drank my vodka cranberry to mask the blush that moved into my cheeks.

He continued to stare at me with a scorching gaze, undressing me without removing a single article of clothing. I pictured him undoing the zipper down my back and yanking my panties off my legs. He would leave my heels on because he liked to see them next to his head when he fucked me into his mattress.

Zeke rubbed the back of his neck, growing more uncomfortable by the second. He wanted to cave and drive home.

I wanted to do the same thing.

But we couldn't.

"It's one of those times when I wish we didn't have any friends." He glanced at the table where everyone was sitting.

"Yeah, me too."

"Or we could take a short intermission so we can fuck."

"Yeah..." That sounded really nice.

He took a large gulp of his drink before he grabbed my hand. "Alright, let's think of something else. Otherwise, I really will fuck you in the bathroom."

"Works for me."

11

He gave me a heated stare as he led me back to the table. "Don't tempt me, baby." He allowed me to slide into the booth first before he sat down. During our absence, Tobias had shown up. His arm was around Jessie's shoulders, and he was whispering into her ear, his nose pressed against her hair. She smiled and moved closer to him, enjoying whatever he said. Rex had his arm around Kayden, and he no longer seemed grossed out by our display of affection.

I had a feeling we were all thinking the same thing.

Chapter Two

Rae

The second we were home, Zeke lifted me into his arms and carried me into the bedroom. I was tossed onto the mattress as he pulled his shirt and jeans off with lightning speed. His chiseled physique was revealed, looking powerful and drop-dead gorgeous. Those strong and sweaty muscles always got me off, even when he didn't touch me. He reached for his boxers next and pulled them off, revealing the best part.

I bit my bottom lip.

"You like that, baby?" He leaned over the bed and held himself on top of me, his blue eyes looking dangerous.

My hands slid up his arms to his biceps, feeling the strength of his sexy body. "Yeah."

"You like that cock?" he pressed.

"I love it."

Zeke pressed his mouth to mine and gave me a kiss so hard it nearly bruised my mouth. His tongue danced with mine, and he felt me up, gripping my tit through my dress while his cock lay on my stomach.

My legs automatically wrapped around his waist, and I pulled him toward me, wanting to feel him stretch me for the hundredth time.

Zeke didn't bother taking off my dress. His fingers found my panties and moved them to the side, allowing himself entry. He played with my clit as he kissed me, and the second he touched me, he was greeted by my wetness. "Always so wet."

"Wet for you."

He growled quietly against my mouth, his arousal increasing. He slipped two fingers inside me and passed through my slickness. His mouth continued to meld with mine, and he pleased me like he did it for a living.

The foreplay was good, but with Zeke, it was also torture. I always wanted to slide into home plate the second things heated up between us. Most women probably needed a few rounds to warm up, but with Zeke, I didn't need that at all. "Fuck me, Zeke."

He growled against my mouth, trapping my bottom lip with his teeth. He slowly pulled his fingers out of me before he sucked them off, his eyes locked with mine.

My nails dug into his wrist.

He grabbed the back of my thong and pulled it down my legs before he tossed it on the floor. Then he pulled me across the bed until my ass hung over the edge. He stood next to the mattress, his hips level with my entrance.

He dug his fingers inside me again, saturating the skin with my slickness. Then he rubbed it down his cock, lubricating himself with my own arousal.

"Stop making me wait." I was begging at this point, feeling no shame for my desperation.

"You can have me whenever you want." He leaned over and kissed me, his lips tasting like heaven. "You know that." The head of his cock pressed against my opening, just as soaked as I was. When he brushed his lips past mine, the scruff from his chin rubbed against my skin. I'd become so used to the rough sensation that I looked forward to it every single embrace.

He widened my legs and tucked my knees against my waist, spreading me as far as I could go. But he didn't thrust into me, choosing to tease me instead.

I grabbed his hips and pulled him inside me, feeling every inch stretch me wide apart until I was moaning uncontrollably. It always hurt just a little bit, but the discomfort was nothing in comparison to the unbridled pleasure. "Oh god...Zeke." I rolled my head and stared up at the ceiling, filled with his entire length inside me. I'd just had sex with him that morning, but it seemed like a lifetime ago.

"You're the sexiest goddamn thing, you know that?" He straightened at the foot of the bed and pulled me farther into him, his cock nearly hitting my cervix. He rested inside me for a moment, enjoying how tight I was around his throbbing dick.

"I'm only sexy because I want to be fucked."

"But you only want to be fucked by me." He grabbed both of my tits and massaged them roughly, his thumb flicking across my nipples, causing pain and pleasure at the same time.

He slowly began to slide in and out, his cock hard like concrete. He moved through my tightness, the muscles of my core contracting with every thrust he made. He closed his hands behind my knees and kept them pinned to my sides, taking advantage of the angle to give me everything he had.

I was in heaven.

Pure heaven.

I rocked with the mattress as he moved inside me, and my fingers wrapped around his wrists just to have something to grab on to. I lay back and watched this gorgeous man fuck me good and slow, taking his time. "Zeke…"

He rocked into me harder, his ass muscles tightening with every thrust. I could see his reflection in the mirrors of the closet. His body was just as nice from behind as it was from the front.

Sweat trickled down his chest as he pounded into me harder, hitting my G-spot with every thrust.

"I'm gonna come..." I could feel it from my fingers to my toes. The explosion was slowly approaching, growing in intensity as it peaked. I closed my eyes as I was swept off into a supernatural experience, my entire body writhing.

He kissed me just before I slipped away. "I love you, baby."

Those words ignited me in an explosive fire. Everything felt good, not just the area between my legs. My body wanted to weep from the pleasure, and my heart wanted to give out in joy. Zeke completed my life in a way no one else ever could, and that knowledge hit me out of nowhere like a speeding car in the dead of night. Zeke was my whole world, the man I was supposed to be with. The loss of my father and my mother didn't weigh on me anymore. Whatever wounds I had, he'd fixed them. "I love you too..." I opened my eyes as the sensation faded away, the pure pleasure slowly wearing off. I kept my eyes on him, my hands digging into his forearms. "God, I love you."

His eyes softened and he leaned over me, his cock still deep within. With a quiet moan, he came inside me, his lips pressed to mine. He breathed through the pleasure and looked at me, the love and devotion evident in his eyes. "I know you do." He pressed a kiss to my forehead before he kissed my lips again. He softened inside me but never pulled out, our mouths moving together in building intensity. One hand dug into my hair, and he deepened the kiss, a new form a foreplay developing. Within minutes, he was hard again, still buried inside me along with his seed. Then he began to move again, just as desperate for me as I was for him.

***

Four days later, I returned to my apartment. All the food was spoiled, and I needed to take out the trash. Now that I spent all my time at Zeke's, I didn't see the point of even keeping the apartment anymore. It was a complete waste of money.

But what would I do with it?

I opened the fridge and realized most of the groceries I'd bought last week had disappeared.

They just vanished.

That was strange...

The front door opened, and Rex walked inside. "Yo, what's up?"

"You can't just walk in like that."

"Why?" he said with complete seriousness. "I saw you come home. Thought I'd say hi."

"And that's fine, but you could knock first."

"Do you normally take off all your clothes the second you get home?" he asked. "I'm a slob, and I don't even do that."

I shut the refrigerator. "Are you taking my food?"

"Huh?"

"My groceries are gone. Have you been taking them?" I crossed my arms over my chest and stared him down.

Rex tried to hide his smile but he couldn't. "What's the big deal? You let them go to waste. I'm just trying to help you out."

"I don't care if you take my food. But I do care about you coming into my apartment without my knowledge. How are you doing that anyway?"

He shrugged. "You know I'm good at picking locks."

"You're breaking in?" I asked incredulously.

"Give me a key, and I won't do it anymore."

"Rex, you have money. You can buy your own groceries."

"And I have a girlfriend," he snapped. "They're damn expensive."

I rolled my eyes and walked to the kitchen table.

"What's the big deal anyway?" He followed me and took a seat.

"No big deal. I guess I'm just in a bad mood today..."

"That time of the month?" He cringed. "No wonder why you aren't staying at Zeke's tonight..."

"No, asshole. I just came to check on the apartment. I guess I'm not sure why I still have it. It's expensive and a waste of money."

Rex stared at me, his features becoming unreadable. "What are you suggesting?"

The thought had crossed my mind a few times since Zeke and I had our long talk. "Is Zeke planning on proposing to me?"

Rex couldn't hide the shock on his face.

"I only ask because I don't want him to. I love him and want to be with him, but I really like the way things are. There's no need to rush into anything serious right now."

Rex breathed a sigh of relief. "That's not on his mind right now, Rae."

"Oh, good. We talked about our relationship after my fight with Ryker, and I wasn't sure where he was at."

Rex looked out the window, his arms across his chest. "Why do you ask?"

"I'm considering asking him if he wants to move in together, but I don't want to go down that route if he is planning on taking it a step further. Obviously, if he asked, I would say yes. But I'd rather wait a while."

Rex nodded like he understood.

"Everything alright?"

"Yeah." He cleared his throat. "Totally fine. Bright as the sun. Why?"

Bright as the sun? "You're just quiet all of a sudden."

"Maybe your love life isn't that interesting. Did you think of that?"

I ignored the jab. "Then I think I'm gonna ask him. I'm there all the time anyway. Safari doesn't even like coming back to the apartment with me anymore. When I tell him it's time to go, he lays on the ground and refuses to move."

"It's probably because of that big backyard."

"Yeah, he loves it. And I know this thing with Zeke is gonna last forever."

"You do?" Rex turned his gaze back to me.

"Yeah...what kind of question is that?"

"I just mean...you really love him, right?"

"Of course." Why was Rex asking me these strange questions? "Where are you going with this?"

"I just wondering. Moving in with someone is a big deal. If you break up, it's an emotional catastrophe."

"We aren't going to break up." There wasn't a doubt in my mind.

"How do you know that?"

I didn't need a reason. Instinctually, it was something I just knew. I couldn't explain it in a way Rex would understand. No one would understand it — except Zeke. "I just do."

—
23

Chapter Three
Rex

I need to talk to you.

Zeke texted back even though he was at work, probably sitting in his office doing paperwork. *No. I already know what you're gonna say and I'm done listening to you. I made up my mind.*

Just shut up and meet me, okay?

No.

Zeke, listen to me.

No response. The dots didn't pop up.

"Fucking asshole." I called his office instead and got his secretary on the line. "Can I talk to Zeke?"

"Uh, do you mean Dr. Hartwick?"

"Yeah, whatever." I forgot he was a doctor sometimes. "Tell him it's Rex."

"Hold please." Click.

I listened to the annoying music over the line until Zeke finally picked up.

"You've crossed a line right now." His threatening voice was quiet over the phone. "I don't take calls at work. Don't call me—"

"Rae is gonna ask you to move in with her."

He fell silent.

"Now, can we meet for a beer or what?"

Zeke sighed into the phone. "Alright. I'll meet you after work."

"Thank you." I hit the end button and slammed my phone down.

***

We sat at a table with our beers in front of us, untouched and frothy.

Zeke spoke first. "When did she say that?"

"Yesterday. She came home to do some stuff around the apartment, and we got to talking..."

Zeke drank his beer, still in his dark blue scrubs. "What else?"

"She said keeping the apartment was a waste of money. Then she asked if you were going to propose."

Zeke's eyes widened. "She did? What did you say?"

"The truth. I said you hadn't mentioned anything like that to me."

"So...does she want me to ask?" The hopefulness was apparent in his voice.

"No. Actually, she said it was too soon and wanted to make sure that's not what you were thinking. Because if it was, then she wasn't going to ask you to move in."

A slight look of disappointment came over his face.

"But she's gonna ask you. I don't know when, maybe today."

Zeke stared into his drink and sighed.

"Everything is going so damn well right now. Just don't tell her. Have her move in with you." It was the best possible solution. Why wouldn't he listen to me?

"Rex, you know I can't do that."

"But—"

"If this was you and Kayden, what would you do?" He looked into my eyes, the confidence obvious.

I shut my mouth because I didn't have an answer. I would never cheat on Kayden. And if I did, I couldn't be a coward and pretend it didn't happen. But I would never know unless I was in the situation myself. "It doesn't matter what I would do."

"You would tell her." He drank his beer again. "I know you would."

"I wouldn't have slept with someone to begin with." It was a low-blow, but it was true. The entire time Kayden and I were apart, she was sleeping around while my dick was tucked into my pants.

Zeke closed his eyes as the insult washed over him. He didn't argue because there was no counterargument to justify what he did. "I wish I could take it back... You have no idea. I didn't enjoy it, and I don't even remember it."

"Did you wear a condom?"

"Come on, Rex. Of course I did."

"But you said you didn't remember so..."

"I remember that part." He crossed his arms and rested them on the table.

"If you really are gonna tell her, you need to do it before you move in with her. Because that would just be a dick move if you waited."

"I know..."

"So...you need to make up your mind."

"I did, Rex."

"Well, you haven't told her, so it sounds like you aren't sure." A week had come and gone, and Zeke hadn't confessed. A part of me hoped he would come to his senses and realize it was a bad idea.

"I am sure. I just…" He ran his fingers through his hair. "I'm just so fucking happy, and I don't want to give it up…if she leaves me."

"Zeke, she's going to leave you." It was the hard truth, and he needed to hear it. "I promise you, she will. She'll leave, and she'll never take you back. You betrayed her, and since you're so high on her list, that means you're going to fall harder than everyone else. Maybe if it was Ryker, she could forgive him. But you're on a pedestal in her eyes. She won't be able to look past the betrayal. She won't be able to look at you the same way. Just listen to me."

He bowed his head in anguish. "And when our wedding day arrives, I'm supposed to look her in the eye and vow to love her forever…when I've lied to her? What kind of man would that make me?"

"Then you need to decide what's more important. Having the woman you love or having your reputation. You can't have both, man."

"It's not about choosing," he argued. "Maybe if this was some other woman, I wouldn't say anything. But this is the love of my life. How could I ever deserve her unless I'm always honest with her?"

I rolled my eyes. "Dude, you're never gonna have the chance to deserve her again once you tell her."

"She loves me." He said it without a syllable of doubt. "She knows I love her. She knows I would never do something like that in any other scenario. She knows — "

"That. Won't. Matter." I slammed my hands down on the table. "It doesn't matter how long you date her. I will always know her better than you. I will always understand her in a way you can't even fathom. I pretty much raised her. You need to trust me on this. The second you tell her, you'll lose her forever. End of story."

Zeke sighed in response.

"There is no other alternative. Do you understand me?"

"Yes, I understand what you're saying, Rex. But I believe in us. And I believe in the values I stand for. What I did was stupid, and I'll own up to it. But it was a difficult situation. She made a lot of stupid choices that caused it in the first place. She's reasonable."

"Not when the love of her life tells her he fucked someone else." I drank the rest of my beer and slammed the glass down, nearly breaking it. "You stuck your cock in someone else's pussy. It's not like you just kissed someone or groped them in the bathroom. Rae could forgive those things. But fucking someone else? Hell no."

Zeke had a dead look in his eyes, like he'd already lost the world.

I shook my head because I knew what he was thinking. "You're still going to do it, aren't you?"

He held my gaze, empty inside. "I have to."

Chapter Four

Rae

Zeke walked in the house just when I finished making dinner. "Damn, that smells good."

"You're talking about me, right?" I winked at him as I finished cooking the vegetables in the frying pan. I was in his boxers and one of his t-shirts, surrounded by his smell even when he wasn't in the house.

"Of course." He came behind me and wrapped his arms around my waist, nuzzling my neck with kisses. "And you look damn fine cooking in my kitchen like this."

"Why, thank you." I rubbed my ass into the front of his scrubs.

He kissed the shell of my ear before he pulled away. "I'm going to take a quick shower. Be back in ten minutes."

"Okay. You don't need to get dressed if you don't want to."

He grinned in his usual sexy way, looking ridiculously handsome without trying. "It's a little cold, so I'll wear some boxers, if that's okay."

"I'll settle."

He greeted Safari with a rub down before he hopped in the shower.

Safari came to my side at the counter, looking up like food might fall off the counter.

"I don't think so, Safari."

He whined.

I knew when I had kids, I would be a terrible mother because I always gave in. I broke off a piece of chicken and dropped it into his mouth.

He gobbled it up with one bite.

"But that's it." I finished the stir-fry and set the plates on the table.

Zeke nearly kept his promise and walked into the kitchen in gray sweatpants. He was shirtless, and since that was the best part, that was fine. He was still slightly damp, so his chest gleamed. "Everything looks good." He sat across from me at the table, his hard chest and sculpted shoulders looked delectable.

"Thanks. My cooking is getting better." I poured the wine and took a sip.

"I've always liked your cooking, baby." He took five bites in the amount of time it took me to take one.

"Thanks. How was your day?"

"I had a patient come in with a bad case of—" He stopped himself like he'd said something wrong. "Nevermind, we're eating dinner."

"I work with bacteria all day. None of your stories could bother me."

He chuckled. "Yeah, that's true. Well, he had eczema that had spread all over his body. Caused bad itching, and now it's all over his face...poor guy. I had to give him a serious dose of steroids to get rid of it."

"How do you not catch anything?" As far as I could tell, Zeke never had skin problems. Not even acne.

He shrugged. "I moisturize."

I rolled my eyes. "You're such a girl."

"Hey, moisturizing is important. I'm not ashamed to admit I've had a few gentlemen's facials."

I stopped eating because I was in shock. "You're being serious right now?"

He pointed to his face. "I'm a handsome guy, alright? I've got to keep up appearances."

33

"I've never had a facial in my life, and my skin looks just fine."

"Well, you're more blessed than the rest of us." He drank his wine and tried not to smile.

"I'm just not as girly, I suppose."

"Oh, you're girly."

"I'm a tomboy, and we both know it."

"When we're in bed together, you're the most feminine and sexy woman I've ever been with. You only wear lacy panties and bras, and your hair is always soft to the touch, and you wear the tallest heels I've ever seen a woman walk in."

"Hey, most of those belong to Jessie."

"Whatever. You look better in them anyway."

That was so untrue, but I didn't argue.

Zeke looked down at his plate and kept eating.

Flirting with him back and forth just made me think about the issue with my apartment. I was here all the time anyway, and I wanted to come home to him every night. There was plenty of room for both Safari and me, and if I were paying half of his mortgage, it would make his life easier too. "There's something I want to ask you."

He stopped eating and gave me his full attention. But he looked reluctant, like I was about to give him some bad news.

"If you aren't ready for this, it's not a big deal at all. I've just been thinking about it lately when I go back to my apartment..." I stirred my stir-fry without taking a bite, suddenly feeling nervous. I'd never asked someone to live with me before. "Would you want to move in together?"

Zeke stared at me with nothing but sorrow. He sighed quietly then ran his fingers through his hair.

That was not the reaction I was expecting. "I just thought since I'm here all the time anyway... But if you aren't on the same page, it's really not a big deal. It doesn't have to be awkward or — "

"Of course I want to live with you." Instead of sounding happy, he seemed defeated.

"Then why do you look like hell right now?"

He pushed his plate aside and didn't look at me, his head bowed toward the table. He dragged his hands down his face, sighing as he did.

What the hell was going on?

"Baby, there's something we need to talk about. I've put it off this week because...I just didn't want to bring it up. But I know I can't wait any longer."

My heart was pounding so hard it actually hurt. My fingertips were numb, and I suddenly felt cold, the shivers getting to me. I swallowed the lump in my throat and tried to appear calm, but I was terrified on the inside. This entire time I thought everything was perfect between us. Obviously, I was wrong. "Okay..."

"The whole thing with Ryker drove me insane. I knew he wanted you back, I told you that and you didn't believe me. I kept my cool, I tried not to get jealous, and I tried to be positive through the whole ordeal..."

Why was he bringing this up now? Ryker was gone for good. There was no point in talking about him.

"But when you didn't tell me when you had dinner with him—"

"I told you I dropped my phone in the toilet."

He held up his hand. "Baby, let me finish. This isn't easy for me. Just let me talk."

"Okay..." I backed off.

"You didn't call me, and when I called you, your phone was off. Rex told me you were having dinner with Ryker, and naturally, I freaked out. I walked into that restaurant and saw you two holding hands over candlelight. I saw him kiss your knuckles like you belonged to him. Something inside me died in that moment. I really thought we were over. I thought you were going back to him and it was only a matter of time before you tracked me down and dumped me."

Why was he throwing this in my face right now?

"I'm saying all of this to explain how I felt that night."

I still didn't understand.

"So, I went out that night and got drunk. And when I say drunk, I mean really drunk. I started off at one bar, and I'm not even sure where I ended up. I was so depressed and angry, and I just wanted to stop feeling like shit..."

I remained quiet and kept my patience, unsure where this was going.

"And…" His voice broke, and he closed his eyes, like he couldn't finish the story. He dragged his hands down his face again, taking a deep breath filled with unbearable pain.

Now I was scared.

I was terrified of what he would say.

I was so scared I wished he would just stop talking.

"And…I slept with someone."

I heard what he said, but I didn't register the meaning. It was so absurd, so ridiculous, I couldn't understand it. My heart stopped beating altogether as time slowed down. I didn't feel any pain at all—I didn't feel anything.

"I don't remember her name. I don't even remember her face."

Fuck, this is real.

He's really saying these words.

This happened.

It's true.

He closed his eyes again and shook his head. "When I came home and saw you, I really thought you were only here to dump me. I thought we were over, Rae. After seeing you with Ryker, I assumed I was old news."

I finally took a breath, a painful one that nearly ruptured my diaphragm. Suddenly, I felt sick to my stomach, imagining his lips on someone else's mouth. I tried to take another breath, but I couldn't remember how to do it. Everything hurt—so fucking much. I gripped the edge of the table because I felt myself tipping, aiming for the floor. My world was shattering into pieces.

He opened his eyes, a film of moisture present. "Rae, she didn't mean anything to me. I hardly even remember it. If I could take it back, I would. I was at my lowest point and made an idiotic mistake."

I couldn't look at him anymore, so I stared at the table. My eyes burned because I wanted to cry, but I wouldn't allow myself to grieve. I wouldn't allow myself to do anything. If I let one part of me break down, everything else would follow. The sensation reminded me of the night I saw Ryker with that woman—but it was so much worse. I never anticipated this kind of agony from Zeke. I trusted him so completely, more than my own brother.

It was a death blow to my heart.

"Rae," he whispered. "I know this is hard to take in. I hate myself for what I did. I hate myself for hurting you. I hate all of this..."

I continued to grip the table like a life raft.

"But you know I would never do anything like this. You know I'm not a cheater. You know I'm completely devoted to you. It was just one horrific mistake."

I couldn't look at him.

"Rae, talk to me."

I hadn't said anything up to this point because I couldn't even breathe. My walls were crashing down around me, and the earth shook beneath my feet. "I just..." Words failed me, and that was all I could get out.

"Rae, I'm so sorry. From the bottom of my heart."

Even though the truth was undeniable, I couldn't feel any anger. All I felt was heartbreak. "I guess I'm in shock..."

"I know..."

After several minutes of silence, I regained my breath and finally straightened in the chair. No matter what I said to myself, I couldn't change the truth. This really happened. Zeke had slept with someone else, and our relationship would never be the same.

Everything was different now.

"Why did you wait so long to tell me?" My voice cracked, and my words came out as a whisper.

"I...I was dreading it. I was going to tell you the second I walked in the door on that terrible day. Then you said you loved me, that you wanted to marry me and you didn't want to be with Ryker. It was everything I dreamed about, and I didn't have the strength to tell you."

I finally looked at him, feeling my heart deflate like a balloon. "How could you not trust me?" Moisture flooded my eyes, and I couldn't stop it. I was losing the battle with my strength and slowly collapsing. "How could you ever think I would do that to you? After everything we've been through..."

"I do trust you, Rae. I just know how you felt about him. I know he was — "

"And you know how I feel about you." My voice escaped as a shout, the rage suddenly gripping me when I least expected it. "I sleep with you every night, Zeke. Maybe I never told you I loved you, but it was obvious in everything I did. How could you think I would betray you like that? Not just as my lover but as my best friend? I would never, ever do that to anyone I cared about."

His eyes slowly began to mirror mine. "When I saw you holding hands—"

"That doesn't mean anything, Zeke. He told me his father died thinking he hated him. He broke down on me. He cried in front of me. I was there for him and took him by the hand like a civil person. Yes, he kissed my knuckles and he probably shouldn't have. But you should have trusted me." I shoved my finger into my chest, hurting myself because I was so angry. "You should have trusted the way I felt about you. So don't you dare blame this on me."

"Rae, I saw you talking close together in the hallway at the bar. I saw you two slow dancing together at that charity gala. And then I saw you two holding hands over dinner. I'm sorry, but it looked pretty damn bad. And if the situation were reversed, you wouldn't put up with that shit. We both know it."

I shook my head, my lips pressed tightly together. "I. Trust. You."

He closed his eyes and sighed. "If I did all those things with Rochelle and she tried to get me back, you would be upset."

"Zeke, I never said you didn't have the right to be mad at Ryker. I never said you didn't have the right to be frustrated by the situation. But you had no right to fuck somebody else." When I said the words, I choked out a sob. "You had no right to turn your back on us. You had no right to stop trusting me..." I covered my mouth with my hand, trying to get myself back to a calm center.

Zeke watched me, his own tears building up. "I'm not making excuses for what I did. I just want you to understand why I did what I did. We know that never would have happened under any other circumstance. I'm not a cheater. Never have been and never will be. And I'm so madly in love with you that I don't even want to be with anyone else. Rae, she meant nothing to me. Absolutely nothing."

"But she was worth breaking my heart over."

He bowed his head and cringed at the insult. "I thought we were over, Rae. I really did."

"And if we were, you would have slept with someone that quickly?"

"I thought you were going to do the same thing with Ryker," he countered.

I covered my face with my hands and took a deep breath, steadying the ache in my lungs. My body was growing weaker by the second. It was hard to believe I woke up that morning happily in the arms of the man I adored. "I can't believe this is happening..."

"I know."

When I looked back on the lovemaking we did all week, I suddenly felt repulsed. "You kissed her then you kissed me...you fucked her then you fucked me. Jesus Christ."

"That's not how it was, Rae."

"Yes, it fucking was. I feel dirty now, disgusting."

"I wore a condom."

I knocked the plate off the table, and it crashed into pieces on the floor. "That's not the point, Zeke."

Safari didn't dart for the plate because he sensed something was seriously wrong. He stayed in the living room and didn't show his face.

Zeke held my gaze, his eyes still watery. "I was going to tell you. I just needed some time to — "

"Debate whether or not to do it."

"No," he said coldly. "In fact, Rex tried to convince me at least a hundred times not to say anything at all."

"What?" I hissed. My own brother would do that to me?

"There's no way you would have found out, Rae. I'll never see that woman again, and Rex would have taken the secret to his grave. The only reason why I told you is because I love you, and I will always be honest with you — even if it hurts."

"How romantic…"

He took a deep breath, breathing through his pain. "That does count for something, Rae. I couldn't go on and not tell you. You're the most important person in the world to me. I will always tell you the truth. You can trust me."

"Trust you?" I snapped. "Would you trust me if I slept with Ryker? Even if it was an accident?"

He shut his mouth, his argument non-existent.

"If you expect me to appreciate your honesty, I never will." I shook my head. "I can't believe this is happening… I can't believe you slept with someone else."

"I know. I wish I could take it back, Rae."

"But you can't."

He sighed. "If you did sleep with Ryker then realized it was a mistake and came back to me, I would have forgiven you. I would have taken you back."

"Bullshit—"

"Yes, I would have. As pathetic as it makes me sound, I'm so goddamn in love with you that I'll do anything to be with you. You're the love of my life, the woman I've always dreamed about. I will do anything and everything to make this work."

"And sleeping with someone else fits in how?" I couldn't control my sarcasm when my anger was the one controlling me.

"Rae, you know I feel like shit."

"And how do you think I feel?" I snapped.

He bowed his head in shame.

I looked out the window, unable to hold his gaze any longer. This house used to be a haven, and now it felt like a prison. All the beautiful memories we made here had been wiped away by his betrayal. Just this morning, I wanted to grab all my things and move in, starting a life with him. Now all of that was gone—like it'd had never happened.

"I know how you feel, Rae."

My eyes turned back to him, unable to believe his audacity.

"That night, I thought you left me for him. I thought you picked him over me. And I've never been so low in my life. I've never been out of my mind like that. I've never gotten that drunk before. It's like a poison in your stomach that won't stop spreading. Obviously, I was wrong for feeling that way. But I do understand it."

I looked away again.

"I'm sorry. I wish I could take it back."

"But you can't," I said quietly. "You never can."

Zeke stared at me across the table, still shirtless. He rested his arms on the surface as he leaned forward. "I love you. You know I do."

48

My eyes remained glued to the backyard.

"Despite what I did, you know that. You know what we have is real. You know what we have is going to last forever. You know what we have is special. It took us so long to come together, so please don't rip us apart."

"You ripped us apart, Zeke."

He didn't react to my venom.

"I know this is hard. I know you're angry, as you have every right to be. I know you want space, as you're entitled to have. But...I know we can work through this. I know we can get past this."

"What if I don't want to get past this?" I turned back to him, feeling my tears double in size.

His eyes matched mine. "I know you do, Rae. We're too good to give up on."

I looked at the table and felt my tears roll down my cheeks.

Zeke sniffed and that's when his tears came loose.

"I can't be with you. Not after this."

—
49

He left his chair and came to my side of the table. He kneeled in front of me, cupping my cheeks and forcing me to look at him. "Rae, we can work through it."

"No." I pushed his arms down and walked away toward the living room so I could finally take a deep breath. "I don't look at you the same way anymore. You made love to me after her... You tainted us."

"Our love is never tainted." He walked up to me, ready to grab me again.

"Stop." I held up my hand and backed into the couch. "Please don't touch me. Don't come near me. Please..."

Zeke listened.

I crossed my arms over my chest, feeling frozen. It felt like the end of the world, the end of my joy. I thought all the pains in my life were over for good. I'd finally found the person I wanted to share my life with, the one person who chased away my demons. But he ended up hurting me more than everything else combined. "I don't feel the same way anymore, Zeke. I know you're sorry, and I know you would take it back if you could, but now every touch feels…wrong. I love you…so much. This hurts more than anything else I've ever endured. But I'll never be able to make love to you and not think about it. I'll never be able to trust you again. I'll never…" Now the tears were falling down my face like a waterfall.

Zeke took a deep breath to steel himself, his wet eyes reflecting the lamp in the living room. "Don't say that. Take some time."

"No…" It didn't matter how much time had passed. This pain would never go away.

"I know you're upset. I understand."

"Zeke, we're done." I wasn't saying it just because I was angry. I was saying it because I meant it. Anything else, I could forgive. But not this. I couldn't be with a man who broke my heart like this. I wasn't sure how I was even going to survive. "I can't move on from this. I can't rebuild a relationship. I can't trust you."

"Rae—"

"I'm sorry." I walked away from him, unsure exactly where I was going. "Safari…"

Safari came down the hallway, rubbing against me because he knew something was wrong.

"Rae." Zeke came after me, following me to the door. "Don't leave like this." He grabbed my arm and pulled me into his chest.

"Don't touch me." I twisted out of his grasp and gave him a venomous look. "Don't make me ask you again."

Safari took a defensive stance, growling at Zeke. He loved Zeke, but the moment I was threatened, he turned on him to protect me.

Zeke stepped back and raised both hands. "Rae, let me take you home. Or at least let me call a cab. Or I'll go and you can stay here." A few tears escaped his eyes, falling down his cheeks. "Don't walk out like this."

"Trust me, there's nothing out there that can hurt me more than the way you just did."

Chapter Five

Rae

I'm not sure how I got back to my apartment.

I think I walked.

Maybe I took a cab.

I don't know.

When I walked inside, I immediately went to the couch, the closest piece of furniture I could get to. I collapsed on the cushions, grabbed the blanket hanging over the back, and felt Safari lay beside me.

After a few breaths, the sobs started.

I cried.

I cried harder than I'd ever cried in my life.

And sadly, I wished Zeke were there to comfort me. He was the person I turned to for everything, the man I considered to be my best friend. But now he wasn't there...and he would never be there again.

Safari whined and licked my face, sensing my sadness just like a human being.

"I'm sorry... I'm okay." I scratched him behind the ear. I sniffed and tried to stifle my tears, but I only cried harder.

Safari moved closer to me and whined again, carrying my pain with me.

The front door opened. "Rae?" Rex's terrified voice echoed in the apartment. "Are you here?" He walked down the hallway and checked the bedrooms because he didn't see me sitting in the dark.

I didn't have the energy to tell him I was there.

He came back, the phone pressed to his ear. "Fuck, she's not here." He glanced at the couch then kept walking. Then he did a double take. "No, she is here. She's on the couch. I didn't see her." He breathed a sigh of relief and gripped the back of his head. "I'll call you later." He hung up.

I knew who he was talking to.

Rex rushed to the couch like I needed emergency intervention. He sat beside me, on the other side of Safari. "Rae..."

I forced myself to stop crying in front of him. He would see my red and splotchy face and make fun of me for it, like always. He would see my pain and feel it too, because we were connected more than most siblings were. "I'm fine. You can go now."

"I'm not leaving." He sat beside me but didn't touch me. "I'm sorry..."

"You should be sorry." I turned on him, feeling angry at the entire world. "You knew and you tried to convince him not to tell me? What kind of brother are you?"

He didn't rise to my anger or seem remotely affected by it. "Because I didn't want to see this." He held up his hand and gestured to my tears. "I didn't want you to go through this..."

I looked away, ashamed for being angry with him.

"I know what Zeke did was wrong and painful. But you know he loves you. You know the situation—"

"Please don't. I just argued with Zeke for an hour... I don't feel like doing it again." I lay down, my head against Safari's side. I was so grateful that I had found Safari in the street that one afternoon. I took him home and made him a part of my family. Ever since then, he'd been my shoulder to cry on— always. "Please go."

Rex rested his hand on my back and rubbed it gently. "No."

"I mean it, Rex. I just want to be alone right now. I just want..." I didn't know what I wanted. The taste of salt filled my mouth from the constant tears. My lips felt dry at the same time. My heart felt like it might shatter into a thousand pieces.

"I'm gonna be here for you — like always."

"I don't want you to be here for me." I was acting like a brat, but I couldn't stop myself. My happiness had been taken away from me. Now I hated everyone in the world. "I just want to be alone. I want to sit in the dark and just...disappear."

***

I didn't go to work the next day. Rex called in sick for me, saying I had the flu.

Rex must have put me in bed at some point because that's where I woke up. Normally, the second I opened my eyes I was out of bed and doing something. But today, I just stared at Safari's fur, watching his chest rise and fall as he snored.

I wasn't sure how long I lay there.

Maybe minutes.

Maybe hours.

Time had no meaning to me anymore.

57

Rex tapped his knuckles on the open door. "Rae, someone is here to see you."

"Tell Zeke to leave," I whispered. "I don't want to see him."

"Not Zeke." Jessie's voice became clear as she walked toward me.

"Just us," Kayden said.

I rolled over and looked at them, feeling both happiness and depression the second I saw their faces. Tears were in Jessie's eyes, and it was obvious Kayden had already cried before she came inside.

"Girl, we're here for you." Jessie wrapped her arm around my shoulder and pulled me into her side.

Kayden sat on the other side and ran her fingers through my hair. "You're going to be okay, Rae. I know it doesn't seem like it right now but you will."

Rex stood in the doorway, watching us bond together.

I closed my eyes, feeling some form of comfort at their affection. "No, it won't be okay. I didn't just lose my boyfriend. I lost my best friend." I lost the most integral person in my life. I lost a family member. It was the most devastating blow I'd ever received.

"That's not true," Jessie said. "You may have lost a boyfriend. But Zeke will always be your friend."

Kayden ran her fingers down my back, her touch comforting me.

"Let's get you in the shower," Jessie said. "Then we'll have some breakfast."

"Don't you guys have work?" I whispered.

"No, not today." Jessie stood up and pulled me to a stand.

"Me neither," Kayden said.

"Isn't it Wednesday?" I muttered.

"It doesn't matter what day it is," Jessie said. "We're here for you — because you're family."

***

I told myself to snap out of it and let this depression disappear. Moping around and crying wasn't me at all. I was devastated over losing Ryker, but I didn't let his absence ruin my life.

But I knew this would be a million times harder.

I had to toughen up and keep going, moving forward. I couldn't cry to myself all day long. I had to go to work and live a normal life.

But it seemed impossible.

I couldn't do it.

Zeke destroyed me.

How could I live without him?

I forced myself to get out of bed, get ready for work, and even made myself swallow a bowl of Cinnamon Toast Crunch. It used to be my favorite cereal, but now I couldn't taste anything.

Rex came over to check on me — like usual. "Are you sure you should go to work?"

"Yes." I could barely talk without wanting to cry. My entire body ached from physical injuries I never actually received. Just putting one foot in front of the other fatigued me. I tried not to think about Zeke, but my concentration only lasted two seconds before he popped back into my mind.

"It's okay if you take another sick day, Rae."

"No...I'm fine." I grabbed my purse and my keys, feeling the burn behind my eyes. "You can stop worrying about me."

"You know I'll never stop worrying about you." He did something unexpected—he hugged me. He wrapped his arms around me and held me against his chest. He pressed my head against his shoulder so I could relax.

I let my brother hold me, but the affection didn't mask the agony deep inside my chest. It didn't matter how long he held me, it wouldn't erase what I'd lost. I pulled away and walked to the door. "I'll see you later..."

"Rae, you don't have to prove anything."

"I'm not trying to prove anything." I managed to open the door but it felt heavier than ever before. "When Ryker dumped me, I went to work. And I'm not gonna let…" I couldn't finish the sentence. "So don't worry about it." I slammed the door behind me even though I wasn't mad.

I was just…lost.

***

The nice thing about work was I had something to do with both my hands and my mind. Working with bacteria, isolating colonies, and growing them in incubators until I had exactly what I needed kept me distracted. I didn't tell Jenny anything, and it was nice to be spoken to like I wasn't a time bomb about to explode.

When the eight hours were over, I wished I could stay forever. I'd always liked my job, but I never wanted to live there before. Now, the idea of returning to my small apartment, something I was about to give up so I could move in with Zeke, made me want to sleep under my desk.

I clocked out and left, but I didn't go home. Instead, I walked the streets, counting the cracks in the sidewalk. The higher the number, the more accomplished I felt. The distraction was keeping me sane, but I knew I couldn't do that forever. It was already dark, and the cold was settling in.

But I kept walking.

My phone vibrated in my pocket for the tenth time, so I pulled it out. Seeing Rex's name was on the screen, I answered without saying hello. I pressed the phone to my ear and kept walking.

"Rae?"

"Hmm?"

"Where the hell are you? You got off work three hours ago."

"I went for a walk…"

"Where?" he snapped.

"Just around…" I glanced up at the street sign on the corner. "On Carver."

He sighed into the phone. "You need to come home. I've got dinner on the table, and it's getting cold."

Rex never cooked anything in his life—unless you counted a peanut butter and jelly sandwich. "You cooked?" I asked incredulously.

"Yes. Now come home and insult it. It's probably not very good."

I wanted to laugh. I couldn't bring myself to do it, but at least I felt the sensation.

When I didn't respond, he spoke again. "You're coming home, right? Please don't make me go out there and hunt you down."

"No... I'll come home."

"Thank you. You want me to stay on the phone with you?"

"No. I'm fine." I hung up without saying goodbye and walked home, my hands in the pockets of my jacket. My hair was in a bun because I didn't care about doing anything with it today. I looked like shit, but I couldn't care less how terrible I looked.

When I walked in the door, Safari immediately greeted me. He licked my hand then stood on his hind legs, his paws against my chest. He whined when he looked at me, greeting me like a concerned friend.

"I'm okay, Safari." I scratched him behind the ears then hugged him, wrapping my arms around the enormous beast that was by my side through every difficult time in my life. He was my true best friend.

Rex set the table then put down a bowl of spaghetti with garlic bread. "You must be starving. Have a seat."

I didn't want to release Safari, but I forced myself to let his fur slip through my fingers. I walked to the table, Safari trailing behind me. I fell into the chair with a thud that slightly hurt my ass, but the pain didn't truly register. Slouching over the table and resting my chin in my palm, I looked at the food without having an appetite.

Rex sat down and made a plate for me. "How was work?"

I grabbed a fork and spun it in my pasta, not looking at him.

Rex didn't press for details. "You don't want to talk, I get it. So, I'll tell you about my day. I ordered a shipment of bowling balls, but for some reason, they thought I made two orders. So, I have way too many balls in the bowling alley. They started to plug up the turning system, so I had to put them in storage." He inhaled his food, getting sauce all over his face. "Wouldn't be that big of a deal, but carrying bowling balls back and forth is exhausting."

I finally took a bite and realized it wasn't half bad.

Rex kept eating as if he wasn't sitting across from a ghost. "At least I'll have some in stock when the ones on the floor get too old or disappear." He grabbed a piece of garlic bread and dipped it into his sauce.

I managed to spit something out. "That's cool..."

"I took Safari for a walk today, and he peed on that same fire hydrant he always pees on." Rex rolled his eyes. "What's with dogs and fire hydrants?"

I shrugged.

He went silent as he chewed his food. "Jessie gave me a haircut today."

I knew he was saying anything that came to mind to fill the silence. "Rex?"

"Hmm?"

I looked at him, seeing the green eyes that were identical to my own. "I know you're trying to help, but you don't need to keep talking to make me feel better. The silence is okay. Honestly, it doesn't make much of a difference anyway." I took another bite of my spaghetti, doing my best to keep eating.

Rex took another bite of his garlic bread, the sadness creeping into his features. "Then what's the best way I can help?"

I didn't have an answer for that. "I don't know... Just being with me is enough."

Chapter Six

Rex

Rae was a mess.

When Ryker walked out with that supermodel, Rae was devastated. She tried to stay strong by keeping busy, going to work every day and hitting the gym. But we all knew she was struggling to get through every single day. It wasn't until three months had passed that she finally returned to her normal self.

But this was a million times worse.

Only partially alive, she moved through the world without any meaning. She forced herself to get ready and go to work every morning, but it was painful to watch. When she was home, she curled up with Safari like he was a stuffed animal.

She was completely and totally devastated.

But Zeke was worse.

I walked into his house without knocking and found him sitting on his couch in the living room, the TV and all the lights out. He sat in the darkness, hardly visible unless you already knew he was there.

I flicked on a few lights so it didn't feel like a cave.

Zeke didn't react at all. I could have been a burglar and he probably wouldn't have cared.

I sat on the other couch and watched him, seeing the pale devastation on his face. He'd been this way since Rae left—not dead but not really alive either. I didn't have the nerve to say I told you so, so I didn't.

"How is she?" Zeke's broken voice cut through the silence. He'd been more worried about her than I was, constantly asking me if she was safe.

"She's...the same. She went to work today."

He stared at the blank TV screen. "That's good..."

"She doesn't say much."

"Has she been eating?"

"When I make her."

Zeke crossed his arms over his chest and sighed. "Does she talk about me?"

"Hasn't mentioned you."

He closed his eyes like my answer was painful. "I want to talk to her, but I know I need to give her some space."

It didn't matter how much time Zeke gave her. Rae would never give him another chance. Even if she wasn't a living corpse, she still wouldn't change her mind. "I think she needs to be alone right now."

"Yeah..." He closed his eyes and took another deep breath. When he opened them, a thin film of moisture coated his eyes.

I didn't judge him for the emotion. If this had happened with Kayden, I'd be just as destroyed. "So...what have you been up to?"

"A friend of mine has been taking my patients at the office. I'm in no shape to work with people right now..."

Since he was a physician, that was probably the best move. "What have you been doing?"

"This." He stared at the TV without blinking, tears still in his eyes. "I can't sleep in my bed. The sheets smell like her..."

"You want me to wash them?"

"No," he said quickly. "No..."

"Is there anything else I can do?" I felt torn. I needed to take care of Rae because she was my sister, the victim in this catastrophe. But I wanted to be there for my best friend too. Despite what he'd done, there wasn't a doubt in my mind that he loved Rae with his whole heart. No one would ever treat her better than he would.

"Just...make sure she's okay. Don't worry about me."

Little did he know, he was in worse shape. Rae was at least going to work every day. "You want me to go by the store and get some groceries?"

"I'm not hungry."

I walked into the kitchen and looked inside the fridge. There was nothing but old lunch meat and two bottles of beer. His cabinets were the same. "I'm gonna go to the store for you. Do you need anything else? Laundry soap?" I walked back into the living room to see him in the exact same spot, starting at the TV.

"No."

"Is it cool if I take your Jeep?"

"Couldn't care less," he whispered.

My heart broke at the sight of my friend, weak and broken on the couch. I walked over to him and placed my hand on his shoulder, knowing a hug was too affectionate for us. I just left my hand there so he could feel some kind of contact. He needed to know I was there even if I didn't have the right words to say it.

Zeke didn't move. "I'm gonna get her back. It might take a while...but I will."

I wasn't an asshole, so I didn't disagree with him. Eventually, he would understand that their relationship was really over. But if that hope was keeping him together, I wasn't going to take that away from him. "Yeah..."

***

"How's Zeke?" Jessie sat across from me at the table, Kayden beside her. They'd been there for Rae, but I insisted on having alone time with my sister too, knowing I was the person she was most comfortable with besides Zeke.

"He's...a mess." I wasn't going to sugarcoat it. "He's terrible. He's worse than Rae. Not even going to work."

"Wow," Kayden whispered. "What about Rae?"

A week had come and gone, and she went to work every day. But she looked like a zombie every morning and every night. "She's the same. Still devastated. She's trying to move forward and get on with her life, but it's not working very well. She had an easier time when Ryker left her. But this time...she's really struggling."

"Poor girl," Jessie said.

"Why the hell did Zeke have to do that?" Kayden demanded. "What the hell was he thinking?"

I shook my head. "It was one bad mistake. We all make mistakes."

"This is Zeke we're talking about," Jessie said. "We all know he's not a cheater. He's got a heart of gold. He wouldn't hurt anyone on purpose, especially Rae. He was just upset over Ryker, and I think he had every right to be upset. Rae was still interacting with Ryker more than she should have been. I think she should forgive Zeke."

"I do too," I said in agreement. "But she won't."

73

"He slept with someone else," Kayden said. "If Zeke was so upset, he should have kicked Ryker's ass. That would have been a more appropriate course of action than to screw a stranger."

"We can't sit around and list all the things Zeke should have done." I didn't like disagreeing with my girlfriend, but I did it anyway. "Because we don't understand how he felt. And besides, what happened is in the past. All we can do is move forward."

"Are they ever going to be in the same room together anymore?" Jessie asked.

"Is our friendship divided now?" Kayden asked. "Will we have to split our time between Rae and Zeke?"

I knew they would never get back together, but I hoped they would pull through this as friends. "They love each other too much to cut each other out. It might take some time, but they'll be friends again. I'm not worried about it."

"Even if they start dating other people?" Jessie asked.

"That's a long way away," I said. "But I think they'll get through that too."

"Wow…" Kayden ran her fingers through her hair, what she usually did when she was nervous. "I can't believe this is happening."

"I can't either," Jessie said. "I really thought they were going to be together forever."

"Me too," I whispered. "I told Zeke not to tell her, but he did it anyway."

"What?" Kayden snapped. "You told him to lie to her?"

"Not lie," I corrected. "Just not go out of his way to tell her."

"You can't be serious." Kayden gave me a fiery look that was hostile yet borderline cute.

"In any other situation, I'd say you should come clean about it." Every person had to own up to their crimes and take their punishment. "But it's different with them. Zeke thought she picked Ryker over him. He thought they were broken up."

"It's still a stupid assumption," Kayden snapped.

"You didn't see them in the restaurant," I argued. "Honestly, I'm totally on Zeke's side for this. Ryker was holding her hands across the table and kissing her knuckles. Frankly, they looked like a couple deeply in love and having a romantic dinner. First, Ryker sent her roses, and then he paid two grand to dance with her at that gala, and he came on to her here at the bar. Zeke put up with a lot of shit. I think he just snapped."

Kayden was quiet because she didn't have an argument against that.

"I agree," Jessie said. "Rae pushed Zeke. We all know he would have never done something like that on his own."

"What roses are you talking about?" Kayden asked.

"Uh..." I never told anyone about them, but now I didn't see the harm. "He sent her roses for her birthday last year."

"Rae never mentioned that," Jessie said.

Since it was so long ago and so much had happened, I just confessed. "Because I threw them away..."

Kayden's jaw dropped. "Rex..."

76

Jessie stared at me in shock. "You never told her?"

"Look." I raised both hands defensively. "This was before she started seeing Zeke, and I knew Ryker would just mess with her head. None of us wanted them to get back together, and if she had seen those flowers, she might have been stupid enough to give him another chance."

Jessie shook her head. "Rex... I can't believe you did that."

"Let's keep that little story between the three of us, alright?" I pointed at both of them before I pointed at myself.

"Hell no, I'm not gonna tell her," Kayden said. "Anything could push her over the edge right now. But what you did was wrong, Rex."

"I know." I would never say otherwise. "I just didn't want her to get back together with him. He was such an asshole to her. She would have gotten her heart broken all over again."

"There's a good chance that's gonna happen anyway," Jessie whispered.

Kayden turned to her. "What do you mean?"

"Yeah?" I asked. "What do you mean?"

She sighed before she spoke. "Guys, it's only a matter of time. Rae is going to mope around for a while, but then she's going to feel lonely, so she's gonna turn to Ryker. They'll start banging again to make her feel better, and then they'll be right back where they were."

"No," I said. "Rae isn't going to hop into bed with Ryker. Not when she's heartbroken over Zeke like this."

"Not right now," Jessie said. "Maybe in a few months when enough time has passed. Come on, she was in love with Ryker, and now Ryker is in love with her. She's not going to sign up on Tinder and go out with a bunch of random dudes. She's going to go for the only other guy she's ever loved."

I dragged my hands down my face because I knew she was right. "Shit."

"Oh no," Kayden whispered.

"I'll have to cock block him." Anytime Ryker wanted to see Rae, I'd be standing in the way. Anytime they were alone together, I would crash their party. Any guy was better than that goddamn asshole.

And Zeke would kill himself.

Chapter Seven

Rae

Two weeks had come and gone.

And I didn't feel any better.

I kept up my daily routine and went to work every day. When I came home, I grabbed Safari and went on a long walk through the park. My head was down most of the time, and I counted the cracks in the sidewalk.

Safari didn't sniff people or chase after squirrels. He always stuck to my side and looked up at me, checking to see if I was okay.

Now that the shock had worn off, I was only left with the truth.

Zeke slept with another woman.

We were broken up.

And now I had to move on...or at least try.

He didn't call me or stop by the apartment. A part of me wanted to talk to him because I missed him, but another part of me hoped we wouldn't speak for a long time. My heart was broken, and it would take forever to heal — if it ever could.

Zeke was the love of my life, and I had been certain we were going to be together forever. The thought of a lifetime with him didn't scare me in the least. He was my best friend, and he would never hurt me.

But then I got a reality check.

I wasn't sure where to go from here. I wasn't even sure if I could ever get over him. How do you move on from the man you pictured yourself marrying? How do you fall in love with your best friend and then fall out of love? I couldn't picture myself dating. I couldn't picture myself sleeping with anyone but Zeke. I couldn't picture any kind of future for myself other than being alone.

At least I had Safari.

When I came home, Rex had dinner on the table like he did every night. I suspected Kayden was helping him because Rex never cooked a damn thing when he lived with me.

"I've got homemade pizza in the oven," Rex said. "Hope you're hungry."

"Where did you learn how to do all this?" I asked as I took off my sweater.

"Kayden and Jessie showed me a few things." He pulled the pan out of the oven, the melted cheese on the pizza smelling exquisite.

Jessie and Kayden came by often, but never when Rex was there. I suspected they were taking shifts. When Jessie and Kayden visited me, Rex spent time with Zeke. And when Rex was here, they were with Zeke.

I knew how lucky I was to have friends like them.

I sat at the table and watched Rex arrange the pizza and the plates. He placed two slices on my plate and set it in front of me. "I appreciate what you're doing, but you don't need to serve me. I'm not disabled, Rex." I didn't want to sound like a bitch, but if he didn't start treating me like I was okay, I would never feel okay.

He would normally make a smartass comment in return, but this time, he didn't. "Gotcha." He took a bite of his pizza, the crust crunching between his teeth. "Sounds like Jessie and Tobias are getting serious."

"Yeah, she told me she really likes him." I remembered when Zeke and I first got together. It was new and exciting. But even toward the end of our relationship, it still felt new and exciting.

"Tobias is a good guy. I think—" The knock on the door silenced him. He dropped his slice on the plate, wiped his fingers on the napkin, and walked to the door. He checked the peephole then sighed.

My heart fell into my stomach because I knew who it was.

Rex paused before he opened the door. "Hey, man. I don't think—"

"Let me talk to her." Zeke's deep voice, broken and hurt, reached my ears. "It's been two weeks. I've given her enough space."

Rex continued to stand in the way, unsure what to do.

"It's okay." My heart made the decision before my brain could realize it was a stupid idea. As much as Zeke had hurt me, I still loved him like crazy. I wanted to forget what he did and just move on.

Rex eyed me, still unsure.

"We can't ignore each other forever," I whispered.

Rex walked out, returning to his apartment across the hall.

Zeke walked inside, looking thinner than the last time I saw him. He shut the door behind him and slowly walked to the table. He took the seat Rex had vacated, pushing his plate to the side. He looked at me with a somber expression, just as heartbroken as I was. His eyes already had a thin film of moisture coating them, and he looked devastated. He stared at me in desperation, like he would give anything to hold me.

Tears burned in my eyes and immediately escaped, falling down my cheeks. Even though he betrayed me, it hurt so much to see him like this, to see him at his lowest point. I'd been by his side through all the hard times in life since we were fifteen. And I'd never seen him this broken.

"Baby..." He reached across the table and grabbed my hand.

I took a deep breath and stopped my tears, knowing the sight only hurt Zeke more.

"These past two weeks have been the worst of my life." His thumb brushed over my knuckles, and his eyes were glued to my face. "I didn't work for the first three days, had someone cover for me. But even when I went back to work, I could barely focus. I've spent all my days and nights in my house, sitting on the couch and staring at the blank TV. Without you, I don't know what to do with myself."

"I know…"

"It hurts so much."

"I know."

"Baby, I can apologize as many times as you want to hear it. I can do whatever you want to make this better. Whatever you want, I'll give it to you. But please give me another chance." He squeezed my hand. "I'll never hurt you again. This I promise you."

My other hand reached for his, clinging to his touch to steady my frantically beating heart. It felt so good, like an addiction I didn't want to break. I wanted more, his hands all over me and his kiss on my lips.

"Talk to me." He squeezed my hands again. "I know you needed space, and I've given you as much as I can. But please end this torture for both of us. End the suffering. You know I'm sorry, and you know why I did what I did. Please forgive me."

I wanted to fall into his arms and forget everything. I wanted to go back to what we had, sleeping in his bed with Safari at our feet. I wanted that passionate love we made every night before bed and every morning before work.

I wanted it more than anything else.

But then I remembered what he did. I pictured him screwing the woman with no face. In my mind, she was blonde, the exact opposite of my features. I imagined him releasing into the condom when he got off, thinking about someone other than me.

And I let go of his hands.

"I can't stop picturing you with her…"

His fingertips opened, as if waiting for me to come back.

"I can't forget what you did. Sometimes, I think I can let it go, but I know I can't…"

"Baby…"

"I know you're sorry. I know you love me. I know it was a terrible mistake. But...it doesn't change anything."

"Don't say that, Rae."

I pulled my hands to my chest, keeping them safe. "You have no idea how much I miss you."

"Yes, I do. Because I miss you more."

I continued forward. "You have no idea how miserable I am."

"Yes, I do," he whispered.

"I want to give this another chance, but I know I can't."

"Yes, you can," he pressed. "It's us we're talking about. We can make this work. I know we can."

"No—"

"Give yourself more time if you need it. Take as much as you need. I'll be here—waiting."

"I don't need more time..."

"Take it anyway." His authoritative voice had returned. "We've both been through a lot emotionally. We're both broken right now. Let's just...take it slow. I'll give you as much time as you need."

"You aren't listening to me..." I wanted to change my mind, but I never would. I didn't want to give Zeke false hope. I didn't want to even tempt myself with false hope. "Zeke, I wish things were different but they aren't. I'll never look at you the same way."

He fell silent, dropping his argument. He pulled his hands away then rubbed his fingers across his chin, a tormented look on his face.

"I just can't..."

He didn't say anything else. "I am listening to you. I'm seeing the look on your face as you say these things to me. I see the same look of love you've always given me, just masked with tears. I see the contradiction, the desire to forgive me as well as the pain of moving on. You're at a crossroads right now, feeling two things at once."

Hot tears burned in my eyes again.

"But I'm not giving up on us. I'll never give up on us."

Tears streaked down my cheeks.

"So, take your time. Do whatever is best for you. But just know that I'm here. I'll always be here when you're ready." He rose from the table and came to my chair, kneeling down so we were eye level.

"Please don't—"

He kissed my tears away, his lips absorbing each drop.

I sucked in the air between my teeth, feeling my stomach tighten.

He looked into my eyes, his own tears showing. "I love you, Rae." His fingers touched my hair, gently massaging me. Silently, he waited for me to say it back, knowing I would cave.

"I love you too…"

He pressed his mouth to mine and gave me a gentle kiss, the kind that breathed new life into me. It felt so good to touch him again, to share the affection I craved so badly. For just an instant, I felt better.

And when he pulled away, I felt worse than before.

***

———
89

Another week had come and gone, and I felt even worse than the first day of the breakup.

Would I ever feel better?

Zeke's kiss set me back, making me feel a new kind of pain.

I missed him even more now.

But then I thought about that woman he screwed and about him getting off to someone besides me. I thought of the fact that all of this was caused by his lack of trust in me. If he'd just known how much I loved him, none of this would have happened.

Rex came by for dinner every night, and the girls stopped by too. They didn't talk about Zeke, always mentioning other things that had no connection to him. Sometimes we played board games, and sometimes we watched sports.

But I wasn't getting any better.

Zeke didn't call or stop by, giving me space like he promised he would.

I hoped I wouldn't see him for a long time. When we were face-to-face, I was so weak. I couldn't resist him. I could have stopped him from kissing me, but I didn't even try.

Didn't even fucking try.

Rex went home after watching the game with me, and then I was alone in the apartment with Safari. Whether I was alone or surrounded by friends, it didn't make a difference. The constant ache in my chest accompanied me no matter what.

That night, I was particularly depressed, tired of sitting in the dark and thinking about Zeke. I just wanted to end the pain, but I didn't know how. Sleeping was the only coping mechanism I had, but I couldn't force my body to sleep more than nine hours a day.

So, I investigated the kitchen.

There was one Corona in the refrigerator and no hard liquor in the cabinets. Rex must have taken everything when he moved, or he'd purposely hid everything so I wouldn't resort to such cowardly measures.

But that didn't mean I couldn't go out and get it.

***

I sat at the bar, sipping my fifth long island iced tea. People and lights began to blur around me, and sounds were distorted and amplified in my ears. One guy hit on me for nearly half an hour and all I could say was, "I'm a lesbian."

The bartender walked over to me, clearly concerned by the amount of alcohol I had pumped into my system. "I think I'm gonna cut you off."

"Nah. I'm fine." I took another drink. "Don't worry about me." I put a twenty on the counter. "Keep them coming, and I'll double it."

He walked away and tended to the other patrons.

I needed to get home anyway since I had work in the morning, but I couldn't bring myself to slide off the stool. I propped my head in my hand and looked down at the counter, feeling the nausea slowly move through my body. I was drunker than I'd ever been, and I knew I would pay for it in the morning.

A man approached the bar, wearing a black t-shirt and dark jeans.

I looked up at him, curious to know who my neighbor was.

He looked just like Ryker.

Man, I really was drunk. Now I was picturing people I didn't want to see. I wondered if the next person who walked over would look like Zeke, and I would burst into tears.

Ryker Look-Alike stared at me for a few seconds.

"Go... Look...elsewhere." It took me forever to say a single sentence because I just couldn't think.

He walked over to me, crowding my space at the bar. "Rae, what are you doing?" He sounded like Ryker too. He turned to the bartender. "Enough for her. Give me her tab."

I tried to push him, but I ended up missing. "Hans Solo, I'm good." I laughed at my own joke even though it didn't make any sense. And then I grabbed my stomach because I felt a bout of nausea once more.

"Rae, I'm taking you home."

"Who are you, and how do you know my name?"

"It's Ryker. And you know that." He pulled out his wallet and left a few hundred dollars on the counter.

"Big shot…"

"Come on." He grabbed me by the arm.

This time, I had the strength to twist away. "No. I'm not falling for it…"

"Falling for what?" His deep voice held his impatience.

"You're gonna get me to your place and try to sleep with me…because that's what Ryker does. Been there, done that. No thanks." I waved him away with my hand. "Scram."

"Rae, I really am just going to take you home. I'm not leaving you alone at a bar when you're like this."

"And I'm not going anywhere with you. I'm probably safer here."

He growled like he wanted to scream at me. "Then I'll call Rex. I'll wait until he comes down and gets you." He pulled out his phone.

I tried to swat it away, but I missed and hit his wrist. "Don't you dare call him."

"Then who?" he asked. "Jessie? Give me your phone, and I'll call her."

"No." I waved down the bartender. "Another, alright?"

The bartender ignored me.

"I'm calling Rex or you're coming with me," Ryker said. "Which one is it gonna be?"

"I live here now." I tried to get the bartender's attention again.

He came over and took the money. "You've been cut off. You should go home."

"No..." I laid my head on the counter even though it was filthy. That's how much I didn't care.

Ryker lifted me from the stool and pulled me into his arms.

I wanted to fight, but I had no energy. I felt sick and weak, my legs numb. My arms wrapped around his neck as his scent entered my nose. He smelled exactly the same as he used to, like fresh soap and cologne.

He carried me to the car and got me in the passenger seat. He held me up as he buckled me in.

"I might throw up in your car..."

He pulled the hair out of my face. "That's alright, sweetheart." He got into the driver's seat and drove away.

"I don't want to go to your place. Take me home."

"Okay, Rae. That's where we're going."

I rested my forehead against the cool glass. "Because I don't want to go there."

"That's fine." He kept his eyes on the road but glanced at me from time to time.

After what seemed like only thirty seconds, he parked the car and carried me up to my apartment. I would have insisted on walking, but I honestly couldn't move. My body gave out on me, and my brain turned off.

He got the keys from my purse then carried me inside. He headed straight to my bedroom and set me on the mattress.

Safari followed us into the room, and once he recognized Ryker, he growled.

Ryker didn't move, watching him carefully.

I reached my hand out and petted Safari. "It's alright, boy. He just gave me a ride."

Safari calmed down, his growls quieting.

Ryker kneeled at the bed and pulled off my heels. Then he pulled the covers over me, tucking me inside. "I'm gonna get some water. Need anything else?"

"Advil..." I rubbed my forehead, feeling the burn of my skin.

"Alright." He disappeared for a moment and returned with the water and pills, placing them on the nightstand. "They're right here, Rae."

"Okay." I couldn't move because everything hurt. "You can go now..."

Ryker didn't move. "I don't think you should be alone right now."

"I'm at home. I'll be fine." I pulled my knees to my chest to fight my stomach ache.

"It's not safe for someone to be alone when they're this drunk," he whispered. "A lot of things could happen. I'm still debating whether I should take you to the hospital."

"No hospital..."

"So, we can do one of two things... I can call Rex or someone else and have them come over here. Or I can stay. Which do you prefer?"

I definitely didn't want to involve anyone else in this. If Rex saw me like this, he would worry. And when I got better, he would yell at me. Jessie and Kayden would feel the same way. "I can handle this on my own. I have Safari."

"Pick, Rae."

"I guess…you." Ryker was the lesser of two evils, by far.

"Alright." He kicked off his shoes then sat on the edge of the bed, preparing to lie down beside me.

Safari jumped on the bed and barked, his teeth bared and a terrifying growl emitting from deep in his throat.

Ryker slowly moved off the bed, taking a pillow and placing it on the floor.

Safari lay beside me, his head facing the floor where he could see Ryker at all times.

Ryker grabbed an extra blanket sitting on my dresser and got as comfortable as possible on the carpet. He fell silent as he stared at the ceiling, probably uncomfortable since he was used to his luxurious bed with expensive sheets. With Safari watching him, he probably didn't dare move a single inch. "Nice to see you too, Safari."

Safari released a quiet growl.

"You really don't have to stay." My eyes felt heavy as they closed, like invisible weights had been placed over my eyelids.

"I know, Rae. I want to stay."

***

The second I opened my eyes, I had to hurl. I rolled over Safari and landed on the floor with a dull thud.

"Shit, Rae." Ryker stirred when I touched his leg. "What the hell are you—"

I moved as quickly as I could and dashed for the bathroom, making it to the toilet just in time. I emptied everything sitting inside my stomach, depositing my soul along with the alcohol and chunks.

Ryker came behind me and grabbed one of my legs. "Lift your knee."

I gripped the bowl and did as he asked.

He slipped a folded towel underneath both of my knees, supplying cushion so I didn't have to kneel on the hard tile.

"Thanks..." I felt another load coming, so I breathed through the pain and waited.

Ryker stood at the counter and opened my drawers until he found a hair tie. He kneeled behind me and gathered my hair in his hand, pulling it into a perfect bun. It was off my neck and out of my face.

"You've done this before?"

He chuckled. "Actually, no." He rubbed my back with his large hand, moving down my spine.

Safari growled from the doorway, his teeth bared again.

"What's your problem?" Ryker snapped. "I'm helping her."

Safari barked.

"Safari." My voice escaped as a whisper, but he quieted down, releasing a few whines. "He's just protective of me..."

"Well, I'm not here to hurt you."

I had a comeback to that, but I left it in my throat. I tensed as I felt the vomit rising again. I threw up in the bowl, gripping the seat for dear life as the nausea blasted through me like a thunderstorm. "Oh, god..."

"It's alright," he whispered. "You'll feel a lot better when it's over." He got a towel from the hallway and ran it under warm water before he returned.

I threw up again, and when the chunks disappeared, I knew that was the last round.

"Here." He handed me the damp cloth.

I wiped my face and then my mouth, removing the signs of bile before I turned around.

"Feel better now?"

"Uh-huh." I flushed the toilet and closed the lid to hold the smell. I leaned back against the side of the tub, feeling sweat on my forehead and the back of my neck. "Can you give me a second?"

"Sure thing." Ryker walked out and shut the door behind him. The second he was gone, Safari barked again.

I rubbed my temple and felt the migraine forming.

"Safari." Ryker's powerful voice rang through the hallway. "Keep it down."

After I mustered enough energy, I stood at the sink and washed my face and brushed my teeth. I rinsed with three rounds of mouth wash until I was certain the taste was truly gone. My face was still warm, so I patted it with cool water, trying to bring my temperature down. Even though I was done hurling, I still felt terrible. At least the pain was a distraction from my heartbreak.

I opened the door and walked down the hallway, spotting Ryker on the couch. Safari sat on the ground right in front of him, watching him like a guard dog with those perceptive black eyes.

"Safari, chill."

Safari lowered his head and rested his chin on his paws, his ears flattening.

Ryker sat in front of the TV, but he didn't turn it on. "You want me to make you something to eat?"

"I'm not hungry." After staring at my puke, the last thing I wanted to do was eat and throw up again.

"You should drink a lot of water. You're even more dehydrated now."

I spotted the clock on the wall and realized it was two in the afternoon. "Oh, shit. You missed work."

He shrugged. "I'm the boss. I can do whatever I want."

"Well, I can't," I snapped. "I didn't even call in sick."

"I took care of it." He patted the seat beside him. "Take a seat."

Just to be stubborn, I didn't. I crossed my arms over my chest and continued to stand even though I was exhausted.

"I take care of you all night and you won't even sit with me?" That arrogant smile and smoldering gaze looked exactly the same as it used to. He tapped the couch again. "Come on, sweetheart."

I sat down, sticking to the opposite side of the couch so we were nowhere near each other. My arms were still across my chest. I was in the jeans and t-shirt I wore the night before, and I looked like hell.

His cockiness died away as he looked at me. His expression softened, just the way it did when he told me he loved me at dinner. "So…you and Zeke broke up?"

"How did you know?" I never mentioned him.

"Well, if I were seeing you, you wouldn't be sleeping alone." His hand rested on the cushion between us, but he didn't try to grab my hand. "He hasn't called. And I've never seen you get that hammered since I've known you…which could only mean one thing."

"That I'm completely and utterly devastated…" I pulled my gaze away from his face because I couldn't stand the look of pity.

"Yeah…I guess."

I felt tears burning in the back of my eyes, but I refused to let them escape.

"Talk to me, sweetheart."

"You don't want to hear about this stuff…"

"Hey." He patted the cushion until I looked at him. "If I didn't want to know, believe me, I wouldn't ask. But I did ask…because I care. Now, tell me what happened."

I took a deep breath so the tears would stay behind my eyes. But I knew once I started talking, they would slowly come free. "That night you and I talked at dinner..."

"Yeah?" he whispered.

"Zeke came to the restaurant and saw us holding hands. He assumed the worst and went out to a bar and hooked up with some girl."

Ryker closed his eyes and cringed.

"He thought I was picking you over him, and he did something really stupid...but I can't forgive him. I love him so much, but I can't let it go. I just see him differently now."

"How long has it been?"

"Two weeks..." The longest two weeks of my life.

"Rae, I don't even know what to say. I'm so sorry." When he said, it seemed like he meant it. But after he confessed to me about how he felt, there was no reason to be sad about my breakup.

"No, you aren't," I whispered. "And that's okay."

He sighed like my words stung him. "When I told you I loved you, I meant it."

I watched the sincerity in his gaze and knew he meant what he said.

"I want you to be happy. I hate seeing you like this. This isn't the woman I know."

I tightened my arms across my chest. "I know…"

He turned to the blank TV and rested his fingertips against his lips, his chest rising and falling with even breaths.

I still couldn't believe he was sitting in my living room. I went out last night to get so wasted I couldn't feel any pain. But then I ran into the last person I wanted to see — besides Zeke.

"I know it's not my place, but I'm gonna say something anyway."

My only response was a stare.

He turned to me, his blue eyes vibrant like they used to be. "Zeke is a good guy. I've known him for a long time. The guy made a bad mistake, but I think you should forgive him. You know he would never do anything like that under any other circumstance."

I couldn't believe Ryker was vouching for Zeke.

"And really, this entire thing is my fault. I asked you to dinner and told you I loved you. He's entitled to be upset."

"But he's not entitled to screw someone," I snapped. "If I slept with you, he'd never forgive me."

His eyes sagged with defeat. "I'm just saying..."

"He could have yelled at me all he wanted. He could have ignored my phone calls for two weeks. He could have even said he needed a break. But to sleep with someone..." I shook my head. "I can't get over that."

Ryker sighed quietly.

"I used to look at him in a different way...but now everything has changed." Tears rolled down my cheeks. "I love him so much, but I can't get back to where we used to be. I don't trust him the way I used to."

"Maybe you should just give it some time—"

"We're done." It didn't matter how many times I said those words, they always hurt.

Ryker bowed his head, finally giving up on his persuasion.

Now that the truth was on the table, I couldn't think of anything else to say. I was grateful Ryker spotted me in that bar and got me home safely, but it didn't feel right having him there. If Rex came home and saw him, he would assume the worst. And then he would tell Zeke, who would assume something was going on when there wasn't. "Thank you for taking care of me…"

"I'll always be here, Rae." He sat forward and rested his elbows on his knees. "I guess I should get going." He rose to his full height and looked down at me, that pitying look still in his eyes. "You know you can call me for anything—even if it's just to talk."

I nodded.

He stood there like he expected something else to happen. His hands moved into the pockets of his jeans.

I didn't touch him, feeling like I was betraying Zeke just for having Ryker inside the apartment. "I'll see you around…"

He knew that was his cue to leave. "See you later, Rae." He walked toward the door and turned around. "And it was nice seeing you too, Safari."

Safari growled in response.

Ryker shut the door behind him and was finally gone.

I breathed a sigh of relief once he was out of my apartment. It felt so good having him sleep in the same room, giving me the best night of sleep I'd gotten in two weeks. Something about having him there made me drift into unremarkable dreams. But that comfort made me feel guilty, like I was doing something I shouldn't.

It was nice of Ryker to take care of me when he could have taken advantage of me instead. He pushed for Zeke when he could have said nothing, but he chose to be honest instead. He'd matured so much since our previous relationship.

Good for him.

Chapter Eight

Rex

When Rae walked in the door, I had tacos sitting at the dining table. Kayden was doing all the prep work for these meals. I just followed the instructions she gave me and had dinner ready by the time Rae came home.

I missed spending time with Kayden since I was busy looking after Rae, but at least I had my nights with my girl. Kayden didn't seem to mind, wanting me to be with Rae as much as possible.

Even though it'd been three weeks, she looked just as terrible as she did on day one of the breakup. Her hair was always up in a bun, she never wore makeup, and her clothes were getting baggier and baggier.

"It's time for a fiesta!" I started doing the Macarena.

"Rex, you really don't need to cook for me every day. I can make food."

I dropped my hands and sat at the table. "We both know you wouldn't eat a damn thing if I weren't here shoving food down your throat. So shut up and just eat."

She sighed but didn't give me any attitude. She sat down and pulled a taco onto her plate, her face looking more slender since she was dropping weight nearly every single day. "I have a favor to ask of you."

"I already do you a favor every single day." I pointed to the plate of tacos, rice, and beans.

"But I never asked you to do this, so it doesn't count."

I finished demolishing one taco before I turned serious. "You know I'll do anything you ask. So, lay it on me."

She was reluctant, like her request would put me in an awkward situation. "I need you to go to Zeke's place and get my things..."

I felt my cheeks grow numb, and my appetite disappeared.

"A lot of my stuff is there, and I don't think I can walk into that house again...at least not right now."

I rested both elbows on the table and stared down at my plate, knowing Zeke would be devastated when I showed up at his door. He was barely holding on right now, and this would just break his already broken heart even more.

"I also think it would make it harder for Zeke if I went myself."

I cleared my throat, finally coming back to the conversation. "Yeah, I'll take care of it."

"He knows where everything is. He can probably pack it up for you, and you can just pick it up."

I nodded. "I'll handle it." I grabbed another taco even though my appetite hadn't returned. I knew this breakup was permanent but going through the steps was still difficult. It'd been three weeks since the day Zeke called me. Enough time had passed for me to get used to the change, but I would never look at either one of them the same as long as they weren't together.

"Thank you." She finished one taco but didn't grab another, clearly not hungry.

I didn't pester her about it, having other problems on my mind.

"How is he?"

"He's the same, Rae. Completely devastated." If it was a competition to see who was more heartbroken, it was a tie. "I've never seen him so low, and I've known him my entire life." I watched her expression across the table, seeing the sadness in her eyes.

"I hate that he's in pain...breaks my heart."

"I hate that you're both in pain." They were my two best friends. "Rae, I really think you should reconsider..."

"Why does everyone keep telling me that?" she whispered. "He cheated on me. As in, slept with another woman. Could you just look the other way if Kayden slept with some other guy?"

My eyes narrowed because Kayden did sleep with someone else. "When we broke up, she slept with all of Seattle. Or did you forget?"

"Not the same thing, Rex. She did that because you dumped her. If she came home to you every night and said she loved you, you would feel differently."

Kayden and I weren't just boyfriend and girlfriend anymore. She was such an integral part of my life that if she were missing, my whole world would come crashing down. "If the situation were reversed, I would forgive her."

"Easy for you to say when you aren't in the situation..."

"Actually it is easy," I said coldly. "Because this is what it comes down to. Either forgive Zeke and spend the rest of your life with the man you truly love, or lose him forever and end up with someone else who you probably will never love as much. That's the truth in black and white."

Rae's expression didn't change. "I don't see him the same way anymore."

"Because you're hurt. But you don't love him less."

"No, I don't," she said in agreement. "But nothing is the same anymore. I can't just go back to what we were because it doesn't exist anymore."

I bowed my head in defeat, wishing I could change the present or change the past. If I'd known how this was going to end, I would have dragged Zeke by the hair and locked him in my apartment until morning. I never thought he would get so drunk that he would do something that stupid.

"I don't want to talk about this anymore…" She excused herself from the table and walked into her room, Safari trailing behind her. His collar jingled when he walked, so you could hear him anywhere in the house. She shut her door a moment later, silently asking me to leave.

Normally, I would take the leftovers back to my place and Kayden and I would devour everything. But now, I didn't want any of it. I would do anything just to put our lives back to the way they were — the way they belonged.

***

Zeke and I watched the game in his living room, but it didn't seem like he was really paying attention. A ridiculous foul was made, but he didn't yell at the TV like he usually would. Ever since the breakup, he'd been a ghost of who he used to be.

115

He always asked about Rae, wanting to make sure she was eating enough, exercising, and going to work every day. He still looked after her without her even realizing it. Just like when they were together, she was his priority.

I hadn't picked up Rae's things yet because I couldn't bring myself to mention it to Zeke. But when Rae asked me again, I knew I had to get it over with. If I didn't, Rae would come herself, and that would be worse for both of them. "There's something I want to talk to you about." I set my beer down because my hands were turning cold.

"Hmm?" He didn't take his eyes off the TV even though he wasn't watching it anyway.

"Rae asked me to pick up her things." I closed my eyes as I finished the sentence so I didn't have to look at his face. But the image in my mind was probably worse than any reaction he could actually give me. When I opened my eyes again, I saw the devastation I'd been prepared to witness.

But it didn't make this easier.

"She asked you to get her things?" When he repeated the question, his voice was weak. He seemed on the verge of tears without watery eyes. His emotions shifted from one place to another dramatically, like he was feeling anguish and indifference at the same time.

"Yeah. I'm sorry, man."

He shook his head. "She sent you to get her things?"

He repeated the question a second time, so I assumed it was rhetorical.

"No." He slammed his beer down. "If she wants her shit, she can come get it."

I'd never seen Zeke turn angry over this breakup, but he'd reached a new level of grief. "Don't be like that, man. She's not doing it to hurt you."

"She's not hurting me. She's sticking a knife in my chest and stabbing me in the heart." He ran his hands over the back of his neck, his head bowed to the floor. "I meant what I said. If she wants her stuff that badly, she can come get it."

"Zeke, that isn't going to get you what you want."

"Yes, it will. She'll have to come here and see the place where we're gonna grow old together. And when she does, she won't have the strength to say no to me again."

It was just going to make things worse. "She's not gonna change her mind, and making her walk into a trap won't help the situation."

"It's not a trap. I know her. It'll be too hard for her."

"Exactly," I said. "Which is why she asked me to moderate. She's already going through hell right now. You don't have to look at her every day."

"I wish I got to look at her every day."

I'd never seen Zeke act so spiteful. "I know you're upset, and I understand that. But don't do something stupid and push her further away. That's not gonna help you out in the long run."

He leaned back into the couch and stared at me with dead eyes. "I can't let her take her things because..." He didn't finish the sentence because the words weren't necessary.

I knew what he was going to say. "Then it'll really be over."

"Yeah..."

"But whether her stuff is here or not, it is over. I hate to say it, but it's true."

He shook his head. "She and I are never over. I don't know how, but I'm gonna fix this. I'm gonna get us back together. I'm gonna marry her...I promise you."

I admired his commitment but it also made me pity him. "So, let me get her things. You can keep working on your plan to fix the two of you. But holding her stuff hostage isn't going to help your cause. It's just gonna push her away."

He sighed. "I don't think I can push her away more than I already have."

I stared at my beer because I couldn't look at him anymore. This wasn't the best friend I was used to seeing. I couldn't remember the last time the guy laughed. He'd been this way for so long I couldn't remember any of the good times.

"I'll pack up her things, but I'm not going to do it right now. I need some time."

"How much time?"

"I don't know...at least a week."

"Does my sister have a lot of crap?" I asked.

"No…I just can't bring myself to do it. You wouldn't understand."

He was right. I wouldn't understand. And I was so grateful that was true.

**

When Rae heard me walk inside, she left the couch and met me by the door. She realized I was empty-handed, and the disappointment flooded her features. "What happened?" She crossed her arms over her chest, her hair a mess in the bun she wore.

"He needs more time."

"More time to what?" she whispered. "Most of my clothes are there. He has my makeup, my clothes, shoes, everything. I've made it without those things for three weeks, but I can't keep washing the same stuff every day."

"I get it."

"Then…what's the hold up?"

"He said he needs a week to pack up your things."

"But it won't take a week." She shifted her weight to one leg, her shirt baggy on her slender frame. "He can just throw everything into a box."

She didn't get it. "It's hard for him to let your things go, Rae. He's just not ready to take that step."

Her eyes softened then filled with moisture.

"So, just give him some more time."

"I'm sorry, but I need my things. I know this is hard, but we've got to move forward. He can keep some stuff until he's ready to give it up. But for now, I can't keep living like this. I need jeans and sweaters. I don't want to buy all that stuff again."

I didn't know what to do. I understood Zeke's request, but I also understood hers. "I'm sure Kayden and Jessie can let you borrow some stuff until he's ready."

"He's the one who ruined this relationship, but I'm the one who has to take hand-me-downs because he's not ready?" Fire burned in her eyes, along with insufferable pain. "That doesn't sound fair to me."

"I know but—"

"Then I'll just go down there and get it myself." She grabbed her only sweater hanging by the door and her purse.

"Whoa, I don't think that's a good idea." I blocked the door so she couldn't get out.

"I've given you a whole week to retrieve my things, but you failed, Rex. I'm a big girl and can take care of it. So, get out of my way before I make you get out of my way." Her attitude was emerging in full force, but she was depressed at the same time. The conflicting emotions made her difficult to handle.

I finally stepped out of the way, not wanting to test her emotions. She was a time-bomb about to go off, and I didn't want to give her another reason to be upset.

She walked out and shut the door behind her, leaving me alone with Safari. She didn't bother locking the door on her way out.

I pulled out my phone and called Zeke.

When he answered, he greeted me with his silence.

"Rae is on her way. She wants her stuff."

The only response I got was the line going dead.

Chapter Nine

Rae

I stood on his doorstep for nearly ten minutes because I couldn't bring myself to knock. It was just too hard to return to the place I considered to be my home. It was overcast, but there wasn't a hint of rain falling from the sky. His front yard was manicured perfectly, and it smelled like pine cones.

Too much of a coward, I didn't knock on the door at all. I considered turning around and just going home, unable to see the look on his face when I packed my things and walked out.

But he opened the door, all the emotions I felt deep inside plastered onto his once handsome face. He leaned against the door as he stared at me, looking weak. He used to be so strong in my eyes, a powerful man with a body comprised of nothing but lean muscle. But now, he just looked hollow.

I didn't step inside, not because I wasn't invited, but because I didn't have the strength to do it.

He stared me down, desperate to hold me and ask me to stay with him. He didn't need to say the words to make it obvious what he was thinking. He bowed his head and looked at the floor as we stood together.

I steeled my nerve and finally walked inside, hearing my shoes tap against the hardwood floor. The sound was familiar because I was used to hearing it every single day that I stayed with him.

He shut the door behind me then stood against the wall, his hands moving into the pockets of his jeans. He wore a gray t-shirt, not filling it out as well as he used to. He had obviously stopped eating and hitting the gym. His blue eyes were no longer magical, but screens that displayed his sorrow.

When I tried to speak, nothing came out. My voice cracked, so I cleared my throat. "I just need to get my things. I'm running out of clothes and stuff." I didn't make eye contact with him because it was just too hard. "You can leave if it makes things easier."

He raised his head and looked me in the eyes, misery etched into his features. "Baby, nothing is going to make this easier."

When he called me baby, I wanted to cry. I missed hearing him call me that every single day, especially when we made love in his enormous bed. I would miss the way his eyes locked with mine when he said the endearment. "Well, I guess I'll get started. Where is everything?"

His eyes didn't water anymore, but he still seemed utterly heartbroken. "Exactly where you left it."

I walked down the hallway and turned my back on him, not wanting to see his expression any longer. His bedroom was exactly how I remembered. It smelled the same too. The bed was made— a weird habit he'd had ever since I could remember. He couldn't leave for work unless the sheets were tucked in and the pillows were arranged. It was something his mother had made him do every day since he was five.

I grabbed a bag and opened my drawer in his dresser, seeing the panties and socks I put on every morning before I went to work.

Zeke followed me and stood in the doorway, his hands in his pockets.

"You're going to watch me?" I whispered.

"It hurts. But I'd rather be with you than not be with you."

I closed my eyes and stopped myself from crying. Stopping the sob fest before it started, I grabbed a handful of clothing and tossed it into the bag. I didn't sort anything because it was pointless. Everything piled on top of each other, weighing down the plastic bag.

Zeke continued to stand there.

I set the bag on top of the bed and entered his walk-in closet. My jeans and shirts were still hanging on my side of the closet, exactly where I left them. His work scrubs and other clothes hung from the opposite side, smelling just like him.

This was even harder than I thought it was going to be.

I took a few tops from the hangers and walked back to the bed. I shoved them inside the bag, letting them wrinkle on top of my socks.

That's when his arms wrapped across my stomach and chest. He pressed his lips against my ear and breathed quietly, his grip hard like steel.

I knew what was going to happen next. "Zeke, no."

He pressed a kiss to my neck, wet and soft. His lips traveled along my shoulders, and he unzipped the front of my sweater as he moved, doing two things at once.

"No..." I shouldn't have come here alone, in this bedroom where we made love for the first time.

He pulled my sweater down my arms then turned me around to face him. "Yes." He cupped my face and kissed me with more passion than he ever had before. His lips devoured mine like they belonged to him once again.

I didn't think about the other woman.

I didn't think about what he had done.

It felt like us again — just the two of us.

My body made its own decisions, and my mouth moved with his, feeling the lips I ached to touch. His tongue danced with mine, familiar and passionate. My hands moved up his chest until I felt his strong shoulders. I was falling into oblivion, feeling good for the first time in weeks.

Zeke grabbed the back of his shirt and pulled it over his head, revealing his chiseled physique. His body was tight and strong like before, just more slender by a few inches. He kissed me again, undoing his jeans and letting them fall to his ankles.

This was a bad idea, but it felt so good I didn't care. My fingers dug into his hair, and I kissed him harder, just wanting to a moment of happiness. I wanted this pain to go away, to feel something besides agony.

He grabbed my top and pulled it over my head, his hand unclasping my bra immediately afterward. He got my jeans undone then laid me on the bed, kissing me as he moved on top of me. His hand yanked my shoes off and pulled down my jeans, getting me undressed as quickly as possible.

More clothes were removed, and we were wrapped together, naked and desperate. His cock lay against my stomach, and he kissed me harder than before, his passion more intense than it'd ever been.

He placed his tip at my entrance and sunk into me, his tongue brushing against mine.

I knew I would feel nothing but bliss for the next twenty minutes. I knew my heart would stop aching and everything would feel good again. Zeke and I would be together, doing what we did best. It would feel like a moment from the past, like reliving a favorite memory.

But when the moment was over, I knew I would feel so much worse.

I would have to start over.

I would have to distance myself all over again.

Every time I tried to sleep, I would think about this night.

It was only going to hurt both of us.

"No." I grabbed his shoulders and pushed him back.

"Rae." He pressed his face to mine and didn't pull out. "I love you."

"I love you too." My response was automatic, my lips doing the thinking. For a second, I gave in again. "But stop."

Zeke clearly didn't want to stop. He wanted to keep going, seducing me until I was so overcome with pleasure that I gave into the desperation we both felt. But he did what I asked and got off me, pulling the buried inches of his cock out. He sat on the edge of the bed and leaned forward, resting his elbows on his knees.

I wanted to cry, but thankfully, I didn't.

I got my clothes on and didn't look at him. The bag was on the floor where it fell, so I grabbed it and returned to the closet, yanking everything off the hangers and shoving it inside the bag. Once it was full of all my possessions, I walked back into his bedroom.

He was dressed, looking more miserable than before.

I had to get out of there.

I walked to the other side of the house, heading for the front door. The walls were closing in and my strength was waning. It would be so easy for me to stay and never leave. But I knew I would regret it later.

I had to keep going.

Zeke followed me, his lips red from kissing me so hard.

I didn't walk out the door even though there was nothing keeping me there.

"Rae, don't leave like this."

"Leave like what?" I held the bag with both hands, ignoring how heavy it was.

"Let me drive you home, at least."

"I can get an Uber." I didn't want him in my apartment. We would just repeat our make out session again.

He kept his arms by his sides but stepped closer to me. There were only a few feet between us, a dangerous proximity. "You kiss me like you can't live without me. You touch me like you love me. You get lost with me instantly…"

The tears were starting up again.

"Please let us work this out, Rae. We have so much to fight for. We can't give up."

They came loose, streaking down my cheeks. "You know I love you, Zeke. You know I love you more than I've ever loved anyone in my life. But...I just can't get over it. I'm sorry. I would never trust you again..."

"Yes, you can." He pushed the bag on the ground and grabbed my hands, holding them against his chest. "You know I would never even look at another woman. What happened between us was a difficult situation, and you know that."

"But what about when we have another fight?" I whispered through my tears. "What about when you get jealous over someone else?"

"Rae, it won't happen again. Ryker is gone, so there's no way it could happen again."

I pulled my hand away so I could wipe away my tears.

"Can you really picture yourself with someone else?"

"No." I couldn't picture my wedding day or my children—not anymore. "Not right now, at least."

"I can't picture myself with anyone else either. Whoever I do marry will never compare to what I have with you. We're both choosing a life of less happiness. It doesn't make any sense, Rae."

"I know it doesn't..."

"Then let's work this out. We can go see a counselor. We can take baby steps. Whatever you need. I'm willing to do anything, you know that."

"I know...but it's not about counseling or taking things slow. It's about...not feeling the same way." I loved him just as much as before, but the connection I once felt was gone. He wasn't high on a pedestal anymore. Now he was on a much lower level, in a danger zone that I couldn't come close to—at least without getting hurt. I pulled my hand away and picked up the bag again. "Zeke, I'm sorry. Everything has changed, and it can't go back to the way it was. I just can't."

He let my hand slip away, his pain burning across his face.

"I wish things were different...you know that."

Now, he was speechless.

"I think we should spend some time apart before we see each other again. Because I need you in my life, Zeke. We promised we would always be friends no matter what happened. Don't break your promise to me." If Zeke threatened to remove me from his life permanently, I may have given in and allowed our relationship another try. Losing our romantic relationship was heartbreaking enough. But if I lost his friendship, something I'd had my entire life, I wouldn't have been able to go on.

"Rae…of course we'll always be friends." He looked at me with hollow eyes. "But we'll never be the kind of friends we were before. I'm never gonna look at you the same. You'll always be my girl. Even if you're married with kids, you'll still be my girl. We can do the best we can but…I'm always going to be in love with you."

And I knew I would always be in love with him.

***

I did a lot of crying that week—just as much as the first week.

But I was still going to work every day, doing laundry, and taking Safari on daily walks through the park.

Instead of thinking about the future, I tried to take it one day at a time.

Baby steps.

All I thought about was what I needed to do at work, how many miles I could walk with Safari that day, and what I was having for dinner.

That's it.

I tried not to think about what Zeke was doing that afternoon. I tried not to look at my phone and hope he would text me. I tried not to think about what he was doing at work. I tried to block him out entirely.

Rex continued to come over every day with dinner, even though it was unnecessary. If I was hungry, I'd make something. Every day I was at work, I usually ate out with Jenny since we took our breaks at the same time. It's wasn't like I'd stopped eating.

Just not as much.

I was in the lab, listening to the radio for the first time in a month. All the love songs always made me think of Zeke, so I couldn't handle it in the beginning. But now, it was easier. I could listen to music without thinking about Zeke during every track.

Jenny was taking her afternoon break, so I was alone with my thoughts, and that was never good. Every time Zeke came into my mind, I forced the thoughts away. I usually switched my focus to Safari and that eliminated the negative thoughts. Safari made me feel happy, with his long tongue and soft fur.

The door at the top of the stairs opened and footsteps thudded as they descended to the bottom floor.

I'd just assumed Jenny was back from her break even though she hadn't been gone long.

"Am I interrupting anything?" Ryker's deep voice came from behind me, confident and suave.

My heart leapt into overdrive when he caught me by surprise. I had just finished a gram stain, so I pulled off my gloves and turned off the burner. Before I could forget where I was in my project, I labeled the microscope slide then washed my hands.

Ryker watched me the entire time.

"No. I was just doing boring science stuff."

"I don't think it's boring. I don't understand it, but I don't think it's boring." He walked to the lab table, wearing his gray suit with a matching tie. He looked like a million bucks with his tailored clothing and styled hair. Instead of being the CEO of a trash company, he should have been in a GQ ad.

"What's up?" Jenny would be back any second, and I didn't want to be questioned about my mysterious relationship with the handsome boss. I'd rather not be seen with him at all costs.

Concern was radiating in his gaze. "Just wanted to see how you were doing."

This man had watched me throw up three times. Fortunately, I was too depressed to be embarrassed. "I'm okay." I wasn't going to pretend I'd put myself back together in the two weeks since I'd seen him.

"You wanna grab a bite after work?"

I wasn't going down this road with Ryker again—not now and not ever. "Ryker, I'm not looking for romance or a hook-up right now." My body had grown numb since Zeke and I broke up a month ago. The only life I felt was when Zeke and I made out and nearly slept together on his bed. But other than that, I was dead inside.

"That's not why I'm asking."

I didn't have time for games. "Yes, it is. I know you."

"You *knew* me," he corrected. "Honestly, I just want to be there for you. You were there for me when I didn't deserve it, and now I'm doing the same for you. I'm here to talk, here to cry on, whatever."

"I have plenty of people for that..."

He walked around the table and came closer to me. "I don't have any tricks up my sleeve. I'm not trying to swoop in now that Zeke is out of the picture. I'm just worried about you and want to help. So, please, have dinner with me."

"I don't know..."

"Come on, nothing fancy. We can go to that taco place down the street. I won't even try to pay for your food. We're just friends."

It seemed like he meant it, so I caved. "Okay, I'll go."

***

I texted Rex when we arrived at the taco shop. *I'm having dinner with a friend so don't wait up.* I didn't want to lie to him, so I didn't. But I wasn't honest either. If I'd even mentioned Ryker's name, Rex would have been down there so fast it wouldn't be funny.

We ordered our food and sat in a booth in the corner. Tons of people were around, and the atmosphere was casual. The fluorescent lights overhead were too bright, and none of the tables looked like they'd been properly cleaned.

It wasn't remotely romantic.

And I loved that.

I picked at my taco then squeezed a lime over the top. Even though the food smelled good, it didn't look appetizing. My need for food fluctuated as time went on. Sometimes, I was starving, but most times, I didn't want to take a single bite.

Ryker ate across from me, his stare off to the side, so he wasn't looking straight at me.

I appreciated it.

If anyone I knew walked in right then, Ryker and I would just look like two friends getting dinner and nothing more.

"So, what have you been doing?" Ryker asked before he took another bite.

"Nothing." It was the sad truth. "I take Safari on a walk every day. But that's about it."

"Good. Getting fresh air is important. When my dad passed away, I started to run at night. It helped me get rid of the anger."

I never knew that. "I finally got my stuff back from Zeke's place. It was really hard."

"I can imagine." He wiped his mouth with a napkin, his scruff thick like he hadn't shaved in a few days.

"He kissed me and things heated up, but I managed to stop it." I wasn't sure why I was telling him this. I hadn't mentioned it to anyone, not even Rex. Words came tumbling out of my mouth. "I knew if I went through with it, it would only make things harder."

"Yeah...you're probably right." If he felt uncomfortable by any of this, he didn't show it. When he looked at me, it seemed to be in a genuinely friendly way. If he was jealous, it didn't seem like it. "It's been a month now, right?"

I nodded.

"And you don't feel any better?"

I shook my head. "I don't think I'm ever going to feel better..."

"Then maybe you should reconsider everything." Ryker pushed for Zeke again, to my astonishment. "You love him. He loves you. The guy made a mistake, and you know he's sorry. Maybe you should forgive him."

"Of course, I forgive him," I whispered. "I love him, and I can't stay mad at him forever. But...I can't be with him anymore." No one would understand my feelings unless the love of their life had cheated on them.

Ryker seemed disappointed with that response. "Let me ask you something. Keep in mind, I'm not asking because it has anything to do with me or how I feel. It's only to prove a point."

I ignored my food and stared at him.

"I was a complete dick to you. I explained what was going on at the time, but at the end of the day, I still broke your heart. If I'd come back to you within a month and asked you to take me back, would you have done it?"

"I...I don't know."

"You would have." His eyes held his confidence, like there was no doubt. "You would have forgiven me, and we would have given the relationship another try."

When I remembered how I felt at the time, I knew he was right. "What's your point?"

"What I did to you is worse than what Zeke did."

"You didn't cheat on me, Ryker."

"But what I did was worse, in my eyes." He threw his napkin down onto his tray. "I pushed you away without explanation, I dumped you, and within a week, I was chasing tail. Zeke would never do something like that because he's not as much of an idiot as I was."

"It's still different..."

He shook his head in annoyance. "You're looking at the situation in black and white. Look at the shades of gray."

I felt my anger rise, but I managed to keep it back. "Ryker, I know you're trying to help, but please stop telling me what to do. Stop telling me how I should feel. Stop simplifying this when you don't have a clue how I feel right now."

He raised his hands in surrender. "You're right. I'll back off."

"Thank you." I sipped my soda and felt the burn of the carbonation down my throat. The moment grew tense, so I stared at the table and avoided his look. It seemed like everyone but Kayden wanted me to go back to Zeke and sweep everything under the rug.

"I have a confession to make."

My eyes found his face.

"I've been making rounds at the bars every night to make sure you aren't there. Can I assume you aren't drinking like that anymore?"

The gesture was sweet. So sweet, it made me feel guilty for scaring him. "No. That was the one time."

"And only time?" he pressed, scolding me like a schoolteacher.

I nodded. "I just didn't want to feel the pain anymore, and I didn't know what else to do."

"There are other coping mechanisms."

"Like?" I'd been depressed for a while and hadn't found a solution.

"Just feel it. Feel it good. Let it kill you. Then once it passes, it's gone."

"Man, that's terrible advice."

He chuckled. "It's the quickest way to feeling better. Take the hit and move on. The longer you wait to feel the worst of it, the longer it's going to last. I held on to my anger for too long and refused to feel the pain. As a result, I lost more than I could afford." The sadness still filled his eyes, but he didn't seem as devastated as before.

Even though I felt terrible, I felt worse for him. "I'm sorry, Ryker."

"It's okay." He cleared his throat. "I'm not talking about me right now. I'm just reminding you that you aren't alone. We all feel like shit sometimes."

"Yeah…" And I knew Zeke felt the same way.

Ryker sipped his soda and didn't eat his last taco, losing his appetite over the discussion. "So, Safari hates me, huh?"

"I'm not sure what's gotten into him. I've never seen him act like that. He's pretty friendly."

"He must know that I hurt you."

"Safari is smart, but I don't think he's that smart."

"I can't think of any other explanation," he said. "He clearly remembers me. He's just very protective of you. Kinda sweet."

"He is sweet." I sighed when I thought about my dog, probably sitting on the kitchen floor staring at the door right this second. "He's gotten me through so much. He sticks to my side every second he's with me. I wouldn't know what to do without him."

"He's a good dog. Makes me want to get one."

"You should."

"I'll have to get rid of my apartment first. No place for a dog."

"Safari didn't seem to mind it." He loved lying on Ryker's comfortable couches, and he particularly loved the king bed in the bedroom.

"Maybe I'll buy a place next to the coast. I've always liked the ocean."

"If I had the money, I would." The water was freezing, but the view was beautiful. Whenever Safari stuck his paws in the ice-cold water, he immediately jumped out. He wasn't as tough as he pretended to be.

"You know, my dad had a sailboat. He left it to me."

"I never knew he sailed." He was a little heavy around the waist and didn't seem nearly as active as Ryker.

"He didn't go often. The boat was an impulse buy that he never used." Ryker chuckled to himself. "My mom was so ticked when he bought it. He named it after her, but she was still annoyed."

"That's sweet." It was the first time I'd smiled in four weeks.

"Anyway, you and Safari want to take it for a spin on Saturday?"

My smile immediately vanished. "Uh..."

He rested his elbows on the table and leaned forward. "Asking as a friend. And only a friend."

Ryker seemed genuine up until this point, encouraging me to get back together with Zeke twice now. It didn't seem like he had a hidden agenda. This wasn't some ploy to get me back.

"Bring your friends. I don't care. You can even bring Zeke if you want."

Just the mere idea gave me anxiety. The three of us would head out to sea, but only two would return. "I don't think it's a good idea to bring Zeke. I don't think it's a good idea to bring anyone, actually."

"Why not?"

I went with the truth because I didn't see the harm. "I know if I tell any of them that we're spending time together, they're going to assume the worst and all hell will break loose."

He chuckled. "Wow. They really hate me, huh?"

"I'm sorry." I didn't sugarcoat it. If Ryker ran into Rex, he needed to be prepared for a fist to the face.

"No, it's okay." His smile faded. "I deserve it. So, what are you going to do? Not take a ride with me because you're afraid they'll find out."

"I'm not afraid of them. I just don't want them to tell Zeke and give him the wrong idea of what's going on between you and me. He doesn't exactly see straight when it comes to you."

Ryker crossed his arms over his chest, looking thoughtful. "I don't mean for this to come out wrong, but what does it matter what he thinks? I mean, you're broken up, and you've said multiple you're never getting back together. It sounds like you're free to do whatever you want. After all, he did sleep with someone."

"Wow, you flipped pretty quickly."

That handsome smile stretched on his lips. "I still think you should give the guy another chance. But I don't think you should have to lie about spending time with me. We're just friends. And if you tell him that, he should believe you. You aren't the kind of person that would lie about something like that."

"Yeah..." But I knew Zeke would be jealous, and I didn't want to hurt him.

"Rex isn't living with you anymore, right?" Ryker asked. "How would he even know what you're doing?"

"He checks on me a lot."

Ryker nodded in understanding. "You still don't have to tell him. Our friendship can be a secret. I won't tell if you don't." He wiggled his eyebrows.

Finally, I laughed. It was the first time my chest relaxed enough to do something other than cry. The ridiculous look on his face made me chuckle enough that the weak muscles in my stomach tensed. "You're my secret friend?"

He shrugged. "I can be your secret friend."

Ryker made me feel better than I expected. For the last five minutes, I didn't think about Zeke at all. It felt so good to talk about sailing and Safari, two things that had nothing to do with Zeke. It was like a breath of fresh air.

But that elation faded away when I realized what I had to say. I didn't want to even talk about it, but it needed to be said. "I want you to know that you and I are never going to get back together either. I just don't want you to hope that's where this is going. Even if I do get over Zeke, it's not gonna happen." I hated myself for being so harsh, but I knew I would hate myself even more if I wasn't.

Ryker's features didn't change. He still had the smile on his face. "Rae, that's perfectly fine. Do I wish things had worked out between us? Absolutely. Do I still have feelings for you? I would be lying if I said I didn't. But I've accepted your decision. However, I don't want to lose you from my life permanently. I'd much rather settle for being your friend, for loving you from a distance, than not having you in my life at all."

My heart ached at his words. They made me feel both good and bad at the same time. "As long as that's the truth, I'm okay with that."

"Great. Now that the awkward and uncomfortable conversation is out of the way...you wanna go sailing?"

"I've never been."

"Never?" he asked, his eyebrow rising. "You've lived in Seattle your whole life and you've never been?"

"Can't say I have."

"Then we have to go. I'll bring some sandwiches, and we'll make a day out of it."

"I don't know anything about sailing so can you handle the ship on your own?"

He rolled his eyes like my words were cute. "Oh, believe me, I can handle the ship on my own."

Chapter Ten

Rex

I got Zeke out of the house and to a bar, somewhere with people. Music played on the speakers overhead and cute girls in heels chatted, eyeing him and hoping he would stop by their table and make a move.

Zeke seemed oblivious to it.

"So…what's new?" I tried not to talk about Rae anymore. It seemed to make things worse.

"I got the oil changed in my Jeep."

Wow, he was the most boring person on the planet now. "You didn't watch the Mariner game last night?"

"I haven't really watched much TV lately."

Then what did he do all day? "Kayden and I were watching America's Funniest Home Videos and — "

A drop-dead gorgeous blonde came to our table and made eyes at Zeke. "Hey, have I seen you somewhere before?"

Zeke looked up at her, not seeming to care about how high her dress was cut or how far her tits were popping out. "I'm a doctor. Maybe you've been to my office." He turned back to his beer and started to peel the label, completely uninterested.

Damn, he had it bad.

The woman didn't lose her confidence. "Oh, maybe that's it. I just got a check-up the other day."

Zeke nodded, even though he wasn't agreeing to anything.

"You're quiet," she noted. "But I like that sort of thing. Can I have your number? Maybe we can grab a pizza."

If a beautiful girl asked me to pizza, I'd have a hard time turning her down — if Kayden wasn't in my life. In fact, the idea of Kayden asking me to get pizza turned me on a bit. With her cute blonde hair and that tiny little mouth...she looked so cute when she ate. Okay, I zoned out there. Back to the conversation.

"I have a girlfriend," Zeke said. "But thanks anyway."

"Oh, my mistake," she said. "I should have known since you're so hot." She walked away and returned to her friends at their table.

"Um..." I rubbed my chin as I tried to find the right words. "You don't have a girlfriend, Zeke. You can go out with her if you want."

"I don't want to go out with her." He stared at his beer again, his elbows resting on the table.

"But you are single—"

"I don't want to be single, Rex." He closed his eyes and curled his hands into fists. "I don't want to be with anyone else. I'm gonna get Rae back, and I'm not touching anyone in the meantime."

This was going to be a tough few months. "I get it, man. But...you aren't getting back together." Since I was his best friend, I had to be real with him. I couldn't let him continue to live in this fantasy. It would just hurt him more in the long run.

"We are."

"Dude—"

155

"I don't know how it's going to happen. I don't know when. But one day, we're gonna end up together. Maybe you think it's hopeless, but I don't. I'm not giving up on her, alright? So stop reminding me that I'm free to fuck whoever I want." He grabbed his beer and slammed it down, almost shattering it. "Because I don't want to fuck anybody."

***

When I walked into my apartment, Kayden was already there. She wore one of my t-shirts and my boxers, looking better in my clothes than I did. She was sitting on the couch reading, her long hair trailing down her front. "How'd it go?"

I shrugged and sat beside her.

She frowned, seeing the sadness on my face. "I'm sorry."

"This whole thing sucks."

"I know." She crawled into my lap and straddled my hips. The second she was on top of me, my cock awakened despite my sorrow. She ran her hands up and down my chest, her nipples pressing through the fabric of my t-shirt.

"I told him not to tell her. But did he listen to me? Nooo."

"They'll get through this."

"I know Rae as well as you do. They're never getting back together."

"I meant, they'll get through it and be friends again." She scooted closer to me, her chest pressed against mine.

My hands moved to her thighs, and I gripped her. "Yeah...maybe."

"They will."

I looked into her green eyes, seeing the sexiest woman I'd ever laid eyes on. "Promise me something."

"Okay."

"Promise me you'll never leave me." I'd never told her I loved her. That was a feeling I'd never been acquainted with. But I knew I never wanted her to walk out on me. I knew I would never hurt her by even looking at another woman. Whatever this feeling was, it was substantial.

She cupped my face, and her eyes softened so much tears began to form. "I promise."

I kissed the corner of her mouth and pulled her into my chest, thankful I had what Zeke lost. I knew what kind of pain he was in because all I had to do was imagine Kayden walking away. She was an integral part of my life, experiencing everything by my side. Now she was a part of me. "You wanna move in with me?" The thought hadn't crossed my mind until that exact moment, but when it did, I knew it was right. She was always there anyway, sleeping in my bed and cooking for me. Every time she went to her apartment, I hated it.

"You're serious?" she whispered.

"Never been more serious in my life."

Tears formed in her eyes and she nearly wept. "Oh my god, I would love to live with you." She wrapped her arms around my neck and squeezed me tightly, her love encasing me. Her joy was infectious.

"Good. I wasn't going to let you say no."

She chuckled. "Would you have captured me and tied me up?"

"Yep. And come to think of it... I think I might do that right now anyway."

"Oh, yeah?" She leaned back and looked at me with a smile.

I squeezed her thighs before I stood, lifting her into the air. "Hell yeah."

***

Kayden was making my favorite breakfast, waffles and tater tots, so I walked across the hall to see if Rae wanted to join us. Like I was back in time, I felt like her guardian that constantly had to check on her. It was a Saturday morning, so I assumed she would spend the entire day in front of the TV.

"Hey, you want some—" I stopped when I saw her in dark jeans with a loose fitting beige sweater. The biggest shock was that her hair was down—and she wore makeup. Foundation was across her skin, and she had a streak of eyeliner under each eye. She pulled a small backpack over her shoulders like she was going somewhere. "Wow, you look nice."

Rae's eyebrows jumped so high they nearly flew off her face. "I've never heard you say that, not once."

159

"I guess I'm just in shock. You've looked like shit for so long—" I shut my mouth when I realized that was a low thing for me to say. "I'm just not used to it."

"Well, my scalp was starting to hurt from always having my hair pulled back. I decided to let it out a little bit." She grabbed Safari's leash. Her dog was in a blue sweater, something else I'd never seen before.

"Where are you going?" I blurted.

"Sailing."

"What?" I heard the word, but I wasn't sure if I'd just imagined it. "Sailing?"

"Yeah. You know, on a boat."

And she was sarcastic again? "You're in a much better mood..."

"Uh..." She shrugged. "I guess I feel better. I still couldn't sleep last night because I kept dreaming about Zeke. So I'm not sure how I feel." She adjusted Safari's sweater then rose to her full height again. "Did you need something?"

"Kayden is making breakfast, and I wanted to invite you over."

"Oh, I'm not hungry. But thanks anyway."

That part hadn't changed. "Who are you going sailing with?" I knew Jessie was far too pampered to sit on a cold boat all day long. And it definitely wasn't Zeke—that I could tell.

"Well, Safari is my first mate." She kneeled down and smothered her dog with kisses and rubs.

I rolled my eyes. "Well, I know the two of you can't commandeer a boat, so there must be someone—"

Someone knocked on the door.

Rae stood and didn't make eye contact with me. "It's open."

The door opened, and my goddamn worst nightmare walked inside.

Ryker.

That fucking piece of shit.

Asshole.

I turned on him, feeling my hands form fists so I could punch him in the face. The last time I saw him, he was sitting across from Rae in that restaurant, holding her hands and kissing them like some douchebag. He was the reason Zeke made the worst mistake of his life. On top of that, he was a shithead to Rae. "Fuck. No." I turned back to Rae, completely livid. "What the hell, Rae? This has got to be a joke. You and Zeke have only been broken up for a month, and you went back to him? He's a son-of-a-bitch."

Ryker put his hands in his pockets and sighed. "Guess I deserved that."

"Shut up, pretty boy." When I turned back to him, I squared my shoulders.

Ryker didn't seem to understand his life was in danger because he was still relaxed.

"Ryker, can you give us a second?" Rae asked.

"Sure." Ryker left the apartment and waited in the hall.

I immediately rounded on her. "You've got to be kidding me right now. This is wrong, just wrong. Zeke is at home crying over you and you're back in bed with Ryker? You're better than this, Rae. Don't treat Zeke like this. And don't trust Ryker."

"First of all, Zeke slept with someone within hours of our supposed breakup. So don't give me that crap."

Technically, that was true. But it was a different situation. "He was devastated, alright? Cut the guy some slack."

"Second of all, Ryker and I are just friends —"

"That fuck."

"No, we aren't." She looked me dead in the eye. "Nothing is gonna happen with Ryker. I'm still heartbroken over Zeke. Nothing has changed. But Ryker makes me feel better. We talk about other things, so I'm not sitting around moping over Zeke all day long. And he doesn't remind me of him like the rest of you."

"Rae, I already see where this is going. You say you're just friends —"

"We are just friends. I told him nothing will ever happen between us—and not just because of Zeke. I'm not gonna start sleeping with him again. I can't picture myself with anyone but Zeke—even now. So seriously, chill out."

"But you know—"

"If Zeke and I can go back to being friends, I don't see why I can't do the same thing with Ryker."

"Because he's a fucking asshole. Did you forget what he did?"

"No," she said calmly. "But I've forgiven him. You can throw a hissy fit all you want, but it's not gonna change anything. So please butt out and stop telling me what to do. I'm a big girl who can make her own decisions."

I was still uneasy about this whole thing. "How do you think Zeke is gonna feel when he hears about this?"

"I said nothing is gonna happen with Ryker. He can either believe me or not believe me. The ball is in his court." She grabbed Safari and headed to the door. "Or you can just not tell him, Rex."

Chapter Eleven

Rae

With the harbor far in the distance, the wind carried us over the waves as we headed out to sea. Ryker wore a long-sleeved white t-shirt with a black jacket. He commanded the ship like it was routine, tying the ropes and moving the sails so we could navigate over the water.

Safari kept running back and forth from one side to the other, practically jumping because he was so excited by what he was looking at. He stared into the water like he might see something interesting. Then he ran to the other side of the bow and looked into the water again, completely adorable in his little sweater.

Ryker anchored the boat in the middle of the sea, providing a great view of the wide open ocean and the land behind us. Then he left the steering wheel and took a seat with me at the front of the fifteen-foot sailboat. "Safari is a natural-born sailor."

Safari was still running around, exploring the water.

"If only he had a captain's hat, he would look complete," I said as I watched my dog move around.

Ryker grabbed the ice chest and set it between us, a large barrier preventing us from touching. "He hasn't growled at me in a few hours. It's a new record."

"I think he's just found something else to do. When we get back to land, he'll be back to his old self."

Ryker chuckled then opened the lid. "Good to know." He pulled out two beers and a couple sandwiches packed in zippered bags. "I hope turkey is okay."

"I'm starving. Couldn't care less what's on it." I grabbed a sandwich from him and opened the wrapping. "Thank you."

"No problem. I also packed a snack for Safari."

I opened my bag of chips and saw Safari sitting at the very tip of the boat, looking out to sea in fascination. "He can eat later." I felt the boat rock gently over the waves as we looked at the scenery before us. It was a sunny day, not a cloud in the sky, but the air on top of the water was freezing. I took a bite of my sandwich. "This is good."

"Thanks. I made it."

"Wow. Maybe you should leave COLLECT and apply to Subway."

He chuckled. "I could be the sandwich maker of the month."

"They have the best cookies too. So, that's always a perk."

He dug into the ice chest and pulled out another bag. "I know you like to have something sweet after every meal."

I eyed the chocolate chip cookies sitting in the plastic bag. "You would be an excellent soccer mom, you know that?"

"Why, thank you." He smiled before he took a bite of his sandwich, looking classically handsome. "That was always my second choice if COLLECT didn't work out."

I didn't realize how hungry I was until the food was placed in front of me. I ate half of it within a minute, truly feeling an appetite for the first time in five weeks. Something about the sun and fresh air made me feel less broken. There wasn't an elephant standing on my chest anymore. But when I went to bed that night, alone, I knew that sensation would return.

"So…Rex seemed pretty upset."

"Just ignore him. That's what I do."

"No, you don't," Ryker said before he took another bite. "He's just looking out for you. Can't really be angry with him for it."

"Yeah, but sometimes he needs to butt out. I know he never will, so I just need to give up on that dream."

Ryker finished his sandwich before I did, which had always been the case when we were dating. "How are things between him and Kayden?"

"Good. He finally admits he has a girlfriend. That's the most progress I've ever seen him make."

"Good for him." Ryker reached into his pocket and pulled out his aviator sunglasses then placed them on the bridge of his nose. He looked like a guy in a cologne ad, sitting on a sailboat on the Pacific. "Kayden is a good fit."

"Yeah, she puts up with his craziness because she loves him... Just not sure why she loves him sometimes."

"Rex is a good guy. His heart is always in the right place."

I talked shit about my brother a lot, but I loved him with my whole heart. When someone said anything mean about him, I turned into a psycho sister. And when someone said something sweet about him, it meant a lot to me. "Yeah...it is."

Ryker rested his arms on his thighs and looked across the water. "Have you seen Zeke lately?"

I knew Zeke was bound to come up in conversation even though I didn't like talking about him. "It's been over a week now."

Ryker turned to me, watching me hold the sandwich without eating it. "I know you don't like to talk about him, but I think it'll help in the long run if you do."

169

"Nothing will help me in the long run." I rolled up the rest of my sandwich in a paper towel and returned it to the plastic bag. "I went to his place to pick up my stuff, but things got out of hand. He kissed me and the clothes fell off...but I stopped it. I knew I would regret it later if I went through with it."

"Regret it how?" He asked the question like the topic didn't make him uncomfortable.

"Just make it harder to move on. I would have had to completely start over."

He shook his head. "Wow. You have some serious strength."

"You have no idea..."

He gave me a look of pity, even though his eyes couldn't be seen.

"I finally got the hell out of there. At the door, I reminded him that we'd promised each other we would always be friends and we needed to keep our promise. He agreed."

"How do you think that's gonna go?"

I sighed because it seemed like an impossible task that couldn't be done. "It's gonna be really hard. It'll take me a long time to truly look at him as just a friend. Eventually, he's gonna start dating again, and I don't know how I'm gonna handle that."

"You could just take him back…"

I ignored the advice, tired of hearing it from anyone. "But I know we'll get through it. I can lose him as a boyfriend, but I could never lose him as a friend. He's too important to me."

Ryker fell silent, like he didn't know what else to say.

"God, breakups suck." I'd been through two massive breakups in a single year, and I couldn't take it anymore. I wondered if it would be better to end up as an old lady with a bunch of cats. Much less heartbreak that way.

"Yeah, they do…but you'll get through it, Rae. You're the strongest chick I know."

"Strength has nothing to do with it. You can't fight an enemy you can't see…" Heartbreak was an emotion that couldn't be physically touched. It just existed in your chest, weighing you down.

"I know I really hurt you, but you got through that, Rae. You can get through this."

I knew I'd hurt Ryker too, so this was a mutual understanding. "How's your mom?"

"She's...alright." He shrugged and stared out at the water. "My brother spends a lot of time with her. I'm around when I can be. It'll take her a long time to get over my father's death. Losing a spouse... I can't even imagine."

"Yeah..."

"But she's taking it one day at a time." He rubbed his left knuckle like he was thinking of an old scar. "I started seeing a therapist."

I tried to hide my surprise so my reaction wouldn't make him uncomfortable. "Oh...that's great."

"I was really against the idea, but my mom kinda gave me a push. It's been helpful."

"Good."

"We talk about my father most of the time. I'm trying to deal with the guilt and the regret."

"It's always good to talk to someone."

"Yeah. You know me, I'm pretty damn stubborn. I told my mom I didn't need mental help. But then I remembered the last time I refused to accept help...and I made a mistake I wish I could take back."

I knew he was talking about me.

"Anyway, it's been helpful. Maybe you should consider it."

"Maybe..." I didn't really want to sit around and talk about Zeke. I already thought about him every hour of every day.

"Or you could always talk to me."

"There isn't much to say. I miss him like crazy, and I'm so angry with him for what he's done to us... But that's it."

He nodded. "Moving on from someone just takes times. You can't speed up the process, unfortunately."

I smiled even though the gesture wasn't exactly appropriate. "When did you get so wise?"

He chuckled. "Well, there's this woman. She walked into my life, refused to take bullshit, and made an honest man out of me. She changed my whole life, and now I can't go back to the way I used to be...at least I don't want to."

My eyes softened, and I looked at the ocean, wanting to see something besides his charming face. "Thanks for being a friend to me during this time. I feel better when I'm with you."

"What a coincidence," he whispered. "I feel better when I'm with you too." He turned to me, a slight smile on his lips. His eyes couldn't be seen through the glasses, but I knew they had softened once they looked at me. His chin was smooth because he had shaved that morning, and he looked like the most harmless man on the planet. His arrogance wasn't as apparent as it used to be. A strong sense of humility had overcome him.

Sometimes, I felt like I wasn't talking to Ryker at all.

But someone else entirely.

Chapter Twelve

Rex

I didn't know what to do.

Should I tell Zeke?

Should I not tell him?

If I did tell him, he would be devastated. But if I didn't and he found out some other way, he would be even worse off. What if he bumped into them in the park or at the bar?

Yeah, I had to tell him.

I hated Ryker so much. Even if they were just friends, I didn't want him anywhere near my sister. He broke her heart like it was worthless. He walked out with some stupid tramp only a week after they broke up.

I'd never forget it.

Zeke and I went out for hot wings after we both got off work. He was still in his dark blue scrubs, but he looked like he'd just rolled out of bed. Exhaustion crept behind his eyes because he wasn't sleeping anymore.

I'd never pitied him so much. "How was work?"

"It was fine." He drank his beer and watched the TV in the corner. "Same old bullshit."

He never spoke about his job that way. He was just in a bad place and projecting his anger onto everything. "How's Rae?"

"She's the same…"

"Has she been eating?" He always asked about her well-being, looking after her through me.

"Yeah. She's been good. Still going to work and stuff…"

"Good," he said with a sigh. "I'm glad she's staying active."

"She put a ridiculous sweater on Safari the other day. Safari isn't the kind of dog meant to wear a sweater."

Zeke chuckled, just a little bit. "Wish I could have seen that."

"I'm sure Safari has ripped it to shreds by now."

"Yeah...I miss him." He stared down into his basket of wings and fries. "I miss Rae like crazy, but I really miss him too. I still sleep with my legs pulled up because I'm used to him being at the foot of the bed. His bowl is still in the kitchen, full of stale dog food."

The confession made me feel worse. "I'm sure Rae would let you borrow him..."

"No. Those two are inseparable."

I dunked a fry into the ketchup and shoved it into my mouth. I wasn't hungry anymore, but I was eating so I had something to do. The weight of my responsibility sat on my shoulders. Zeke needed to know about Ryker, but I didn't want to be the messenger. "Zeke...there's something I gotta tell you. And you aren't gonna like it."

Zeke looked at me, his blue eyes narrowing in defense. "Fuck... Please don't tell me Rae is seeing someone. I just can't handle that right now. I can't, okay? So...anything but that I can handle."

I cringed because he'd hit the nail right on the head.

He saw the painful truth written all over my face. "Fuck." He ran his fingers through his hair, the anger stretching across his face.

"I went to her place on Saturday, and she told me she was going sailing with—"

"Please don't say Ryker."

I sighed in response.

"Fuck. Fuck. Fuck." He dragged his hands down his face and released a growl that could have come from a bear. "God fucking dammit. I should kill him. I should cut him into pieces and drop his limbs in the harbor."

Mental note, don't piss off Zeke.

"I told her she shouldn't go down this road again and—"

"What did she say?"

I left out the jab she made about Zeke sleeping with someone immediately after they broke up. "She said they're just friends, and they're never getting back together. She said she made that clear to him. And she doesn't see why they can't be friends…since you and her are friends too."

Zeke's hostility waned after I finished speaking. "She said they're just friends?"

I nodded.

"And they're never getting back together?"

I nodded again. "I'm just afraid that's how it'll start. It'll lead to other things down the road…"

Zeke stared across the restaurant, looking at the wall with a stoic expression. He didn't even blink because he was so absorbed in his thoughts.

I patiently waited for him to say something else, to snap and flip the table over.

"If she says they're just friends, then they're just friends."

My eyebrow rose because I couldn't hide my surprise.

"I didn't trust her when I should have. But I trust her now. If she says they're only friends, I believe her."

This calm acceptance was the last reaction I expected. I knew Rae was being honest when she said she and Ryker were only friends. But it would only be a matter of time before Ryker left the friend zone and ventured back into the boyfriend zone. But I wasn't going to tell Zeke that and ruin this Zen moment he was experiencing.

"Eventually, Ryker might try to make something happen," Zeke said, mainly to himself. "But for now, I'm okay. I have time to get Rae back. I have time to make this work."

I didn't disagree with him, knowing this sense of hope was all he had left to hold on to. And as a friend, I would never take that away from him.

At least not right now.

Chapter Thirteen

Rae

Rex had formed a new habit of walking into my apartment without knocking. "Hey, what's up?"

"I don't just walk into your place," I reminded him.

He pointed to the door. "Does your door not lock?" If he was speaking to me like a smartass, then he must have known I was feeling a little better.

"Does your brain not work?" I countered.

He rolled his eyes and ignored my final jab. "We're going out tonight—all of us. I hope you join us."

I knew what the word *all* meant. The last time I saw Zeke was two weeks ago. We'd broken up for six weeks, and it felt like an eternity. I wasn't sure how I could be around him and not run my hands all over his body. I wasn't sure how I could watch other women look at him without being jealous.

"Rae?" He narrowed his eyes on my face when I didn't say anything.

I promised we would remain friends, and I need to make that happen. Of course, I wanted to see Zeke again. I just didn't want to ache the entire time. "Yeah, I'll be there."

"Good. That was the only answer I was going to accept." He helped himself to a beer from my fridge and sat with me at the table. "So...how was sailing?" He could barely keep the rage out of his tone.

"Good. Saw a pod of orcas swim by."

He drank his beer, still annoyed. "That's not that cool..."

"And saw some seals too. Safari went crazy over that. I had to stop him from jumping in the water."

"Oh..." He rested his elbows on the table and didn't look at me.

"And nothing happened, like I said. Ryker and I had lunch on the boat and did some talking. That was about it."

"I still don't like this, Rae. Ryker was an ass to you."

"I know he was. But I've forgiven him."

"But you won't forgive Zeke?" Rex snapped.

"I have forgiven Zeke. I just can't get back together with him. You know that."

"But you have no problem hanging out with that piece of shit?"

"As friends, no. I'm not getting back together with Ryker either. There's no law that says I can't be with friends him."

"Wish there was..." Rex took another drink of his beer, still in a sour mood.

"Rex, you need to let it go."

"Fuck no. If Kayden pulled that shit, would you *let it go*?"

I couldn't deny that I would probably be just as protective. "Nothing you say is gonna change what's happening, so I suggest you just accept it."

"Well, I don't want to see his asshole face."

"Then stop barging into my apartment and sticking your nose where it doesn't belong. We talked about this already, Rex."

"No." He held up his finger like he was about to make a point. "I said I would stay out of your dating life. You aren't dating Ryker, so I'm technically not doing anything wrong. So, ha!" He lowered his hand, victory in his eyes.

I rolled my eyes. This conversation was so stupid, it was actually painful. "Where are we going tonight?"

"They just opened that new sports bar downtown. Tobias has nothing but good things to say about it."

"Cool. I think the Wizards are playing the Thunder tonight. Should be a good game."

"You wanna get a bet going?" he asked.

"If you're gonna bet against the Wizards."

"You know they suck, Rae."

"Hey, I'm loyal. I'm never betting against them."

He extended his hand. "Hundred bucks?"

I took his hand without blinking an eye. "Hundred bucks, it is."

He grinned. "Hell yeah. I'm gonna take Kayden out somewhere nice with that money. And I'm gonna get some good loving afterward."

I swallowed the bile that rose up my throat. "Good to know."

***

I was sitting on the couch when Kayden and Jessie walked inside without knocking, just the way Rex did.

"The Pink Ladies are here." Jessie held a black dress on a hanger, silver heels in her other hand.

Kayden had a thick bag over her shoulder, probably full of hair and makeup supplies. "And we're here to make you look good."

As usual, I was sitting on my butt doing nothing. I looked like hell. "Please come in…"

"You know that door is always open for us." Jessie turned the hanger and showed off the dress. "What do you think?"

"It's tight and kinda slutty." I set my book down, Safari's chin resting on my thigh.

"Exactly," Kayden said. "Which is perfect for you."

"Excuse me?" I asked. "When have I ever been slutty?"

"You aren't," Jessie said. "Which is why you need to be a little slutty. We're ready to get you back in the game."

I stood up and put my hands on my hips. "I'm all about getting a makeover. I look like hell, and we all know it. But I'm not getting back into any game, alright? I'm not dating anyone for a long time, so don't even think about pushing me in that direction."

"Alright, we feel ya." Jessie extended her wrist and showed off the pumps. "But it's time for you to be beautiful again. Show the world that you still got it."

I smiled, appreciating the gesture. "Well...thanks."

"Now get your ass up," Kayden said. "We've got a lot to do. When was the last time you shaved?"

I fell silent because I couldn't even remember.

Jessie nearly gasped. "We really need to get to work."

***

When I looked in the mirror, I hardly recognized myself. With dark eyeshadow and some magical handiwork from Jessie, I looked like I was about to hit the runway. The dress was a size smaller than what I normally wore because I'd lost a significant amount of weight in the past six weeks. The heels were four inches tall, and I wasn't used to walking in heels anymore. My body had been shaved, and perfume had been lathered onto my skin. I looked like a Barbie doll — with brown hair.

"You look so good." Jessie admired her handiwork proudly. "This will really get you back on your feet."

"You look hot as hell, Rae," Jessie said. "Zeke is gonna drool all over you."

I didn't want him to drool all over me. "You don't think it's a little much?"

"Not at all," Jessie said. "You used to dress like this all the time. Looks like you forgot."

I was used to wearing the same jeans and sweater everywhere I went, not caring about my appearance at all. "Honestly, you guys don't think I look like I'm trying too hard?" They were both dressed in heels and dresses, but they looked natural.

"Would we ever steer you wrong?" Jessie asked.

"Never," Kayden said. "So let's go out and have a good time."

***

There was already a crowd at the bar when we walked inside. The popularity of the new place had caught on, and the enormous TV that took up the entire back wall played the basketball game.

I immediately spotted Zeke with Rex at the bar, in his dark jeans that hung low on his hips and a green t-shirt that hugged his nice arms. His chin was cleanly shaven, and his hair was a little shorter like he'd recently had it cut. "Ugh..."

"What?" Jessie asked. "You knew he was going to be here."

"But he looks so hot." I tried to get a grip on myself and keep my legs closed.

"Zeke always looks hot," Kayden said. "Just ignore it."

"How am I supposed to accomplish that?" I asked.

"He's gonna think you look hot too, so don't worry." Jessie gave me a gentle push forward, and we walked up to the counter.

My heart was beating a million miles an hour.

I could hardly breathe.

I missed him.

Missed him like crazy.

My hands were shaking.

Before I knew it, we'd arrived. Rex turned to me first, unable to hide his surprise. "Wow, you look like a girl," he blurted. "I'm not used to this."

"Yeah, thanks," I said sarcastically. I turned to Zeke, seeing him stare at me with the same desperation that I felt in my entire body. I wanted to wrap my arms around him and stay that way forever.

Everyone fell quiet as we silently stared at each other.

Zeke looked sexy and strong, and I couldn't help but think of our nights sleeping together. I missed the feel of his wide chest when I was settled on top of him, warm throughout the night. I missed his kisses. I missed the way he felt inside me. I missed everything.

Zeke was clearly thinking the same thing, the declaration in his eyes. "What can I get you ladies?" he asked all of us, but only looking at me.

I'd backed off the drinking since that horrific night Ryker took me home. "I'll just have a water."

Zeke didn't question me about it. "Jess? A cosmo?"

"Yes, please," she said. "Make it a double."

"Coming right up." Zeke turned around and spoke to the bartender.

Rex gave me a sad look, like he knew how difficult this was for me.

"Let's go snag a table." Kayden hooked her arm through mine, and we found a booth with a great view of the TV. We scooted inside, and to my misfortune, Zeke happened to sit right across from me when he sat down.

"You're just going to have water?" Jessie asked incredulously.

"For now." I couldn't lay off the alcohol forever.

"I'm getting you a gin and tonic when you're done with that," Jessie said. "Loosen you up."

"Leave her be." Rex kept his eyes on the TV when he spoke, clearly speaking to Jessie without actually looking at her. Rex never told Jessie what to do, but he'd made an exception this one time.

Jessie didn't argue with him.

"So, where's Tobias?" I tried not to look at Zeke across from me, feeling his scorching stare on my face.

"He'll be here after the game," Jessie explained. "He's working right now. You know, sports agent."

"He has the coolest job ever," Rex said. "Seriously."

Zeke drank his beer and looked at the TV in his line of sight, finally pulling his gaze away from my face.

Kayden did a slight drumroll on the table. "So, Rex and I have some great news…"

———

191

"Oh my god." Jessie covered her mouth. "You're pregnant."

"What?" Rex almost knocked his beer over. "Pregnant? Wait...no." He turned to Kayden. "No, right? God, please tell me no."

Kayden rolled her eyes. "No, I'm not pregnant. But Rex and I are moving in together."

"Really?" It was the best news I'd heard in six weeks. I wasn't sure where things were going for the two of them, and I was glad Rex was taking their relationship to a more serious level. He was clueless when it came to women, and I was afraid he was going to do something stupid to drive Kayden away. "That makes me so happy..."

"Congrats, man." Zeke clanked his beer against Rex's, a genuine smile on his face. "That's great."

"Thanks," Rex said. "It's like having a really hot maid that you can sleep with."

Kayden shot him a glare.

"But more romantic than that," Rex said quickly.

"Whose apartment are you gonna stay at?" Jessie asked.

"Mine," Rex said. "You know, since Rae is—" He fell silent then masked the awkwardness by drinking his beer.

I stared into my glass of water and counted the ice cubes. Going back to being friends with Zeke was much harder than I thought it was going to be. Would I always want him like this? Would I always need him like this?

***

Jessie went outside to meet Tobias, Kayden went to the bathroom, and Rex went to the bar to get another beer—all at the same time, which resulted in Zeke and I being alone together at the table.

Not awkward at all.

He stared into his beer before he looked at me, his eyes locking to mine. "You look really beautiful tonight, Rae."

This was what I was afraid of. Having this kind of conversation. "Thanks. Jessie and Kayden wanted to give me a makeover. I didn't argue with them because, you know, they always win."

When he chuckled, it was forced. "I'm just glad to see that you look better. Seem a little happier."

"I guess a little…but not by much. What about you?"

Zeke looked down into his glass and never answered my question. "Rex told me you've been spending time with Ryker." There wasn't an edge to his tone. He didn't even seem mad about it.

I guess I should have known Rex would tell him. "It's not what you think—"

"He said you guys were just friends. If you say there's nothing going on, I believe you." He sat straight and looked at me again, his blue eyes no longer vibrant like they used to be. There was a permanent dullness to them, making them almost gray.

That was the last thing I expected him to say.

"So, there's nothing going on, right?" He heard what Rex said, but he wanted to hear me say it to his face.

"Of course not, Zeke."

Relief stretched across his face even though he did his best to hide it.

"I'm not in that place. And I won't be in that place for a very long time."

He nodded in understanding. "You guys went sailing or something?"

"Yeah. His father left him his boat. We went out for the day. Safari came along even though he hates Ryker."

"He hates Ryker?" Zeke asked.

"Anytime they're in the same room together, Safari growls at him."

Zeke wore a true smile. "That's one loyal dog."

"I can tell he misses you..." Sometimes he'd whine at the door, not because he wants to go outside, but because he wants to go to Zeke's place. Safari was like a child we had together, but I got full custody in the end.

"I was just telling Rex how much I miss him."

"You can always come by and see him. Take him for a walk or something..."

"Yeah, I might do that if it's okay with you."

"Of course." I would never be annoyed about someone wanting to spend time with Safari. He loved the attention.

He drank his beer and swallowed, his Adam's apple moving. His hard jaw and handsome features were irresistible at the moment. Those lips looked kissable, and his eyes were so easy to fall into. Sometimes, I preferred it when he had scruff on his face, and other times, I preferred the clean look, like what he had now.

"Can I say something?" he whispered. "I'm only gonna say it once, and you don't need to say anything. But I want to say it anyway."

"Okay..." I knew where this was going, but I guess I shouldn't have been surprised. I was just sitting there thinking about how much I missed him.

"I miss you...like crazy." He sighed as he looked at me, his eyes full of sorrow.

It was nice to hear because I felt the exact same way. "I miss you too."

He moved his hands forward across the table but stopped himself when he realized it wasn't a good idea. He pulled them back and hid them in his lap, no longer tempted to grab me.

Rex returned with another beer. "Where did the other two go?"

I forced myself to stop staring at Zeke and answer my brother's question. "Kayden is in the bathroom. Jessie went outside to meet Tobias."

"Oh, okay." Oblivious to what he'd just interrupted, Rex drank his beer and watched the TV. "Oh, come on. You're really gonna call a technical on that? Zeke, did you see that shit?"

Zeke reluctantly pulled his gaze away from my face. "Yeah...bullshit."

***

"Thanks for the ride home, man." Rex carried Kayden in his arms, his sweatshirt covering her legs so no one could see up her dress. He fished his keys out of his pocket with one hand and got the door unlocked.

"No problem." Zeke opened the door so Rex could get inside easier.

Rex carried Kayden into the bedroom then returned. "You wanna hit the course tomorrow? Some guy at work gave me two passes to the country club."

"Cool," Zeke said. "Yeah, I'll be there."

"Alright." Rex eyed both of us, suddenly realizing we would be alone together once he shut the door. "Uh…good night." The door closed and his footsteps disappeared as he walked down the hallway and joined Kayden in the bedroom.

Now, we were alone in the hallway, and I suddenly felt vulnerable. I wanted to invite him to join me in bed just so I could get some sleep. The last time I slept the entire night without having a nightmare was when Ryker stayed with me. If Zeke were next to me, all I'd think about were unicorns and Fruity Pebbles.

Zeke placed his hands in his pockets and slowly walked to my door. "Need help getting inside?"

I had two sips of wine and nothing else but water. I was the soberest person of the bunch. "No, I got it."

"Alright." He continued to stand in front of me even though there was no reason to stay. He eyed my door before he turned his gaze on me again, his look fiery with longing. He didn't act on it, but his need for affection was palpable.

I was sure he could feel the same thing from me.

"I've been going through a really hard time," he whispered. "I can't believe it's been six weeks."

"I know..."

"Feels like a lifetime."

"It does."

He bowed his head and looked at the ground. "I haven't been sleeping much. Thinking about canceling my gym membership because I never use it. The house feels like a prison now, haunted by our memories." He didn't seem to be talking to me as a lover, but as a friend. Whenever he had a problem, he always opened up to me, and I did the same for him.

"I haven't been sleeping either. Safari helps but...not enough."

"And I know you haven't been eating as much as you should." He raised his head and eyed my waistline.

Guilty, I just shrugged.

"Would it be too much to ask to hold you?" He straightened and pulled his hands out of his pockets, wanting to make a move before I even agreed to it.

I knew I should say no, but I was so weak. I missed him like crazy and still felt as heartbroken as the day I walked out of his house. These past six weeks had been the worst of my life.

"I won't try anything else," he whispered. "I promise."

When he gave an offer I couldn't refuse, I took it. "Okay…"

He moved into my body, his hands circling my petite waistline. Then he pulled me into his chest, nestling me just the way he used. His face moved into the crook of my neck and he breathed a sigh of relief once we were connected.

It felt so good.

My hands moved around his neck, and I closed my eyes, letting his scent wash over me and elicit beautiful memories that I would never forget. I memorized the way his hands felt on my back, strong and warm. Even though it was cold and my shoes were painful on my feet, I wanted to stay like that forever.

I never wanted to let go.

His lips were against my neck, but he didn't kiss me, like he'd promised. His hands stayed in appropriate zones, and he didn't beg me to take him back. He seemed to finally accept the fact we weren't getting back together.

Somehow, that made me feel worse.

We were really over.

After ten minutes, he pulled away, clearly forcing himself to break apart from me. "Well...I guess this is good night—"

"You want to stay over?" I blurted out the question without thinking, my emotions doing all the talking.

Zeke couldn't hide his surprise—or his joy.

"Just to sleep... I haven't slept well in so long. I just thought we could both, you know. I don't know—"

"I'd love to."

This was probably a stupid idea, but I couldn't stop myself. I pulled out my keys and got the door unlocked.

Safari immediately greeted us in the entryway, and when he saw Zeke, he climbed up his body and whined in joy.

"Hey, boy." Zeke kneeled down and scratched him behind the ears, just the way he liked. "I missed you too."

Safari whined again and shook his tail happily.

Zeke patted him on the butt before he rose to his full height, a smile on his lips as he looked down at Safari.

I walked into my bedroom, the hole that I'd been sleeping in every night. I grabbed some clothes to change into without turning on the light and walked into the bathroom where I could undress in private. He'd seen me naked hundreds of times, but everything was different now.

When I was ready for bed, I walked back into my room. Zeke was under the covers, in his t-shirt and boxers. He looked at home in my bed, like he'd never left. Safari sat at the end, happy that things seemed to be back to normal.

I got under the sheets and moved to his side of the bed, greeted by his natural heat. My arm circled his waist, and he turned his body into me, holding me close with his lips resting against my forehead.

I knew the joy was fleeting, but I was so happy I wanted to cry.

I closed my eyes and felt the tears form under my eyelids.

Zeke ran his hand over my thigh then grabbed my knee before he hiked it over his waist, bringing us closer together. He wasn't hard like I expected him to be. He seemed content to just be with me, sharing my bed. "I love you, Rae."

Two tears came loose. "I love you too."

He pressed his lips to each one and absorbed them, the salty moisture sticking to his mouth. One hand moved into my hair, and he positioned himself against me again, his lips returning to my forehead.

After a few moments of silence, I began to drift. When I fell into a deep sleep, the nightmares didn't come for me. I didn't think about anything at all, actually. And that was the greatest gift Zeke could have given to me.

***

When I woke up the next morning, I actually felt good. I wasn't exhausted from waking up five times during the night like usual. Like I did when Zeke and I were together, I woke up happy and ready to turn a new leaf.

Zeke was already awake. His eyes were open, and he was watching me sleep before I opened my eyes. "Morning."

"Morning." We were in the exact same position as we were before we fell asleep. My leg was wrapped around his hip, and my arm was still locked around his neck. This time, I did feel his morning wood.

And I really missed that too.

The past six weeks had left me in a serious dry spell, but I'd been too depressed to feel aroused. Now that Zeke was in my bed, I wouldn't mind feeling him inside me, getting me off. But I knew that was a step neither one of us should take.

"I haven't slept that well since the day you left." The hair had already regrown along his chin, a light scruff of brown.

"Neither have I." That wasn't completely true, but if I told him Ryker slept over, it would've sounded far worse than it really was.

I wanted to stay like that as long as possible, but my bladder was about to explode. "I'm sorry, but I need to pee."

He smiled, his usual response when I did something cute. "Alright. I'll make some coffee." He got out of bed and pulled on his jeans, keeping his back to me so I wouldn't see him try to zip up his pants over his hard-on.

After I went to the bathroom and did my business, I walked into the kitchen. The TV was on the sports channel, the air smelled like coffee, and Zeke stood at the counter as he sipped his mug. When he had that sleepy look in his eyes, he looked so perfectly sexy. It was effortless, which just made him even cuter.

I poured myself a cup, blowing over the surface so it wouldn't be too hot when I drank it.

Zeke came to my side, his mug still in his hand. "Wizards lost last night."

"Damn. I owe Rex a hundred bucks."

He chuckled. "You remained loyal to your team. That's more important than losing a hundred bucks."

My clutch was on the counter where I left it, my phone right beside it. I left it there last night because there was no one important I needed to stay connected to. My phone vibrated with a text message even though it was only ten in the morning on a Sunday.

It was from Ryker. *This made me think of you.* It was a picture of a German shepherd in a ridiculous sweater, yellow with blue strips.

Zeke clearly saw the message because he looked down once it vibrated. Like he was trying to prove something to me, he turned around and faced the TV again, knowing it was from Ryker but refusing to read it.

I turned my phone off and ignored the message, not wanting to make Zeke jealous when he was already struggling. "When we went sailing, I had Safari wear this sweater—"

"You don't have to explain anything, Rae. If you're just friends, you're just friends. I trust you." There was no anger or bitterness, just the calm Zeke I woke up to that morning. He was trying to prove to me that he wouldn't repeat past mistakes.

But it was too late for that.

The door opened, and Rex barged inside like any other day. "Hey, do you have any—" He stopped when he saw Zeke standing at the counter drinking coffee in the clothes he wore yesterday. Rex's eyes widened, and a ridiculous smile stretched across his lips as he jumped to inaccurate conclusions. "Uh... I was just... I gotta go." He tiptoed backward to the door. When he shut it behind him, he was as quiet as possible even though we were staring at him.

Zeke pretended nothing happened. "You wanna take Safari for a walk and get some breakfast?"

I'd already crossed a line when I asked him to stay over, and it seemed like I was sinking further into the hole I'd made for myself. So I couldn't say no. Waking up with him felt so nice. I was on a high I didn't want to lose—not yet. "Sure."

***

Like nothing had happened six weeks ago, we took Safari on a walk around the park, Zeke holding his leash. Safari was happier than usual, excited that the three of us were together again. Like a child that wanted his divorced parents back together, he wanted to be the same family we used to be.

"I need to stop by the ATM and get some cash."

"To give to Rex?" he asked, holding the leash and walking beside me.

"Unfortunately."

"Don't give him a dime."

"A bet is a bet. I honor my debts."

"You let that terror live with you for almost a year," he reminded me. "Rent free, and he ate everything in the kitchen. Not to mention, he trashed your apartment. So, technically, he's the one who should be paying you."

Anyone would agree with that argument. "He doesn't owe me anything. He's been paying me back over the last six weeks. He makes me dinner every single day and checks on me." In fact, he'd been really sweet despite the fact he was stuck in the middle of this breakup.

Zeke nodded in understanding. "I guess that's true."

"So, I'll give him the hundred bucks. I'll get it back after the next game."

"I admire you for always betting on the Wizards. But maybe you should bet less money next time."

"Yeah… I'm figuring that out." After we took Safari for a walk, we went to a diner that had patio seating for Safari. We sat down and ordered our food, sitting across from each other like a married couple taking their dog for a walk.

How I wished that were the case.

Zeke ordered an omelet with a side of biscuits and gravy, and I ordered a short stack with powdered sugar and cinnamon. The second the food was placed in front of me, I went to town. I devoured everything, finally having a real appetite.

The corner of his mouth rose in a smile before he sipped his coffee.

"What?"

"Nothing." He returned his gaze to his food and kept eating. "Can I slip something for Safari under the table?"

"Why are you asking me? You just do it anyway when I'm not looking." When Zeke made dinner in the kitchen, he always dropped scraps on purpose. He was definitely the fun dad, and I was the hardass mom.

He smiled in guilt then dropped a few chunks. Safari opened his massive jaws and got everything inside in a single bite. Then Zeke patted him under the table, scratching him behind the ears. "I thought he was looking a little thinner..."

"Yes. He's lost some weight since he's only been eating dog food." I gave him a pointed stare, full of accusation.

Zeke didn't deny it. "I guess I'm the good cop."

"Bad cop, in my opinion. I don't want Safari to be fat."

"He was never fat, just...muscular." He peeked down over the table. "Right, man?"

I sipped my coffee and felt the pain leave my chest. It was such a relaxing day, one where I didn't spend my afternoon crying. Zeke and I were together again, and I felt like I'd been transported back to the past, living in a beautiful memory.

"Like your food?" he asked.

"Yeah. Why?"

"Well, there's nothing left." He looked at my completely empty plate. "Instead of making fun of Safari, maybe you should look at yourself."

"Did you just call me fat?" I asked incredulously.

He smiled. "I guess so. But it's a sexy kind of fat. You know, curves in all the right places."

I felt warmth shoot through my body. I missed the way we would flirt back and forth, and the flirting that always led to awesome sex where our bodies were covered in slippery sweat. Fortunately, the check came and the moment was dispelled. Zeke laid the cash on the table. Since I only had the hundred bucks I was supposed to give to Rex, I let him pay for it.

We left the diner and walked back to the apartment, and with every step closer to the door, I felt dread over saying goodbye. I didn't want this beautiful day to end. Even though I was so hurt by what he'd done, being with Zeke was comforting.

I opened the door and allowed Safari inside, but I purposely shut it again so we stayed in the hallway. That was my cue to Zeke that the day was over, that my weakness had gone on long enough.

Zeke didn't seem disappointed. "I should get going. Supposed to hit the green with Rex in an hour."

I was grateful he made this easy on me. He could have opened up the conversation that I didn't want to have, but he didn't. He seemed to understand this day didn't really mean anything. It was just a break from the pain. "Make sure you kick his ass."

"Always do." He smiled at me, the longing forming in his eyes. He didn't move to touch me again, just loving me with his eyes. "I guess I'll see you later."

"Yeah…"

He stood in front of me the same way he did last night, waiting for some kind of invitation for physical contact.

All I did was nod.

Zeke moved into my body and wrapped his powerful arms around me, hugging me tightly and filling my stomach with butterflies. His smell overpowered me, making me feel both alive and dead at the same time.

I could do this all day.

After a few minutes, he pulled away, his arms reluctant to let me go. "Until next time."

Chapter Fourteen

Rex

I didn't slow down in time and knocked over his bag that contained all his clubs. They toppled over and fell onto the grass, his expensive gear slamming to the earth. His prized driver flew out the farthest. "What happened?"

Zeke sighed and picked up his clubs. "You knocked over my shit, that's what happened."

"No." I righted his bag and helped him drop the clubs inside. "With Rae. Did you guys...you know?" It was difficult for me to say the actual words because, you know, she was my sister. The mere idea grossed me out.

"No." He pulled out the driver and snagged a white golf ball from the pouch. "Even better."

"Better than sex?" Nothing was better than sex. I would know, I'd had a lot of it. "So, you got back together?"

"Not that good." He set the ball on the tee and tested his grip on the handle. "She asked me to sleep over. So, we cuddled in her bed then went to breakfast in the morning."

Was I missing something? "And that's better than sex?"

"To me, it is." He lined up the shot then whacked the ball hard, sending it flying over the green toward the hole far in the distance.

"How so?"

"We aren't back together. But it's gonna happen. She just needs more time to get over what happened."

"She said that?"

"No. But it's obvious. At first, I wasn't sure. We hadn't talked or seen each other much. But when she asked me to sleep over, I knew things were going to be okay. If she really couldn't forgive me, she wouldn't want me alone in her apartment. She wouldn't want me to touch her and hold her all night. But she pretty much begged me to."

"Honestly, I think you're jumping to conclusions."

"Yeah? I don't think so." He stepped away from the tee so I could prepare my shot. "I know her, Rex. I know what she's thinking even if she doesn't say it. We're getting back together. I have to keep my distance and give her space, but when she's ready, she'll come to me."

"Well, I hope you're right. Really, I do." I set the ball down and grabbed the perfect club. "I just want things to get back to normal. Nothing has felt right since you guys broke up. The whole group dynamic is off. I can't hang out with you and Rae at the same time, so I have to keep going back and forth."

"Yeah, I know. But everything will be back to normal in no time."

***

I carried the box into the apartment and set it on the counter. "Damn, this is heavy. What the hell is in here?"

"Shoes." Kayden walked in behind me, carrying some of her clothes on hangers.

"Then you have a lot of shoes." My shoulders and back were sore from carrying all of her crap. "Might need to get a bigger place since you've brought an entire store with you."

"Maybe we should get married and buy a house." She looked up at me like her comment wasn't terrifying.

Marriage wasn't on my mind — at all. Investing in real estate with a woman — also not on my mind. "Uh...I hope you aren't expecting a proposal. Honestly, that's the last thing on my mind right now." All I knew was I wanted her there with me every night. But beyond that, the future was unseen.

She smiled, like my response didn't offend her at all. "That's fine, Rex. Just wanted to test the waters and see where you're at."

"I hope you figured it out."

"I did. And living together is fine — for now. We'll see where it goes." She carried the clothes into the bedroom down the hall, her ass shaking from left to right as she sauntered with those gorgeous hips.

My heart finally slowed down.

217

Rae walked through the open door. "I heard all the racket and decided to pop in."

"Do you knock?" I countered.

She rolled her eyes and opened the box on the counter. "You're one to talk." She rifled through the contents until she pulled out a pair of black pumps. "Wait a sec, these are mine. I've been looking everywhere for these." She set them on the counter and examined them for scuff marks.

"Well, Kayden looks better in them."

Rae smacked my arm.

I wanted to ask her about Zeke, but I knew I shouldn't bring it up. Zeke said they were going to work out but she still needed more space. If I bombarded her with questions, it might chase her off. "What are you doing tonight?"

"No plans. Thought I would help you guys out."

"Lame."

She placed one hand on her hip, giving me attitude. "Or I could sit on my ass across the hall and not help."

"Alright. You aren't lame."

"Thank you."

Kayden returned to the kitchen. "Hey, Rae."

Rae held up the pumps. "Thanks for returning these, by the way."

Kayden had a counterattack. "Thanks for giving me back that Louis Vuitton dress I let you borrow last week."

A guilty look stretched across her face. "I'll go get that now…" When she turned around to walk out the door, she nearly ran into Zeke. Dressed in running shorts and a t-shirt, he was there to help us move the rest of Kayden's things. His eyes locked on Rae, and Rae stared back at him.

I could feel the chemistry between them—which was saying something because I was pretty clueless.

Rae cleared her voice, clearly caught off guard. "Hi."

Zeke's voice was deep, like usual. "Hey. Here to help out?"

"Yeah," Rae answered. "And go through Kayden's stuff to see what I want to borrow."

He chuckled, his face lighting up the instant he was in her presence—like always. "Ulterior motive… I respect that."

"I was just going to get something I borrowed from Kayden. I'll be right back." Rae moved around him, doing her best to not touch him. But she brushed against his arm anyway, tensing as she moved.

Zeke stared at her the whole time, obviously feeling her slip by. When she was gone, he walked farther into the room, his eyes directed out the window deep in thought. A quiet sigh escaped his lips, his blue eyes still bright from his interaction with Rae.

Kayden stood at the counter, eyeing Zeke and looking a little awkward. "So...how are things going between you guys?"

"Haven't seen her since I slept over on Saturday." Zeke kept his voice down so Rae wouldn't overhear him.

"I think she's coming around," Kayden said. "When we went out to the bar, she couldn't stop talking about how hot you looked."

Zeke grinned, flattered by the comment. "Good to know."

Rae walked back into the room with the black dress on the hanger. "I was going to give it back..."

Kayden snatched it from her. "I can smell your bullshit, Rae. Just own up to it."

"Well, you were never going to give me back my heels," Rae countered.

"You're right, I wasn't." Kayden's sassiness came out in full force. "But they're so damn cute, I just couldn't give them up."

Rae sighed. "Alright, you can keep them. But I may need to borrow them in the future."

Kayden smiled in victory. "I'm so glad we're best friends forever."

I couldn't imagine borrowing something of Zeke's — other than his Jeep. "Don't try to borrow any of my things, man. I don't share clothes."

"Like your skinny shit would fit me anyway," Zeke countered.

Rae laughed. "Good comeback."

Now my eyes narrowed on her face. "He just insulted your brother."

"I know," she said. "Good for him." She walked out of the apartment and headed to the U-Haul outside on the street. Just as I did when Kayden walked down the hallway, Zeke turned his eyes to her ass and stared at it until she could no longer be seen.

"Dude," I snapped. "Could you not pull that shit right in front of me?"

"Get over it, man. That's my future wife. I'm gonna stare at her ass all I want. It's not like I'm getting any right now. Gotta take what I can get." He left the apartment and walked down to the street to join Rae.

Kayden smiled when they were gone. "They're gonna get back together. I can tell."

"Yeah?"

"Yeah. Did you see the way Rae was staring at him? She's still head over heels."

Maybe I didn't need to be so worried about Ryker after all. "I don't pay much attention, honestly."

"And Zeke is still hung up on her. It might take some time, but they'll be a couple again soon enough. And things will be back to normal."

222

I liked the sound of that. "I hope you're right. I miss when all of us would hang out. Seems like a lifetime ago."

She rubbed my arm. "Don't worry. We just need to be patient."

"Yeah...I guess so."

Rae walked in carrying a box and placed it on the counter. She read the label in black ink along the side of the box. "You keep all your magazines?" She cocked her head so she could read it clearly.

"Just wedding magazines." Kayden said it nonchalantly, like those words wouldn't give me a panic attack.

"Oh, gotcha." As a woman, Rae apparently understood.

Zeke came in behind her, carrying a large box. His eyes went to Rae's ass immediately before he set the box on the ground. "There's not much left in the truck. Are we getting dinner after this? Starving."

"We'll treat you guys to Mega Shake as a thank you," I offered.

"Cheap ass," Zeke teased.

"Didn't realize your wallet was so tight," Rae jabbed. "Poor Kayden..."

"Fine," I snapped. "No Mega Shake for either of you."

"Oh no," Zeke said sarcastically. "Where am I gonna find five dollars to pay for my food?"

Rae's cheeks reddened as she laughed. She hadn't smiled like that in over six weeks.

I didn't have a comeback, so I just rolled my eyes and walked out.

"I'm sure we can find five bucks in change on the street," Rae said. "You know, since Mr. Rich won't stretch out his wallet."

I shook my head and growled under my breath. "Assholes..."

***

I sat across from Kayden and popped a few fries into my mouth.

Rae sat across from Zeke, her hair pulled back in a bun. She wore a white tank top with black dirt spots on the front from the old boxes. Whenever Zeke's gaze was turned down, she looked at him.

And the second she looked away, he took the opportunity to stare at her.

They should just knock it off and get back together. Their silent flirting was starting to get annoying.

"Watch the game last night?" Zeke asked her.

"No," Rae admitted. "Taking a short hiatus from sports right now."

"Why?" Zeke asked.

"Because I have a gambling problem." She threw a glare at me. "I'm down a hundred bucks because of that asshole."

"Hey," I snapped. "This asshole didn't force you to bet anything."

Zeke chuckled, his eyes still on Rae. "Maybe you need to stop gambling."

"It's so hard," she said. "Once the shit talking starts, I have to put my money where my mouth is."

"Maybe bet five bucks instead," Zeke said. "To Rex, that's like a hundred bucks anyway."

I grabbed a handful of fries and threw them in his face.

With quick reflexes, he opened his mouth and caught a few. "Thanks, man." He chewed the pile then swallowed.

Damn, now I had less fries, and I was still hungry.

Like Kayden could read my mind, she grabbed her basket of fries and dropped a few back onto my plate. Then she picked up her burger again and kept eating.

That was something I treasured about our relationship. I was the man, and I was supposed to take care of her, but she did thoughtful things for me all the time. She knew I had a big appetite, and she never let me go hungry. There was always food on the table, coffee in the morning, and clean towels hanging in the bathroom. Not to mention, there was always lingerie packed in the drawers.

Rae opened her mouth and leaned back. "Hit me."

Zeke grabbed a fry and tossed it in her mouth. "Goal!"

"Yes." She chewed it then opened her mouth again. "Hit me again."

Zeke picked up on her trick long before I did. "You're just trying to eat all my fries."

"Damn." She closed her mouth and leaned forward again. "I was hoping no one would figure that out."

"I know you too well." Zeke turned his gaze back to his food, breaking their eye contact.

I turned to the people sitting a few tables over from us, looking about the same age. It was one woman with three guys, and she was picking at her fries, talking quietly to the man sitting across from her, who was eyeing her tits so hard his eyes were about to pop out of his head. When she reached over to grab his soda, she knocked over her basket of fries.

"Geez, you're so clumsy," the guy on her right said.

"Want me to order you another, baby?" the guy who'd just checked out her rack asked.

"No. This is fine." She scooped up the basket and the fries and then continued to eat them like nothing happened.

I cringed and turned back to Rae. "That's so gross."

"What's so gross about it?" Rae asked. "You think the kitchen in the back is pristine clean? It's a diner."

"I know it's not the Ritz in here," I countered. "But I sure hope the kitchen is cleaner than this tile floor that was installed thirty years ago."

"Food is food," Rae said. "I couldn't care less."

"Well, you're just gross." I didn't eat shit off the ground, and I would judge Kayden if she did. But I knew my sister had always been off the spectrum of normalcy.

Zeke grabbed his burger and trained his eyes on her. "I think it's sexy."

"Me eating food off the ground?" she asked incredulously.

"I guess," he said. "But I think anything you do is sexy."

Chapter Fifteen

Rae

I was at home, on the couch with Safari, when Ryker called.

I stared at his name on the screen for a few seconds before I answered. "Hey."

"Hey." His deep and sexy voice came through the phone, innately arrogant like always. "What are the two of you doing tonight?"

"I'm looking sexy in my pajamas with my ass parked on the couch. Safari is a stud like always."

"Wow, that does sound sexy," he said in complete seriousness. "I hope you dress like that when you come with me to the Wizards game tonight."

I heard what he said, but I couldn't get a grip on my bearings. I slowly stood, letting Safari slide off me. "What's that supposed to mean?"

"It means I have courtside seats to the game tonight—and I want you to come with me."

"Say what?"

"You heard me right."

"No freaking way."

He chuckled into the phone. "Yep. It's true."

"How did you pull that off?"

"You know, same old story. I know a guy who knows a guy…"

"And you want to take me?"

"Of course," he said with complete seriousness. "No one else I'd rather go with. But there will be no gambling. I'm not taking cash from a lady."

"Good. Because I'm kinda broke from all the bets I made with Rex."

"In that case, I'll buy you a chili dog."

I remembered when we got chili dogs on our very first date. I taunted him about giving him a blow job, and the tease tortured him until he dropped me off that night. Sometimes memories came flooding back, times when I was in love with Ryker and I didn't even realize it. "Are you sure you don't want to take someone else? You could really get laid with seats like that."

"I get laid with or without seats," he said, cocky as usual. "But I want to take you. So, I'll pick you up in an hour. Sorry, but Safari can't come."

"That's alright. Rex will watch him." I got off the phone then showered and got ready as fast as I could. Even though I lived close to the stadium, I never went to games because they were usually too expensive, so this was a big deal for me.

I put on jeans and my favorite jersey then walked across the hall and knocked on the door.

Rex answered, looking irritated the second he saw my face. "Yes?"

"I'm gonna be out for the night, so can you keep an eye on Safari?"

"I'm not your maid," he barked.

"You look like one."

His eyes narrowed. "You want me to watch your dog?"

"You don't need to watch him. Just let him out to pee in a few hours."

"Nah." He walked across the hall and opened my door. "Come on, boy."

Safari walked right past me into Rex's apartment.

Rex followed him back across the threshold. "We like having him around. Much better company than you are. Where are you going, by the way?"

"To a Wizards game." I crossed my arms over my chest, knowing exactly how jealous he would be. "Courtside, baby."

"What?" His mouth dropped. "Right in front of the cheerleaders?"

Not an incentive for me, but whatever. "Yep."

"What the hell? Zeke is gonna take you instead of me? What a shithead."

"Uh...I'm not going with Zeke."

Rex's face fell when he understood my meaning. "Oh."

"Ryker will be here any minute." I tried to speed things along to make this less awkward. "So, I'll see you later. Keep an eye out for a friendly face on TV." I turned around so I wouldn't have to look at him anymore.

At that moment, Ryker appeared down the hallway, dressed in a black t-shirt and jeans — like usual. "You ready for this?" He didn't spot Rex in the open doorway yet, his eyes on me and my jersey. "Need a jacket?"

"No, I'm good. It'll be warm on the court with the players." I locked the door to my apartment, aware of Rex still staring at us.

Ryker finally noticed him. He looked at him with his unreadably stoic expression, seeming unaffected by my brother's presence. "Long time, no see, huh?" He placed his hands in his pockets, wearing his handsome smile.

Rex's only response was a glare.

Man, this was awkward. I tried to keep the moment light. "Thanks for looking after Safari." I shoved my keys in my purse then walked down the hall with Ryker.

Rex stared at us the entire time, his eyes smoldering with hatred.

When we were out of earshot, Ryker sighed. "Wow. That guy still hates me, huh?"

"Honestly, I think he's always going to hate you."

Ryker shrugged it off. "Eh, whatever. I'll butter him up eventually."

***

"Can you believe this?" If I stuck my foot out, I would actually be touching the inside of the court. Sweat gleamed from the players' bodies, and I could actually smell it. They were playing Cleveland, and LeBron looked even bigger in real life. "This is amazing."

Ryker sipped his beer and smiled. "I can't believe it either. Way better than watching it at home."

"I hope they lose control of the ball and come toppling this way."

Ryker raised both eyebrows. "Man, I really hope not. If LeBron jumped on you, he'd snap you in half."

"It'd be worth it."

He chuckled then picked up his basket of nachos from underneath the seat. He popped one into his mouth and watched the players run back and forth. "Anything new with you?"

Ryker and I hadn't seen each other in over a week, and in that time period, a lot had happened. We sent each other random text messages every day with pictures of dogs in ugly sweaters, but we didn't discuss anything real.

"Not really."

"What's been going on with Zeke?"

I had no idea what I was doing with Zeke. I was still so angry at him, but I couldn't keep my distance. "Well...I did something really stupid."

"Uh-oh," he said with a grin. "That doesn't sound good..."

"We were all hanging out, and I asked him to sleep over."

Ryker popped another chip into his mouth, keeping his thoughts a mystery.

"Then we got breakfast the next morning and took Safari on a walk. After that, we went back to being friends again."

"You guys had sex but didn't get back together?"

"No," I said quickly. "We just slept together. We didn't even kiss. I'm just so exhausted from not getting enough sleep, and I missed him so...I had a moment of weakness."

Ryker's shoulders immediately relaxed. "Oh, I see."

"And now we're back to being friends, but I still miss him... I'm so confused. I don't want to take him, back but I can't stop thinking about him." I talked to Ryker about my relationship problems more than I did with my own girlfriends. Somehow, he'd turned into a confidant that I shared everything with.

"You want to know what I think?"

My eyes followed the ball on the court, listening to him the entire time. "I guess."

"I think you're just postponing the inevitable. You love the guy, so just take him back. No one is going to judge you for it."

"But I can't forget what he did. I love him and miss him, but once I think about him and that woman, I push him away again. It's a vicious cycle that will never go away."

"Maybe you need more time to forgive him. But I don't see why you can't be with him during that time."

Maybe I was being irrational, but it really seemed like no one understood how I was feeling. "He slept with another woman. I don't think we can move on from that."

"But you obviously can't move on from him," Ryker pointed out. "So what's the lesser of two evils?"

"That's not how I want to think of my relationship."

"You may have to." He tossed a few more chips into his mouth, his eyes on the game. The second quarter ended, and we went into halftime.

"What about you? Have you been seeing anyone?"

He placed the nachos under his chair again. "No."

"Not even a date?"

He shook his head. "Nope."

I wondered if he was still waiting for the possibility of getting back together with me. I told him it was never going to happen, but perhaps he didn't believe me. He had encouraged me to go back to Zeke, so that didn't exactly add up. "Not even hooking up with a regular?"

"No." He eyed the players as they retreated to their places at the benches. "I had meaningless sex for a while, and it just made me feel worse. I'm just not in the mood to pick up a woman for a late-night fuck. Honestly, I miss the sex we used to have."

I stared at the court and tried to ignore the inappropriate statement he just made.

"Sorry if that makes you uncomfortable. But I'm being honest."

"No, it's okay. It really was good sex." There was no denying that we both enjoyed it on a spiritual level.

"Anything besides that is...mediocre."

"Maybe it's because we had a connection."

"Yeah," he said in agreement. "I think it's because we loved each other — even though I was too much of a shithead to admit it."

I crossed my legs and adjusted myself in my seat, wanting to do something with my body.

He turned to me, examining my face. "You asked, right?"

I nodded. "You're right, I did. Does that mean you aren't trying to date?"

"I've had no interest. My days are pretty routine. I go to work, hit the gym, and then come home. Sometimes, I go out with some friends, but I'm not looking for tail."

Ryker was a sexual person so going through a long-term dry spell didn't sound like him. "And you just use your hand all the time?" It was an inappropriate question to ask, but I did it anyway.

"Yeah. In the shower every afternoon. It took some getting used to, but now I'm comfortable with it." His eyes darkened like he was thinking of something arousing. "What about you?"

"I've had no sex life since the day Zeke and I broke up — not even by myself."

"You retired the vibrator?" he asked with a smile.

"I think the batteries are dead. Not sure."

"That's a long time to go without a release," he said. "Not like you."

I used to be really sexual when we were together. After he dumped me, I went through a dry spell that lasted longer than the dust bowl. But when I got over it and started seeing Zeke, I picked it up again. Now, I was back in the desert, having no sexual appetite at all. "I've been too miserable."

"Actually, you seem a little better. I think you've come a long way since I found you in that bar."

I was so grateful Ryker was the only person who knew about that incident. "I do feel better. But I'm still pretty lost right now."

"What's the worst thing that could happen if you take back Zeke?" he asked. "You push him away from time to time when you remember what he did? It's not like he's going to make that same mistake twice."

"I don't want to be in a relationship unless it feels right. And right now, it doesn't."

He sipped his beer and watched the TV in the corner. They were doing the kiss cam, where the camera focused on couples in the audience and waited for them to kiss on live TV. "Hmm... I've never seen them do that at a basketball game."

"Me neither."

The camera moved between the different couples, and of course, it landed on us — because that was my luck.

Ryker smiled then turned to me, wiggling his eyebrows.

I laughed but didn't lean forward, having no intention of kissing on live television.

The crowd cheered, trying to get us to kiss, and the camera stayed on us.

Ryker shrugged, suggesting we just kiss so the camera would move on.

Zeke was probably at home watching the game, and there was a good chance he could see us right this second. And even if that wasn't a possibility, I couldn't kiss Ryker. I didn't want to give him the wrong idea of where this friendship could lead.

Ryker recognized my discomfort so he held up his hand. "How about a high-five? It's a kiss with our hands."

I smiled at the suggestion then clapped my hand against his. "I can do that."

The camera finally moved on, and the focus was taken off of us.

"Crisis averted." He drank his beer, all the women staring at him now that they knew he was available.

"If Rex saw us kiss, I would never hear the end of it."

"You're never gonna hear the end of it anyway," he said. "He wanted to tell me off then and there."

"Ignore him. He'll get over it."

"Not only do I have to deal with Safari, but now I have to deal with your brother too. But I guess I deserve it. I was a huge punk."

I didn't think Ryker needed to beat himself up forever. "I've forgiven you, so don't worry about it."

"Yeah?" he asked. "So, if Zeke wasn't in the picture, would I have a chance?" He turned his beautiful blue eyes on me, watching every reaction.

He asked me this question once before, when we were at dinner together. "I don't know."

"Yes, you do," he said quietly. "And I want an answer."

Spending time with Ryker felt oddly normal, like I was with a good friend. I was still attracted to him, feeling the knots deep in my stomach. He'd changed a lot over the course of eight months, becoming exactly who I wanted back when we were together. "I think so."

He nodded, a slow smile stretching his lips. "Good to know."

"But that doesn't mean anything will ever happen."

"That's perfectly okay," he said. "But I wanted to know that answer—for myself."

***

"You didn't need to walk me to my door."

"Are you kidding me?" he asked, his hands in his pockets. "It's one in the morning, and Safari isn't here to make sure you're safe. So the job falls on my shoulders."

"Rex taught me how to break a man's nose, so I think I'm okay."

"I know how to kill a man with a single fist." He walked to the door then leaned against the frame.

Across the hall, Rex's door shifted and a shadow of footsteps could be seen under the door.

I knew Rex was watching us. "Rex, we know you're there," I said with a loud voice.

After a bit more shuffling, the door opened. Rex stepped out with a garbage bag that was half empty. "Just came out to drop this in the trash chute..." Safari came out behind him and immediately growled once he looked at Ryker. Rex smiled and patted him on the head. "Good dog."

I got my door unlocked and snapped my fingers. "Inside."

Safari walked between Ryker and I, growling at Ryker the entire time.

"Such a drama queen..." I shut the door so Safari's growls could no longer be heard. "Sorry about that."

"Maybe I need to bring him treats," Ryker said. "A bone or something."

"Or maybe you should go back in time and not be an asshole," Rex jabbed. "Safari wouldn't have a problem with you then."

Ryker wasn't the type of man to take shit from anyone, but he held his tongue. He gave Rex a threatening look but that was the worst of it. "Why don't you make yourself busy and dump that empty trash bag instead of spying on your sister?"

"I'm not spying," Rex said defensively. "Just making sure there are no creeps in the building." He walked to the end of the hall where the trash chute was located.

Ryker turned back to me, still looking annoyed. "Thanks for coming to the game with me."

"No, thank you. I've never sat that close to the court before."

"Well, if I get more tickets, you'll be the first to know."

"Awesome."

Ryker's eyes moved to Rex, who was coming back up the hallway. "Well, I should get going before I punch your brother. Good night."

"Good night."

Ryker turned around and walked away, his hands still in his pockets. His powerful shoulders looked strong as he walked away, the muscles rippling under his t-shirt. When he turned into the stairwell, he disappeared.

"Stop spending time with him." Rex's bossy voice came into my ear. "Zeke acts like it doesn't bother him, but I know it pisses him the hell off."

"How ironic," I said sarcastically. "It pissed me the hell off when he fucked some bimbo. Looks like we have something in common." I glared at Rex hard, standing my ground and ignoring his obnoxious insult.

Rex's argument died in his mouth. He didn't know what to say to that. But he kept up his look of hatred, frustrated that this situation wasn't going the way he wanted. His prejudice against Ryker would always be there — even when we were old and gray. "He's the reason you and Zeke aren't together anymore. So, you shouldn't be spending time with him."

"No, Zeke is the reason we aren't together anymore." Zeke had the right to be as angry as he wanted when he saw me with Ryker, but he didn't have the right to pull his dick out of his pants.

"I'm on Zeke's side for this one, Rae. If you hadn't kept spending time with Ryker, none of this would have happened. You're in the wrong. You should have been more respectful toward Zeke."

I placed my hands on my hips, feeling my anger boil. "Shut up, Rex."

"No. I'm telling you the truth even if you don't want to hear it. Frankly, you're lucky Zeke is still hanging around. If it were me, I'd move on. I wouldn't want to be with someone who won't admit their faults but point out mine like I'm a criminal." He walked into his apartment and slammed the door.

Then I walked into mine and did the same.

***

I was just about to take my lunch break when my phone lit up with a message from Zeke. *Lunch?*

I probably shouldn't spend more alone time with him than necessary, but seeing his name on my screen sent chills down my spine. The butterflies exploded in my stomach and all I wanted to do was be with him—right this second. *Sure.*

Pizza?

Okay.

I left the lab and walked to the pizzeria that we always went to. Zeke already had a booth when I walked inside, his order number sitting at the edge of the table. Two fountain drinks were on the table. Zeke knew I liked cherry cola, so he already had it ready.

Even in scrubs, he looked sexy as hell. The muscles of his chest were noticeable in the deep curve of his shirt. His chin was covered with hair because he hadn't shaved in a few days. And today, his eyes seemed to be brighter than usual.

I slid onto the chair and hid my disappointment that I wasn't greeted with a hug. "Hey."

"I ordered a combination. Should be out any moment."

"Great. I'm starving." I sipped my soda so my nerves would die down.

He stared at me with a look that I was used to, like he missed me but wouldn't say it out loud. "How's work?" He hid behind the question, talking about something generic that wouldn't make either one of us uncomfortable.

"Pretty boring. I've had to do paperwork all day."

"Does sound boring," he said with a smile. "But once that paperwork is done, it'll be interesting again."

"How's the office?"

"Today was Jessica's last day. She just left for maternity leave and everyone is pretty excited about it."

"Wow, good for her." I saw her at an office party when she was just a few months along.

"So, I have a temp in for the next three months. Jessica is a great admin so I'm gonna miss her while she's gone."

"I bet."

"I have a feeling I'll be at the office a little later than usual."

"Hopefully not by much." I knew Zeke loved his job, but his life didn't revolve around it. He had a well-rounded life, an existence not based on any single thing.

"Worst case scenario, I can have the games on the TV while I finish up in my office. So, it won't be too bad."

"True." I didn't have a TV in my lab, just two desktop computers.

"So, had fun at the game last night?"

Of course, Rex told him. "Yeah. I've never sat that close before."

"I couldn't believe it when I saw you on TV. When I saw Ryker beside you, I realized it was really you."

So maybe Rex didn't tell him anything. And Zeke did see the kiss cam moment, so thankfully Ryker and I only shared a high-five. That would have eaten Zeke alive. "Ryker got the tickets from some guy he knows. Asked me to come along."

Zeke nodded but didn't say anything.

It didn't seem like Zeke was mad about the situation, not the way Rex implied. Maybe he really did trust me. Maybe he really was trying to prove something to me.

The pizza arrived, and Zeke took three enormous slices. He ate as much as he wanted but still stayed in perfect shape. Sometimes it annoyed me, but since I was the one who got to enjoy him, my jealousy faded away.

But when I realized he wasn't mine anymore, I felt like shit.

I missed him so much.

This was so hard.

Could I really keep doing this? Keep him at a distance?

Could I ever truly just be his friend?

"What's Safari up to?" he asked after he finished his first slice.

"Being cute, like usual. I took him on a walk this morning, and he tried to chase a squirrel. Thankfully, I had a good grip on the leash. But my coffee went flying everywhere."

He cringed. "Hopefully, there were no victims in the mess."

"I almost hit a jogger, but he got out of the way in time. But Safari caught a little of it, so he smells like coffee."

Zeke chuckled. "There are worst things to smell like."

"I'll give him a bath when I get home. It was easier to do that at your place since I could just spray him with a hose."

"You're still welcome to do that."

That was a red flag. Zeke's house only made me think of beautiful nights when we slept in each other's arms. Being there would make me melt into a puddle on the floor, and I would be powerless not to do something stupid. "I should probably take him in for a haircut anyway…"

Zeke grabbed another slice of pizza and didn't press the matter. "So, have you stopped gambling?"

"Ryker won't take any of my money, so I'm safe with him."

"I wouldn't take any either, so you're in the clear. But steer away from Rex. He'll run you dry."

"I know. He already has." He lived in my apartment for almost a year, rent free. And then I gave him a huge loan for his failing business.

Zeke chuckled. "You need to make a good bet so you can get all your money back. And then never bet him again."

"That's a lot harder than it sounds." Even when a team was favored to win, that didn't mean anything.

"Maybe Tobias could help."

"Maybe."

"Things seem to be getting serious with him and Jess," he said. "At least, that's what he tells me."

"I don't know if serious is the right word. She's just glad the sex is good. You know her, she doesn't look far into the future about stuff like that."

"Well, I think he's smitten. Hopefully, he doesn't get his heart stepped on."

"There's a good chance of that happening." Jessie was a notorious heartbreaker. All the men wanted her, but never got her. And when they did, she usually dropped them pretty quick. Unpredictable and free, there was no telling what she wanted.

We finished the pizza together, just like old times, and before I knew it, I had to head back to work. "Well, I should get going."

"Yeah, me too." Zeke left the table and threw our trash away before he walked outside with me. Even though it was a cool day, he didn't wear a jacket. But with arms like that, he really didn't need one. "I guess I'll see you later. Maybe all of us can do something fun this weekend."

"Yeah..." I wanted him to hug me. But I also didn't want him to hug me. Damn, I didn't know what I wanted. "I'll see what the girls are up to."

"Cool." He gave me a handsome smile before he turned around and walked off, his office in the opposite direction of COLLECT.

I watched him go, staring at the fine piece of ass. And I had a feeling he knew I was staring at it.

***

I didn't know if it was because of my conversation with Ryker, but my sexuality had been awakened. I couldn't sleep because I kept dreaming about Zeke doing amazing things to my body, making me writhe underneath him while he pounded into me. My hands gripped the sheets, and I woke up in a sweat.

When the dream faded away, I tried to go back to sleep but the area between my legs burned. My nipples were so hard they chafed against my t-shirt. I tossed and turned, trying to shake the feelings out of my body.

I considered touching myself. I used to do it all the time. But once Ryker came into my life, using my vibrator was a rare occurrence. And then when I got together with Zeke, I stopped altogether.

I couldn't go back to that.

If I thought about Zeke, it would just depress me because my imagination wasn't as good as the real thing. It would remind me I was alone, missing the man I loved. I couldn't think about anyone else because that would just feel like a betrayal even though I wasn't seeing Zeke anymore. Ryker always turned me on, but that felt even worse. I couldn't think of an old ex so I could stop thinking about my current ex.

So what should I do?

I tried getting comfortable enough to go to sleep, but that didn't work.

My mind kept picturing Zeke shirtless and sexy.

My nub was throbbing.

Could I go over there for a booty call?

Would that cross a line?

Would I just be playing games?

Ugh, I didn't know what to do.

Since I couldn't sleep, I threw on sweatpants and a hoodie, left Safari asleep on the bed, and walked out of the apartment. It was three in the morning, so there was no possibility of Zeke still being awake. It was a bad idea, but I kept walking.

I took a cab to his place and stood on the sidewalk, seeing all the lights off in the windows. I walked up the path right to his door, staring at the beautiful white door that led to the entrance of his home.

This was a bad idea.

Where would it lead?

Could we have a one-night stand? Was that even possible for us?

Was that insensitive of me?

Without realizing it, my knuckles had already collided with the wood. I knocked three times, knowing he would hear it since he always left his bedroom door open so he could hear everything throughout the house.

I always felt so safe with him.

A moment later, his footsteps hit the hardwood floor as he approached. I pulled my hood down so he could see my face when he looked through the peephole. The door opened and Zeke looked down at me, in only his boxers. His hair was messy, his eyes were lidded and sleepy, and he looked sexy as hell.

Now I definitely couldn't back down.

He stared at me with concerned eyes, unsure why I was standing on his doorstep at three in the morning.

"I can't sleep, and I keep thinking about you..." Once I tried to explain why I was there, I suddenly felt self-conscious. I was asking for a hook-up, and I definitely didn't look sexy doing it in a baggy sweater, sweatpants, and no make-up. "I just want one night, you know. I'm just so horny, and I don't know what to do about it."

He grabbed my hand and pulled me inside the house, locking the door behind me. His hands cupped my face and he kissed me, just the way he used to when we didn't see each other for over a day. With desperation and longing, he devoured me, slowly guiding me down the hallway and up to his bedroom.

The second I felt his lips, I was in heaven. I melted and swooned, my legs turning to Jell-O and my heartbeat racing to a terrifying level. My hands felt his powerful chest, recognizing the heartbeat that had become my lullaby over the past eight months. My lips were throbbing from our hard kisses, but I wanted more.

He pressed me against the foot of the bed then pulled my sweater over my head. I was still in my nightshirt without a bra, and he tossed that aside as well. His arms circled my body, and he kissed my neck and shoulders, his teeth nipping at me from time to time. He gripped my sweatpants and pulled them down, letting them fall to my knees.

I didn't think twice about what I was doing. I just wanted him without any concern of the consequences. Tomorrow morning, I would feel terrible after what I did tonight, but I didn't care. I would worry about that later.

He got my panties off then positioned me on the bed, laying his massive body on top of mine, his cock hard and ready for me. His mouth pressed against mine again, kissing me like we were back in time. His knees separated my thighs, and he pinned me underneath him, aggressively taking me like he never had before.

My nails trailed down his back, remembering the feeling of every single muscle and groove. His smell washed over me, and I basked in our memories, taken to a time when I was on the verge of moving into this very house.

The head of his cock pressed against my entrance, and with a single shove, he thrust inside me.

It felt so good I wanted to cry.

I hadn't felt him inside me, his length and his girth, for far too long. My body clenched around him in longing, adoring the sensation of him between my legs. My nails dug into him harder as I fell into the euphoria we shared. "Oh, god..."

He stopped kissing me as he savored the feeling of our bodies joined together, breathing into my mouth quietly as his throbbing cock stretched me. "Baby..." He dug one hand into my hair and began to rock into me, still breathing into my mouth.

I never wanted this to end.

His headboard tapped against the wall as he slammed into me, his thrusts setting a hard pace. He slid in and out of my slickness, knowing just how soaked I was the instant I arrived on his doorstep. His eyes locked to mine as he moved, telling me he loved me with just his look.

And I said it back.

Within minutes, he hit me in the right spot and made me convulse, tears forming in my eyes because the orgasm felt so amazing. I wasn't sure if it was the satisfaction or the connection, but one of the two made me crumble apart.

The sensation felt amazing, but there was something else I also looked forward to. I missed the way he used to come inside me, to dump all of his seed as far into me as he could. It made me feel owned, possessed. I hadn't felt that sensation in so long, and I needed it now. "I want you to come inside me, Zeke."

He kissed the corner of my mouth as he kept thrusting. "I was going to anyway." He gave a few final pumps before he released with a moan, coming longer and harder than he ever had before. His seed felt heavy, having more than weight than ever before. When he finished, he remained inside me, kissing me gently along the mouth.

All the aches and pains in my body went away, leaving me relaxed and even happy.

Zeke slowly pulled out of me then positioned me against his body, cuddling with me under the sheets of his enormous bed. It felt just the way it used to, except without Safari at the bottom. The sheets smelled like him — smelled like home.

We both had work in a few hours, so we drifted off immediately, exhausted and fulfilled from the intense lovemaking. His lips found my shoulder, and he gave me a gentle kiss just before I slipped away. "I love you, Rae."

I said it back automatically, my mouth making all the calls. "I love you too."

Chapter Sixteen

Rex

The second I got off work, Zeke called me. "What's up, pimple popper?"

Zeke ignored the insult. "Are you free right now? We need to talk."

"Dude, I'm always free for you."

"Good. Hot wings?"

"Anything is good for me."

"Alright. Meet you there in five." He hung up.

I walked down the block and headed to the wing place while I called Kayden.

"Hey." Her feminine and sexy voice came through the phone, sounding like an angel without even trying—a Victoria's Secret angel. "Are you on your way home?"

"Actually, I'm having an early dinner with Zeke. He asked me to meet him."

"Oh, okay. Then I'll make something light for dinner."

"Thanks, baby." I felt like the center of her universe in all the good ways. She always made sure there was a hot meal on the table. But the second I left my socks on the ground, she turned on me quicker than a snake. "I'll be home later."

"Alright. See you then." She hung up.

I walked into the place just as the conversation ended, and I found Zeke already sitting at a table. Wings, fries, and beers were on the table. But the thing that stood out the most was his enormous grin.

"What?" I sat in the chair across from him. "You had sex or something?" Obviously, he didn't, so there had to be a different reason.

"As a matter of fact…"

Rage rushed through me quicker than I could form the words I was about to say. "What the fuck? What about Rae? You said you were getting back together."

He rolled his eyes and drank his beer. "You're such an idiot, Rex."

"What?" I asked, still clueless.

"Rae is the woman I slept with. Geez, you're dense sometimes."

"Oh…" Actually, that made more sense. "Wait, that's great! Are you guys back together?"

"Technically, no. But pretty much. I think she'll take me back in a week or so."

"Dude, you're gonna have to start from the beginning. How did this happen?"

"We had lunch together yesterday and everything was normal… Well, as normal as it could be. I saw her with Ryker at the game the night before, and he didn't try to kiss her during that kiss cam stunt. We talked about a few other things and went our separate ways."

"Okay…this is really boring so far."

Zeke ignored that last comment. "And around three am last night, she showed up on my doorstep."

"Really?" What the hell was she doing up at three in the morning?

"She said she was horny and wanted a one-night stand."

Now I wanted to throw up. I usually liked hearing Zeke's stories because they were about sexy ladies. But when they were about my sister, they just sucked.

"And obviously, I gave it to her. She slept over, but she slipped out when I was in the shower — probably because she didn't want to have the conversation."

"What conversation?"

"You know, about where we stand."

"Oh…are you gonna have that conversation?"

"Not necessarily. I know where we're at."

"Which is…?" This just sounded confusing to me.

"She needs a little more time, but she'll be back." He tossed a fry in his mouth then sipped his beer.

"How do you know this?"

"Why would she stop by for a booty call if she was really intent on moving on from me? When she came to get her stuff, I made a move on her, and she turned me down. She said it would just make it harder for her to move on. But then she comes to my place, in the dead of night, and asks me to make love to her. Trust me, I know her. We're getting back together. I just don't know when that will officially happen."

I sincerely hoped he was right. "Good. The sooner that happens, the sooner everything can go back to normal."

"And Ryker will stop sniffing around…"

When I saw him the other night, I wanted to break his face. I hated looking at him. He was an arrogant asshole that didn't deserve Rae's compassion. "If she slept with you, I'm pretty sure that means she's not interested in sleeping with him."

"I know," he said with confidence. "But I'll be glad when he's gone for good."

"That makes two of us. Actually, three. Safari hates him too."

Zeke smiled. "I miss that dog almost as much as I miss Rae—almost."

"I've been training him to attack Ryker, but he still won't do it. Just growls at him."

Zeke laughed. "That would be awesome if Safari tore him to pieces. I'd certainly get a kick out of it."

"Yeah, me too." I finally scarfed down some food and drank my beer. "Why don't you just ask Rae to take you back instead of waiting around?"

"Doesn't work. The harder I try, the more I push her away. I've got to let her come to me."

"Man...chicks are confusing."

"Is Kayden?"

I guess in the beginning she was. I didn't have a clue how she felt about me. Rae was the one who had to break everything down for me. "Not really. Now that we're living together, she's pretty forthcoming about what she wants. If she wants sex, she tells me. If she wants me to clean up after myself, she tells me. She's pretty bossy, actually."

"Good for her. I remember she used to be shy around you."

Those days were long gone. "She has no problem being herself now."

"So, who asked who to move in?"

"I asked her." It was a spontaneous decision. When she was sitting in my lap, I didn't think twice about it. The question just popped out.

"Does that mean you've dropped the L word?"

"Absolutely not." The L word was for people like Zeke and Rae, not me.

"You're gonna live with this woman but you don't love her?" he asked incredulously.

"Look, I like her. That's not enough?"

"But you want her around 24/7. That must mean your feelings go beyond general liking."

"Not for me, man." I didn't have deep feelings about anything.

He leaned back in his chair, watching me with a serious gaze. "Then what made you ask her to move in?"

I shrugged.

"Rex," he pressed. "Come on, it's me. You can tell me anything."

"I don't know... I don't like it when she's not with me. When she's not in my bed, I feel alone. When I'm not with her, I'm always thinking about her. If we live together, then I'm guaranteed to see her every day. Plus, I know she's safe with me. No one is gonna break into her apartment and hurt her. As long as I'm around, no one will ever touch her. It just made the most sense."

Zeke's eyes softened.

"What?"

"Nothing." He tried to hide his smile.

"Stop looking at me like that."

"Like what?" Now he really couldn't stop smiling.

"What the hell does that look mean?" I demanded.

"Come on, man." He scratched his chin before he moved his hand back to his mug. "It's so obvious."

"What's obvious?"

"Dude, you love her."

"Nah."

"Did you hear what you just said?" he asked. "You pretty much declared your undying love for this woman."

"Did not."

"Did too. What's the big deal? Why don't you tell her?"

"Because..."

"Because why?" he pressed.

"I just... I just don't want to." I suddenly became uncomfortable, even with Zeke. This was something I never mentioned, not even to Rae. It bothered me so much I refused to allow myself to admit there was a problem at all.

His voice softened. "Is it because of your dad?"

I raised an eyebrow, surprised he figured it out.

"I can tell Rae has some abandonment issues too. I think the reason she's overreacting to this whole thing is because me sleeping with that girl felt like I was leaving her. And she hasn't been able to forgive me because she's just afraid of me leaving in the future. There's no shame in that. We all have our baggage."

Since he guessed it right, I didn't disagree. "I'm afraid Kayden might leave one day. So I don't want to...you know."

"Dude, she's not going anywhere. That woman is head over heels in love with you."

I knew she was. I saw it every day.

"Tell her, man. I'm sure she already knows anyway."

"I'll think about it."

When Zeke got what he wanted, he backed off. "Okay. But I'm putting a timer on this. If you don't do it quick enough, I'm telling her for you."

"That's really romantic..."

"Since it's really coming from you, it will be."

Chapter Seventeen

Rae

"Are you serious?" Jessie was so engrossed in my news she actually forgot about her drink. Kayden did too. "You slept with Zeke?"

"Yeah..." The worst part was, I didn't regret it. It felt so good to get off, to have amazing sex with the man I dreamt about every single night. "And then I snuck out when he was in the shower the next morning."

"You just bailed?" Jessie's voice rose an octave.

"Without saying goodbye?" Kayden asked. "Girl, that's so skanky."

"I know, I know." My behavior wasn't exactly graceful. "I told him I just wanted to hook up, so I didn't want to see him in the morning and have him kiss me and make me coffee...and have that conversation about where we are."

"And you think he's not going to ask you later?" Jessie asked.

"Well, we haven't spoken in two days," I said. "I guess I'm off the hook."

"Wow," Kayden said. "I'm surprised he's playing it cool."

"I'm not," Jessie said. "He got laid, so he's happy."

"But you are going to have the conversation, right?" Kayden pressed, giving me an evil look.

"I don't know..." I still wasn't sure what I wanted. I wasn't sure if we could get back together and move on from what happened. After what he did, I was still crushed. The only reason why I hadn't completely walked away from him was because I was madly in love with him.

"Just take him back," Kayden said. "You obviously want to."

"Yeah," Jessie said. "It's pretty obvious."

"But you guys were there," I reminded them. "He slept with someone else."

"And she didn't mean anything to him," Jessie said. "He saw you making out with Ryker in the middle of an expensive restaurant while you were holding hands—"

"We weren't making out," I interrupted.

"Whatever," Jessie countered. "You put him through a lot of bullshit with Ryker. I can't blame the guy for being so jealous he snapped."

I turned to Kayden, who was on my side initially. "You don't think I should take him back, right?"

"I didn't before, but now I think you should," Kayden said, twirling her hair.

"What changed your mind?" I asked, knowing Kayden was stubborn and didn't change her mind about anything.

"Because it's you guys," she said quietly. "Come on, you guys are both head over heels. Zeke isn't an asshole like Ryker. The guy made a mistake that he would never repeat. He's not a cheater or a liar."

"And you know what else?" Jessie said. "He's the one who came clean about it. He could have kept the secret forever and you never would have known about it. Even Rex, your brother, told him not to say anything."

"But he respected you too much to lie," Kayden said. "Come on, that's the kind of man you want to spend your life with. He's loyal and honest."

I found myself outsmarted and outnumbered.

"And if you slept with him," Jessie said. "Then that means you love him more than you hate him."

"True," Kayden said. "So, it seems like you're not getting back together with him only out of principle."

"That's not it at all," I whispered. I wasn't being stubborn for the sake of it. Honestly, I was just confused.

"Just end this nightmare so both of you will be happy," Jessie said. "That's what I think."

"Me too," Kayden said. "If Rex and I were in this situation, I would take him back instantly."

I knew that too well. She was obsessed with my brother, something I tried to forget about when we were hanging out.

"So?" Jessie pressed. "What are you going to do?"

"I don't know," I said. "Do I have to decide right now?"

Kayden turned to the bar. "You should since Zeke and Rex just walked in."

I glanced in her direction and saw Zeke in a dark green t-shirt, his arms looking as amazing as they felt the other night. His dark jeans hugged his tight ass, and those blue eyes lit up the place. All the women were looking in his direction, recognizing a hunky man when they saw one.

"Ugh. Who invited them?"

"Not me," Jessie said.

"Not me either," Kayden said. "But this is our favorite bar. It's not that much of a coincidence."

"Ugh," I repeated. "He looks so hot. This is killing me."

"Girl, just go get your man." Jessie gave my arm a gentle smack. "We all know it's gonna happen, so just do it already. Don't wait another two weeks. Life is too short for that."

After thinking things over in my head, I scooted out of the booth. "Okay, I'm gonna do it."

"Yes!" Kayden raised her hands in the air.

"You go get some." Jessie swatted my ass playfully.

I wanted to keep Zeke away, but I knew I couldn't. My anger dimmed the longer I missed him, and I couldn't fight it anymore. Maybe what he did paled in comparison to what we had. It'd been two months since that horrible breakup, and I'd finally had enough time to come to terms with his mistake. Perhaps it was time to move on.

I walked across the room and migrated around the groups of people talking with drinks in their hands. By the time I reached the guys, they had just gotten their drinks and were looking at the TV where a game was being broadcasted.

I placed my hand on Zeke's shoulder, feeling the electricity surge up my arm.

When Zeke turned, he wore the same expression he always gave when he looked at me. There was a smile mixed with something else, a special look he never gave anyone else—not even Rochelle. "Hey." He didn't mention our hookup two nights ago, and it didn't seem like he was going to.

"Hi."

Rex stood there awkwardly, knowing this was a greeting he shouldn't be a part of.

Now that I was going to say what I went over there to say, I felt my nerves get to me. My hands were shaking and my heels suddenly felt uncomfortable. I couldn't catch my breath no matter how hard I tried. "I've been thinking a lot and...I don't want to live without you anymore." That was all I could muster myself to say. And that was all I needed to say.

Zeke's smile dropped, and his eyes softened. "Neither do I."

"So...can we start over?" Without even realizing it, tears bubbled in my eyes.

His hands cupped my face, and he kissed me gently on the mouth, the exact opposite of the way he had kissed me two nights before. His fingertips reached my hair, and his touch felt soothing. Everything felt right the instant we touched. "I don't want to start over. I want to pick up exactly where we left off." His arms circled my waist, and he pulled me into his chest, hugging me near the crowded bar while music played in the background. He traced his lips against my hairline, his smell washing over me like waves from the ocean. It felt surreal.

"I'm sorry I—"

"Don't apologize, baby. Let's just move forward and spend the rest of our lives together."

"Okay. That sounds good to me."

Rex was still standing there, and he finally said something. "My god! Took you guys long enough. I'm so glad we can go back to normal now."

Zeke didn't take his eyes off me. "Me too."

Rex finally walked away and joined the girls at the table, giving us some privacy.

"Want to get out of here?" he asked.

"We have the rest of our lives," I whispered. "It can wait."

He smiled. "True. And we already got some hot action the other night."

My cheeks blushed at the memory, the way I pretty much demanded sex from him in the middle of the night.

He wrapped his arm around my waist and walked me back to the table, looking like the happiest guy in the world. His fingers dug tightly into my side with excitement and his powerful body felt comforting next to mine.

We scooted into the booth, and his arm immediately draped over my shoulders.

Jessie held her straw to her mouth but didn't take a drink because she was smiling. "That's better."

"Much better." Kayden scooted next to Rex and placed her hand on his thigh.

Rex shook his head. "I never thought I'd want you to make out with my sister so much."

"Well, you're in for a treat," Zeke said. "There's gonna be a lot of making out."

"Good for me." I glanced at Zeke's mouth, excited to kiss it later.

Rex cringed. "Nevermind. I'm not too excited about it anymore."

"Don't tease them." Kayden smacked his thigh. "You can give them one night to be however they want to be."

"Yeah, I guess," Rex said. "But I'm only doing it because I love you."

Kayden tried to grab her drink but nearly knocked it over instead. Her eyes were wide like golf balls, and she stopped breathing.

Jessie stiffened at the sound of the endearment. She was in the middle of sipping her drink when she stopped to nearly spit it out.

I hoped Rex would grow up to be a man, but I didn't think he'd really do it.

Rex clearly had no idea what he'd just said because he was looking at the entrance. "Tobias just walked in. Jess, things are still going well?"

Kayden was still in shock by what Rex had said, but now, she seemed confused about his comment toward Tobias.

"Uh, Rex?" I asked.

"What?" he said, looking at me with a slight hint of annoyance.

"Uh...do you know what you just said?" My brother was so clueless he didn't even notice his own actions.

"Yeah," he said like a smartass. "I said Tobias is here. Do we hate Tobias now?"

"No." Kayden finally found her voice, her eyes returning to normal. "You just told me you loved me."

"What?" Rex asked incredulously. "No, I didn't."

"Yeah, you did," Zeke said. "We all heard it, man."

"Did not," Rex argued. "I think I would know."

"Obviously, you don't," Jessie said. "You just blurted it out two minutes ago."

"You guys need to lay off the drinks," Rex said. "Because there's no way in hell I said that."

Zeke rolled his eyes. "Grow a pair and just admit it. You love Kayden."

"Whatever," Rex said.

I figured out what Rex was really doing. It took me a few minutes to crack the code, but once I did, everything made sense. "Kayden, he knows what he said. He wanted to tell you, but he wanted it to be so casual that he wouldn't have to put his heart on the line. Because in the end, he's scared you're going to leave him someday, the way our father left us."

Rex turned to me with an expression I couldn't read.

Kayden turned her body and wrapped her arms around his shoulders. "I love you too, Rex. I'm never going anywhere." She buried her face into his neck and held him, ignoring the fact we were all there and staring.

Rex lowered his gaze and wrapped his long arms around her, encompassing her effortlessly. Then he placed a kiss against her hairline, giving her the kind of affection I'd never seen him give in my life.

Jessie turned to me. "Aww..."

"They really are cute together," I whispered.

"Today has been a great day for couples," Jessie said. "I have a feeling Tobias is gonna give me some serious lovin'. Excuse me." She scooted out of the booth and fixed her already perfect hair. Then she strutted across the room right toward Tobias, making every other guy jealous that she was taken.

Zeke pressed his face to mine. "I'm gonna give you some good lovin' tonight too."

"You better."

***

Zeke and Rex went to the bathroom, so the girls and I stood at a table while we waited. "I think we're gonna take off." I wasn't sure what I was more excited about, having sex in Zeke's bed or going to sleep in it. It would feel like home all over again, the place where I was supposed to be.

"I'm surprised you lasted so long." Jessie stood with Tobias, his arm around her petite waistline.

"Me too," Kayden said. "I figured you'd be getting it on right about now."

"Oh, we will." I already knew I wanted to be on top for our first rendezvous.

"You get him, girl." Jessie finished the rest of her drink before she placed the empty glass on the table.

Tobias smiled like he was impressed. "You drink more than anyone I know, but you're never drunk. What's that about?"

"Because ladies never get drunk." She batted her eyelashes and gave him a flirtatious smile.

When he looked down at her, he took a peek at her cleavage line. "Let's go back to my place."

I glanced at the bathroom and saw the guys return, laughing about something. "They're on their way, so we can all go home and get some."

"Excellent," Kayden said. "I'm so glad I never have to go home alone again."

Zeke came to my side, a look of love reflected in his eyes. "Ready to go?"

"Even if they aren't ready to go," Rex said to Kayden. "I'm ready to go."

"Yeah, me too," Kayden said with a chuckle.

"Can we go by my place and pick up Safari?" My dog should have been the last thing on my mind, but he would be so happy to return to Zeke's place.

Zeke smiled. "Absolutely." Just when he turned away from the table, he nearly bumped into a blonde that appeared out of nowhere. "Excuse me."

She didn't get out of the way. "Zeke, right?" She had bright blue eyes, just like Zeke's, a pretty face, and a body that rivaled Jessie's. If she wasn't sure of his name, then she obviously didn't know him very well. Perhaps she was a patient.

"Yeah," he said. "I'm sorry, do I know you?"

"Yeah." She lowered her voice so the rest of us couldn't hear. "We hooked up about two months ago. Remember, we were at the Raging Bull with Denise before we headed back to my apartment?"

God, I felt sick.

She was the woman.

The other woman.

Everyone else heard what she said and they turned pale white. Jessie's eyes immediately darted to my face. Kayden automatically covered her mouth with her hand, silencing a gasp.

Zeke was completely caught off guard. "Uh..."

"I've been looking for you everywhere," she continued. "I had a lot of fun that night. Denise did too."

Who the hell is Denise?

Didn't she see his arm around my waist?

I wanted to punch her teeth out.

Zeke cleared his throat, still shocked. "I have a girlfriend." That was the only thing he could spit out.

"Oh..." She finally looked at me, noticing me beside him. "Well, Denise and I had fun with you, so I'm always open to a threesome again." She pulled out a napkin with her number already written on the material. "Give me a call if you want." She left it on the table before she walked away, her dress so short her ass pretty much hung out.

All the happiness left my body.

I felt like I might throw up.

So it wasn't just one woman.

It was two.

Two fucking women.

Now I didn't want his hands on me. I never wanted him to touch me again. He went out that night and fucked two women at the same time while I slept in his bed and waited for him to come home. I told Ryker I wanted to marry Zeke, and at that very moment, he was in bed with two women.

Fucking asshole.

I pushed his arm off my waist, feeling dirty.

Zeke immediately turned back to me. "Rae, listen —"

"You lied to me." I tried to keep my voice steady, but it escaped as a scream. "You fucking lied to me."

"What?" he asked blankly, having no idea what I was talking about.

"You said there was only one woman. Clearly, there were two."

"Apparently," he said. "But I honestly don't remember —"

"You can remember one woman but not two?" I shrieked. "You're so full of it." I pushed him in the chest then stormed off, wanting to get out of that bar as fast as I could. I wasn't heartbroken like last time. Now I was just furious. For the past two months, I'd been miserable without Zeke and I just wanted to be with him again. But now, I just thought of him as a pig.

When I was outside, he caught up to me. "Rae, hold on."

I twisted away from his grasp. "Don't. Touch. Me."

He kept his hands to himself but walked with me. "I honestly don't remember. I didn't lie to you."

"You're lying to me right now."

"Rae, I'm serious. Why would I tell you I slept with someone else to begin with if I was just going to lie about part of the story? Calm down and think rationally."

"Fuck you, Zeke. I'm beyond rational right now."

He kept walking beside me, his pace slower than mine so I could keep up with him in my heels. "The past is in the past. Yeah, it happened. But we're two months into the future now. We love each other, and we want to be together. You can forgive me for sleeping with one woman. Why does two make a difference?"

I stopped walking, shocked by the bullshit he just fed me. "Are you serious right now? You think two women is the same as one woman?"

"It was at the same time, so it's one act," he argued. "It wasn't like it was two different nights."

I held my hand in his face. "Just stop talking."

"Rae, I'm sorry. I'll apologize as many times as you need to hear it. But I really didn't remember."

"Did you even wear a condom?"

"Of course I did."

"So you remember that part, but you don't remember there being two women?" That didn't seem possible to me.

"You have no idea how much I drank that night."

"So you may not have worn something?"

"No, I did," he said firmly. "Even if I didn't, I got tested and I'm clean. You know I would never put you in jeopardy like that."

I was too pissed to care about that piece of information. "I'm done, Zeke. I'm actually done this time. This isn't going to work."

"Don't say that." He maneuvered in front of me, forcing me to stop. "I understand you're mad right now and that's okay. You're entitled to be pissed off. But I didn't lie to you. And this doesn't change anything. I've already explained my point of view from that night. We both know I would never do anything like that again."

I tried to get around him. "I don't care, Zeke."

He grabbed me and forced me to stand still. "How would you feel if I slept with someone during these past two months?"

"I couldn't care less." He was single and could do whatever he wanted.

"Bullshit, Rae. If I even looked at someone, you would be upset. And you would have every right because we're still together... even if we aren't together. If you let Ryker even touch your hand, I would be pissed off. I've been faithful to you even though I technically didn't have to be, okay? I'm loyal. I'm honest. And I'm so fucking in love with you. That counts for something."

I shook my head, still livid. "You're a pig, Zeke. A goddamn pig."

The fire left his eyes, and he looked wounded. "Rae, you know how I was before I got with Rochelle. Yes, I had threesomes. You know I had foursomes. You know I'd pick up a girl on a Saturday night and then never see her again. I was playing the field because I couldn't have the one woman I actually wanted. I'm not a pig, Rae. I'm a man like every other guy in the world. But I happily said goodbye to all that when I finally got you. You know I'm not a pig, so don't call me that. You know how I feel about you. So please, let's just leave that night in the past and move on. Let's just forget that horrific nightmare and be happy together. Let's carry on."

I crossed my arms over my chest, not even remotely tempted by that option. "No."

He sighed loudly, showing his frustration as well as his pain. "Less than ten minutes ago, you were happy. You were looking at me the way you used to. And not even forty-eight hours ago, you were on my doorstep asking me to make love to you. Let's go back to that."

"I can't. I feel nothing but disgust toward you." I stepped away, needing more space.

293

He dragged his hands down his face, showing his anger. "Rae, there's nothing more I can do. You know I love you. You know I'm sorry. One woman or two, it doesn't make a difference to me. That night happened because you were with Ryker — plain and simple. I can't keep taking all the blame for this."

I shook my head. "I can't believe you're turning this around on me and making excuses."

"I'm not making excuses at all," he snapped. "I'm just telling you that as much as I love you, I can't keep doing this. We're together or we aren't together. No more back and forth, no more asking me to sleep over, no more flipping on me. This is the moment of truth. You either forgive me and give me a clean slate and we move on, or you don't and we're done. What's it gonna be?"

"You're giving me an ultimatum?"

"I guess," he said. "I know you've been through a rough time, but I can promise you, what you felt these past two months, I've felt it a million times more. I can't keep doing this to myself. I've apologized and done everything I possibly could to make this right. If this is over, then I need to move on instead of letting my heart get stomped on every day. So, what's it gonna be?"

Tears burned in the back of my eyes, full of frustration and heartbreak.

"Pick, Rae." His eyes burned into mine, needing an answer.

"I..."

"What?" he pressed.

A tear rolled down my cheek. "We're over."

Zeke took a deep breath but hid his pain. His eyes didn't water like they did before. His shoulders were just as straight, and he held himself upright despite the agony surging in his veins. He finally gave a slight nod of calm acceptance. "Okay. We're over."

Chapter Eighteen

Rae

Somehow, I arrived at Ryker's building.

My feet carried me down the blocks of Seattle, and I felt numb the entire time. The cold didn't bother me despite the fact I only wore a short dress and heels. The agony is what got to me—the rage. I couldn't look at Zeke in the same way, not after what he did. One woman was difficult enough, but two…it was unthinkable.

I rode the elevator to his floor without even thinking twice about it. I couldn't remember the code to get inside because it'd been so long. But even if I did, I had no right to walk inside. So I hit the buzzer.

His deep voice came through the intercom. "Who is it?"

I opened my mouth, but no words came out. I had to clear my throat before the word could form on my tongue. "Rae."

The doors opened immediately, revealing his luxurious apartment with the amazing views of Seattle in the background. The Space Needle was so close I could actually see through the windows.

Ryker came out of the other living room in a black t-shirt and dark jeans. He walked right up to me, the line between the apartment and the elevator in between us. His eyes examined my face, knowing I had just hit rock bottom. "Sweetheart, what happened?"

I crossed the threshold and moved into his chest, feeling the hardness of his body the second I collided with him. The doors shut behind me, and I inhaled his scent, recognizing his body soap from the shower. My arms circled his waist, and I treasured the affection, needing something to get me by.

His arms circled my waist and he pressed his forehead to mine, his eyes closed.

"I just kept walking...and this is where I ended up."

"There are worse places," he whispered.

My arms rested on his, and I closed my eyes. "Can I stay here?"

He brushed his lips across my hairline, gently kissing me. "You know you can stay here forever." He scooped me into his arms effortlessly and carried me into his bedroom. He set me on the bed and kneeled before me, slipping off my heels that were now scuffed up from walking so far. He gave my feet a quick massage before he rose to his full height and opened his drawers. He pulled out a pair of boxers and a t-shirt before he set them on the bed. "I'll give you a minute." He walked out and shut the bedroom door behind him.

I grabbed the shirt and felt the fabric in my fingertips, remembering the nights I used to wear his shirts to bed. I was on these very sheets when I locked eyes with him and told him I loved him. And that was the last time we ever slept together.

I got dressed and left my dress and heels on his dresser. His bed looked so comfy, despite the thoughts of all the women who'd come and gone since I left. I moved to my side of the bed, the right side, and pulled the sheets to my shoulder.

Ryker gently knocked on the door before he entered the bedroom. He spotted me under the covers before he pulled his shirt over his head and dropped his jeans on the floor. He pulled on a pair of sweatpants before he turned off the lamp on the nightstand and got into bed beside me.

He stayed on his side and didn't venture onto mine.

I hadn't slept in this bed in so long, but it felt exactly the way it used to. The sheets smelled like his body soap and shampoo.

He tucked his arms behind his head and looked up at the ceiling, the lights from the city shining through the floor-to-ceiling windows. "What happened, sweetheart?"

"Zeke and I are over." Saying the words out loud hurt more than they ever had—because I knew they were true. We would never get back together. We wouldn't move in together and start a life.

He turned his head and looked at me, his blue eyes bright despite the darkness. "Why?"

"I decided to take him back because I missed him. And within ten minutes, the slut he slept with started talking to him...and it turns out there was another woman too. So he had a threesome that night but claims he doesn't remember."

Ryker didn't look triumphant at all. He looked just as sad as I felt.

"He says he doesn't remember, but I don't believe him. And even if he's telling the truth, I can't forgive him. It was hard enough with one woman...but two?" I shook my head and pulled the sheets against my chest. "It doesn't matter how much I love him. I'll never look at him the same."

Ryker said nothing, allowing me to do all the talking.

"He told me I was overreacting, that I needed to let it go and just move on. Then he said he couldn't handle my indecisiveness so he forced me to make a decision then and there, to either forgive him or forget him. So...I chose to forget him."

Ryker snaked his hand under the sheets until he found my hand next to the pillow. He interlocked our fingers and brushed his thumb over my knuckles, comforting me the only way he knew how.

"So...we're really over."

"I'm sorry, Rae."

"I know you are." I knew he truly cared about my pain, my sorrow. Even if that made it possible for him to have another chance with me, he was sad things didn't work out with Zeke. He cared more about my happiness than his own.

Ryker pulled his hand away then scooted closer to me across the bed. His arms wrapped around my waist, and he rested his head on the same pillow, our faces nearly touching. He closed his eyes and ran his fingers through my hair.

Somehow, he calmed me enough so I could fall asleep. I closed my eyes and slipped away, blanketed by the comfort of Ryker's presence. For a short period of time, I felt safe like nothing could hurt me. But I knew once I woke up the following morning, the pain would return in full force.

And I would have to deal with it.

When I woke up the following morning, I was still wrapped in Ryker's arms. His eyes were open and he was watching me, his lids heavy with sleep. His hair was messy from laying his head against the pillow all night.

"Morning, sweetheart."

"Morning."

"How'd you sleep?"

"Pretty good, actually." I didn't wake up once in the middle of the night with a nightmare.

"Great. I'm gonna make some breakfast." He pulled away, taking his comfort and warmth with him.

I stayed in bed because I didn't have the energy to get up. The same pain sat on top of my chest, weighing heavily on my entire frame. Every breath was harder than the last because I was still so angry with Zeke.

I hoped I wouldn't always be angry with him.

A ringing cell phone came to my ears, and a moment later, I heard Ryker's voice. "Hey, man. Yeah, she's here."

Who was he talking to?

"Yeah, she's fine. Bye."

Was he talking to Zeke? Or Rex? I hopped out of bed and walked into the kitchen. Ryker had a pot of coffee going and eggs in the frying pan. His cell phone sat on the counter, the screen still lit up. "Who were you talking to?"

He divided the eggs between two plates then set the dirty pan in the sink. "Rex called me. Just wanted to know if you were here."

"Oh..." He'd probably called me, but my phone was buried in the bottom of my purse—abandoned on the couch.

"And he still hates me," he said with a chuckle. He poured two mugs of coffee and set the kitchen table with two forks. "Sit down and have some breakfast."

I didn't have an appetite, but since he went through the trouble of cooking me something, I sat down and did my best. The window was right next to the table, overlooking the city. It was a cloudless day, bright and sunny. There hadn't been much rain this week, which was a nice change.

Ryker sat across from me, still looking glorious with his shirt off. He seemed to be in better shape than before, his muscles carefully outlined as if they were carved out of stone. His skin was flawless, fair and smooth.

I felt his eyes on my face, so I quickly looked away.

"Like what you see?" he asked with a smile.

"You look like you're in better shape." I decided to be honest instead of pretending I hadn't been staring.

"Was I in bad shape before?"

I laughed because it was absurd. "Not at all. You just look...bigger."

"I've been working out a lot over the past few months. Gives me something to do."

"I haven't been working out at all...but I never work out."

"Not true. You jog."

"That's just because Safari needs to go on walks."

He sipped his coffee. "It's still better than nothing."

I took a few bites of my eggs, my stomach still indifferent. "Thanks for breakfast."

"Thanks for eating. I know you aren't hungry."

Ryker knew me too well.

"Now what?"

"I don't know what you mean." It was difficult for me to think about the future.

"With you and Zeke. If it's really over, then what?"

"We'll always be friends." That was something I could count on no matter what. Zeke and I respected each other far too much to turn our backs on our friendship. Maybe our relationship didn't work, but our friendship would last forever.

"You think you can handle that?"

"Yeah." It would take some time to get used to, but one day, everything would be back to normal.

He finished his eggs and sipped his coffee, his shoulders broad and powerful. He set his mug down and looked me in the eye. "When can I ask you out?"

The forward question caught me off guard. I told Ryker nothing would happen between us, but he obviously didn't believe me. "I said we would never get back together."

"But you also slept in my bed last night. And you told me if Zeke weren't in the picture, you might give me another chance. Clearly, Zeke is officially gone. I did the right thing and tried to steer you back to him, but it didn't work. I was a good guy because that's what you deserved. But now, things are different, Rae. So, I'll ask again. When can I make a move?"

Now that Zeke had hurt me so much, I knew we couldn't get back together. But I couldn't go back to Ryker either. My heart wasn't in the right place. I could lie to myself and say I was over Zeke, but even I knew that was bullshit. "I'm not ready, Ryker."

"That's fine. When do you think you will be?"

I didn't have an answer for that either. "I don't know. Maybe never..."

His eyes fell in sadness. "How about this? If you ever start to feel differently, you just let me know. Until that moment comes, I'll only be your friend. Does that sound fair?"

Very fair. "Yeah."

"Alright." He grabbed his mug and took another sip, acting casual like he didn't just put me on the spot.

Chapter Nineteen

Rex

Zeke sat across from me at his dining table, the French doors opened to the backyard where the sun shined on the grass. He slouched forward with his elbows resting on the surface, a permanent frown on his face. His eyes were full of hostility, and he looked like he wanted to hit someone — even me.

I'd been meaning to say something for the last ten minutes but couldn't think of anything helpful. My best friend was in a deeper hole than he was before, and any second now, he was about to lose control altogether. "So, you really said all that to her?"

"Damn right I did." He clenched his jaw. "I get she's mad. It's okay to be mad, alright? But to dump me again, going back and forth all the time, it's just bullshit. It's time for that little princess to start taking responsibility for her actions too. None of this shit would have happened if she wasn't up on Ryker all the time."

He'd never said anything mean about Rae, so I knew he was really ticked. "She's not up on Ryker."

"Oh, come on." His eyes shined with rage. "She'll forgive him for the stunt he pulled, but she won't even think of forgiving me. We both know she loved Ryker more than she ever loved me. I give up, man. I officially give up."

"She didn't love him more than you." She never told me that, but I knew it was true. "And she did take you back. But then—"

"That stupid cunt ruined everything."

Maybe I should take all the knives out of the kitchen. He was about to stab someone. "She picked you over him, remember? Let's not forget that happened."

Zeke looked out the window, his jaw clenched.

"And I can't believe you said that to her." Making her choose right then and there didn't sound like a smart idea. She ended up at Ryker's for the night.

"I'm not babying her anymore," he snapped. "I did what I did. I won't make excuses for it. But I'm not gonna keep kissing her ass. If she wants me, I'm here. But if she doesn't, then I'm moving on."

I didn't believe that—not for a second.

He must have known because he lowered his gaze, not making eye contact with me. "I know how she is. If I try to win her back or convince her to be with me, it just pushes her away. This cold-hearted distance is better. It'll make her rethink her decisions."

"Are you sure about that?"

"She came back to me the first time, right?" he said. "I didn't chase her. I let her come to me."

"But is that gonna work a second time?"

He sighed and dragged his hands down his face. "Fuck, I don't know. I don't know what to do. I'm so pissed at her, but goddammit, I love her. I love her more than any other guy will love her. I just want to grab all her shit and make her move in with me. I wanna get married, have kids, all that stupid stuff. I'm still stuck in this warzone when it comes to her. I'm never gonna get over her. We both know it."

Yeah, probably not. "Well…maybe this isn't the best time, but I need to tell you something."

He closed his eyes for a moment. "What?"

"She slept at Ryker's last night."

He didn't react at all.

"I couldn't get a hold of her, so I called him this morning. He told me she stayed over."

Zeke ran his fingers through his hair and sighed, but he didn't flip the table over.

"Are you okay?"

"Yeah." He cleared his throat. "I'm fine."

I wasn't sure how he was fine right now. If Rae slept over there, she probably slept with him.

Zeke responded to my unsaid statement. "She didn't have sex with him."

"What makes you so sure?"

He looked out the window again. "She wouldn't do that. I know her."

After being told off like she had been, I would be surprised if she didn't sleep with Ryker.

"She was mad, but not mad enough to do that." He seemed certain about it, like there was no possibility Rae would get involved with him again.

Since he seemed so sure, I didn't try to tell him otherwise. Besides, it might kill him. "Then what are you going to do now? I really don't think ignoring her is going to work this time."

"I didn't ignore her last time."

"You know what I mean."

He shrugged when he couldn't find the words. "I never thought I'd say this, but damn, I wish I'd listened to you."

I couldn't force a smile. "I know."

"This whole thing is so stupid. We should be together right now."

"I'm very wise, I know."

Zeke rubbed his temple as if he had a migraine. "I really don't know where to go from here. Not a clue."

"I wouldn't mind killing Ryker."

He chuckled. "Yeah. But I don't think that would help me get Rae back."

"But you would feel better."

"Yeah...for a while." His playfulness died away when he came back to reality.

Zeke and Rae were so screwed up, and I didn't have any hope for them. They finally hit rock bottom and there was no way for them to come back from that. I wouldn't have been surprised if Rae ended up with Ryker, getting married and having kids. Then Zeke would end up with someone else... It was all pretty depressing. I didn't like thinking about it. But then an idea came to me. "I think I know what you should do...but you aren't going to like it."

"Well, you were right about me not telling her in the first place, so I have an open mind."

"Well...I think you should start seeing someone."

Zeke gave me a blank look, like he didn't understand what I said.

"Not for real. Just pretend. Someone super, super hot. Someone really chill, athletic, and just awesome."

"What's that going to do?"

"Dude, it'll make Rae so jealous she'll come crawling back."

"Or it'll just push her further into Ryker's arms."

"Yeah, that could happen..." Rae would probably be upset and do something stupid, like sleep with Ryker. But that was a risk he had to take. "But when she realizes how awesome this chick is, she'll know she's the real deal...that you're probably going to marry her someday. And if she doesn't do something now while she still has the chance, she'll lose you forever."

Zeke was reluctant, like I expected him to be. "If she really thought I had a girlfriend, she wouldn't try to win me back. When I was with Rochelle, she never told me how she felt."

"But that was different. Now she sees you as hers. You'll always be hers, you know?"

"I guess," he admitted.

"I'm telling you, it would work."

"I don't know..." He shook his head. "I don't want to play games with her."

"And what are you doing now?" I snapped. "You're messing with her head as we speak."

"This is different. This will hurt her."

"Dude, you've gotta hurt her. Make her understand that you aren't going to wait around forever. Make her realize she has to forget the past and move on if she wants you for the rest of her life. I think this plan is pretty solid."

"I don't even know a chick like that."

"I do."

He rolled his eyes. "Do not say Kayden."

"I wasn't. You think I'd pimp out my lady?"

"Honestly, yeah—at least for me."

"Nope, not even you." Just the idea of Kayden touching someone besides me made my blood boil. "What about Zoey's friend Monica? That chick is so damn hot. Remember?"

"Oh, yeah…" Zeke nodded when realized who I was talking about. "Yeah, she is. But I'm not gonna be able to convince her to be my fake girlfriend. I'm sure she has more important things to do."

"Or she could be your real girlfriend."

He shook his head. "I'll pass."

"You just said she was hot."

"Yeah, she is. But she's not Rae."

Because she was better than Rae. "I'm sure Zoey would help us out. She was pretty bummed when you guys broke up."

"Man, my whole family was torn apart. My mom still calls me every day and asks if I got her back yet."

"Seriously? Did you tell her what happened?"

He nodded.

"You told your mom about your one-night stand?" I couldn't even tell Rae something like that, let alone my own mother.

"Rex, you know I'm close with my family. I don't tell my mom everything about my personal life, but she wanted to know why we broke up...so I told her. I was pretty upset at the time, and I needed someone to talk to."

"Such a mama's boy..." I rolled my eyes.

Zeke didn't seem offended. "So, I don't think that will work."

"I think it will. We can give her a few hundred bucks or something. It'll only take, like, two weeks of her time."

"You think I can get Rae back that quickly?" he asked incredulously.

"With Monica, hell yeah. But you've got to be serious about it. You've got to make it seem like you're really over Rae and you're doing your own thing now."

Zeke sighed like that was impossible.

"I'm serious."

"Yeah, I know."

"And you've got to be prepared for Rae to hook up with Ryker. It's a serious possibility."

The blood drained from his face.

"Can you accept that?"

He still looked sick. "I don't know…"

"If you think about it, you'd be even."

"This isn't a game, Rex."

"You're right. It's a war." Zeke got her back once, but she'd slipped away. And now it would be even harder to get her back a second time. "If you don't do this, she's going to sleep with him again anyway. At least this will get you back together."

Zeke was quiet.

"So, you want to go through with this?"

Zeke still didn't have an answer, his jaw tense.

"Come on, man."

He finally agreed. "I guess it's worth a shot."

"That's the spirit," I said. "But if she brings Ryker around, you've got to be so damn cool, alright?"

"Yeah, I know."

"That will bother Rae more than anything else."

"Or just confuse her."

"No. It'll put her on the right path to where she should be. She'll kick Ryker to the curb and beg you to take her back. And then this nightmare will finally be over."

Chapter Twenty

Rae

A week went by, and Zeke didn't contact me.

Not that I expected he would.

Okay, I expected it a little...

Rex and Kayden were coming over for the game, and I debated inviting Zeke. I knew that if none of these relationship problems were occurring, I would invite him in a heartbeat—because he was my friend. So, I pulled out my phone and typed the message. *Rex and Kayden are coming over to watch the game if you want to stop by.* Before I thought too much about it, I hit send.

The three dots didn't appear.

For an hour and a half.

Then he finally wrote back. *I'll be there.* That was all he said. As impossible as it was, I felt his indifference through the phone.

I wanted to write something back to break the ice, but I couldn't think of anything good to say. So I just let it be, knowing our first interaction would be awkward, bordering on painful. But we had to get through it.

An hour later, there was a knock on my door. There were still forty-five minutes until the game started, but perhaps Zeke decided to come early so we could talk in private. "It's open." I got off the couch and walked into the kitchen.

Ryker opened the door with a bag of groceries in his hand. "Hey. Thought I'd stop by and cook dinner."

Safari took a defensive stand and growled viciously.

"Safari, chill." I walked over to him and gave him a gentle pat on the nose. "Stop growling at him."

"I think I know what might help..." Ryker pulled a dog bone out of the bag and handed it over. "Truce?"

Safari snatched it out of his hand and walked away to enjoy it in the living room.

"I think I'm softening him up." He set the groceries on the counter.

"Maybe, but I wouldn't mind him. He'd never actually bite you."

"I don't know..." Ryker pulled out the chicken and vegetables.

I watched him unpack the food and tried to think of something smart to say. People were coming over, and I didn't necessarily want Zeke to see Ryker. We were really done so I could do whatever I wanted, but I didn't want to parade it around him. "Actually, I invited people over to watch the game..."

"Oh, really?" He put everything in the fridge. "It'll still be good tomorrow, so I'll whip up something then."

I should've invited him to stay because it was rude not to, but I couldn't bring myself to do it.

Ryker leaned against the counter, obviously having no intention of leaving. "How was work?"

"It was okay. Just bacteria and fungi, the usual."

He smiled even though he didn't seem that interested. "You're such a cute nerd."

"I may be cute, but I'm not a nerd."

The door opened again, and Zeke walked inside with a case of beer.

Oh, god.

Zeke spotted Ryker but didn't react whatsoever. "I got Blue Moon. Thought I'd change it up again." He opened the fridge and placed the case inside before he grabbed a bottle. "You want one, man?" He held it out to Ryker.

I couldn't believe what I was seeing.

Ryker couldn't believe it either. He kept staring at him like he thought it was a joke. "Uh, sure." Ryker took the bottle and twisted off the cap.

Did Zeke just call Ryker man?

"You want one, Rae?" He grabbed another beer from the top shelf.

"Yeah, sure," I answered.

He tossed it to me, refraining from touching me.

The second I grabbed the bottle, I felt hurt. "Why are you here so early? The game doesn't start for an hour."

"No." He eyed his watch. "It started five minutes ago."

"Are you sure?" I raised an eyebrow.

Ryker pulled out his phone. "Yeah, the Wizards are winning."

"Oh..." How did I get that mixed up? I hoped Rex and Kayden would be there soon. Otherwise, it would just be me stuck with the two of them...my exes. "Let me put it on." I walked into the living room and hit the button on the remote.

"How's your trash empire?" Zeke asked in the kitchen.

Were they actually talking?

Ryker was caught off guard by Zeke's interest. "Pretty much the same. People don't recycle enough."

"We're pretty green at my office. People don't take it seriously though."

I still couldn't believe this.

"Catch the Mariner game yesterday?"

"Yeah," Ryker said. "I'm glad we won. Couldn't handle another loss."

Were they friends again?

I walked back into the kitchen. "You were right, the game is on."

"Told ya." Zeke drank his beer and walked past both of us, acting like it was a year in the past. Back when Zeke and I were just friends, and Ryker was the one I was dating.

Once he was out of sight, Ryker turned to me with a questioning look.

I only shrugged in response. "I'm gonna go get Rex. Be right back."

"Alright." Ryker walked into the living room and sat on the other couch.

I practically ran across the hall and broke down the door with my fists.

"What?" Rex asked the second he opened the door. "What's with the drumming?"

"The game is on now so come over."

"I think Kayden and I are gonna stay here. We have leftover tacos —"

"You guys are coming over. I've got Ryker and Zeke both in there right now, and it's the most awkward thing in the world."

Rex couldn't hide his surprise. "Why is Ryker there?"

"I don't know. He just stopped by."

"We're coming." Kayden met me at the door. "Rex, we have to go now. We can have sex later."

Rex glared at her, his eyes narrowing. "It better include a blowjob now."

"Like you don't get enough of those from me already." She walked across the hall and entered my apartment. "Get your ass over here."

I was so grateful Kayden turned into a hardass with him. I joined her in the apartment, Rex right behind me. Once we were inside, I felt a little less terrified of the arrangement I was in. There hadn't been any punches, and everything was oddly calm—but that's what frightened me.

Rex sat on the couch beside Zeke, giving Ryker a look of pure hatred.

Ryker smiled then held up his beer. "How's it going?"

"Pretty terrible since you're still breathing," Rex countered.

Zeke tried not to laugh.

"Rex." I put my hands on my hips and gave him a look our mother used to give us.

He didn't apologize, but at least he turned to the TV.

Kayden took the last seat on the couch, both of them silently supporting Zeke and sticking to his side of the room.

I sat on the couch with Ryker, leaving a few feet between us.

Safari grabbed his bone off the floor and walked to Zeke. He laid down right at his feet, returning to chewing his bone.

His choice was pretty clear.

Ryker drank his beer and pretended this wasn't uncomfortable at all.

Zeke didn't seem to care in the least. "Ryker, do you have a dog?"

Ryker was as surprised by the engaging question as I was. "Not yet. But I'm thinking of getting one. I'll need to move to the suburbs first."

"My neighborhood is nice. It's really quiet and close to the coast." Zeke rested his beer on his thigh. "There's this pretty rad place that just went up for sale around the corner from my place. You should check it out."

Was Zeke really giving Ryker advice about real estate? And close to where he lived?

"Thanks for the tip." Ryker subtly turned to me, giving me a questioning look.

Again, I just shrugged in response.

"Hey, Rex," Zeke said. "You want to make the game interesting?"

"What are you thinking?" Rex asked.

"Hundred bucks on the Wizards," Zeke said. "Are you in?"

Rex looked at Zeke like he was an idiot. "I just took that bet from Rae and cleaned her out."

"I know," Zeke said. "She's not allowed to gamble anymore, so I'm gonna get her cash back."

"Dude, the Wizards aren't gonna win," Rex said. "I don't mind taking money from my sister, but it would be weird taking money from you."

"Ouch," I hissed.

"Because you're family," he reminded me. "So, it's kind of a compliment."

"Believe me," I said sarcastically. "It's not a compliment."

Ryker turned to me, his handsome smile on his face.

I leaned farther away from him on the couch, not wanting anyone to think I was hooking up with Ryker. Zeke pissed me off and pushed me away, but I couldn't do something like that so soon. It wouldn't be right.

The Wizards scored three three-pointers in a row, and Zeke sighed in triumph. "I want a single crisp one hundred dollar bill." He leaned down and rubbed Safari's head. "And throw a dog bone in there for me."

***

The Wizards won, and Rex reluctantly handed over the cash. "This sucks."

"I know," I said. "I remember when I had to open my own wallet."

"Now that my work here is done, I'm gonna take off." He tossed his beer bottles in the recycling bin then walked up to me and raised his hand in the air.

I stared at it blankly, having no idea what he was doing.

"Thanks for having me over. High-five."

High-five?

When I left him hanging, he grabbed my wrist and tapped it against his palm. "See you later. Bye, Ryker. Let me know if you check out the place. My realtor is awesome." He walked out without further conversation, buoyant and borderline happy.

What the hell was going on?

"She owes me a blowjob." Rex wrapped his arm around Kayden. "So, we're gonna go. Peace out." He held up a peace sign with his fingers then left the apartment.

When I was alone with Ryker, I finally wore my thoughts on my sleeve. "I have no idea what just happened…"

"I'm not sure either." Ryker tossed his empty bottle in the recycling bin then leaned against the counter. "It's like Zeke and I are friends again. Strange."

"Just last week, we were back together. And now, he doesn't care?"

Ryker shrugged. "Maybe he's given up and just accepts it. Technically, you haven't really been together in two months, so it's not like this is sudden for either of you."

"I guess..." I just couldn't believe how quickly he'd moved on. He went back to being my friend like he'd never loved me. He didn't look at me the way he used to, with undying affection in his eyes. At the bar, he seemed like he wanted to hold me forever and never let me go. And now...it was pure indifference.

"Does that bother you?" Ryker watched me closely, analyzing my features.

"I don't know... I'm just not used to it."

"You know, it's not too late," he said. "I'm sure you could still talk to him about working things out..."

"He slept with two women, Ryker."

He shrugged. "Yeah, it was shitty. But his heart is in the right place, and if you ask me, that's more important."

"You're pushing for him again?"

He held up both hands. "I'm not pushing for anything. I just want you to have what you want. That's all. Believe me, I wish I were what you wanted." He nodded to the couch. "Right here, right now."

My cheeks reddened, and a smile formed on my lips.

"I'm just being a good guy right now. But believe me, I can't wait to be a bad guy again." He walked back into the living room and watched Safari play with the bone he brought for him. "So, you want to watch something else or should I go?"

I didn't want to be alone. Ryker was good company. He made me smile and laugh more than anyone else. "No. I want you to stay."

"Great. So, what should we watch?"

Chapter Twenty-One

Rex

"Dude, you did a phenomenal job last night."

Zeke stared at the TV, his face full of unspoken rage.

"How did you do it?"

"I took a Xanax before I went over."

"Xanax?" Was that a drug or something?

"It's a med that forces you to relax."

"And you drank after you took it?" I wasn't bright, but I knew that wasn't the smart thing to do.

He shrugged. "Whatever. Didn't really care at the time."

"But you handled that well. I could tell Rae was totally confused. Ryker too."

"Yeah." He dragged his hands down his face. "This better work, Rex. I can't stand seeing Ryker even sit on the couch with her. She should be mine right now. Everyone knows it."

"I know, man. We've just got to be patient."

The girls finally walked inside, Zoey with her light brown hair like Zeke's, and Monica looking like a *Sports Illustrated* model with her jet black hair, green eyes, and smokin' body. "They're here."

Zeke sighed. "I can't believe I'm doing this…"

"It'll be worth it. Trust me."

Zoey walked up first and hugged me. "Hey, Rex. Long time, no see."

"We need to hang out more often," I said. "Just because you're the cuter sibling."

Zoey smiled. "You have an excellent point, Rex."

Monica walked up to me next, curvy and perfect. "Haven't seen you around. How have you been?"

I didn't hug her or shake her hand. Somehow, it felt wrong since I found her attractive. Kayden would kick my ass if I even touched this woman. "Uh…I have a girlfriend." I assumed I was supposed to be upfront about that information with pretty girls. I wasn't totally sure since I'd never done the relationship thing before, but it was probably best if I put that out there.

She chuckled. "Okay. Good to know…" She hugged Zeke next, and Zeke barely touched her with his hands, acting like he was doing something wrong. Once they pulled away, he relaxed and sat down.

"So." Zoey led the conversation, usually being the one in charge. "I talked to Monica about everything, and she's on board."

"Really?" Zeke couldn't hide his surprise. "Because you really don't need to help me out." He looked at Monica, his arms across his chest. "I'm sure you have better things to do —"

"You've been in love with Rae since you were sixteen," Monica interrupted. "I remember seeing the way you looked at her and hoping some man would look at me that way."

I was sure every man did.

"We need to make this work," Zoey said. "You're thirty years old, and you aren't married. I'm not having kids anytime soon, so you need to get on that. Mom is driving me crazy."

"Believe me, I'd be making babies with her right now if I could," Zeke said with a straight face.

I cringed automatically.

337

"So, we're gonna do this," Zoey said. "Monica is gonna make Rae so jealous it won't even be funny. Rae will get over your little mishap, and everything will be back to normal. We need Rae to come back because she's the only girlfriend of yours I've ever liked."

"Well, you've only met Rochelle," Zeke reminded her.

"Yeah," Zoey said coldly. "And she was *not* a good fit."

Even though Rochelle was long gone, I actually felt bad for her.

Zeke didn't stand up for Rochelle like he normally would have. He must have understood there was no point now that so much time had passed. "So, when do we begin?"

"I think you shouldn't see Rae for at least two weeks," Zoey said. "That way, when you bring Monica around, it's not so sudden. And we need to start flooding your Facebook with pictures of you guys."

"I'm hardly on Facebook," Zeke said.

"Monica will post things and tag you," Zoey said. "That's even better because it doesn't look like you're flaunting it. And Monica is awesome at basketball. She used to play in high school and a little in college."

"So?" Zeke asked.

"Dude, that will drive Rae crazy," I said. "Basketball is her thing. That's perfect." The ground beneath Rae's feet was going to shake— and shake hard. "She's gonna be in for a surprise. We can't tell any of the girls about this plan. We've got to make it genuine."

"What about Kayden?" Zeke asked.

I shook my head. "We can't tell her either. Their reactions to seeing you two together have to be authentic. And all I'm gonna tell Kayden is you started seeing Monica but haven't told me much about her because I haven't seen you—because you're too busy with your new girlfriend."

"I don't think we should call her my girlfriend," Zeke said. "Too serious."

"Yeah, you might be right," I said in agreement. "I guess we just won't put a label on it."

Monica ran her hand up his arm. "I'm excited for this plan. If there's an opportunity to kiss you, I'm going for it."

Zeke let her touch him, but he didn't seem thrilled about the kissing part. Normally, he would've smiled and said something cocky, but now, he was silent.

"This is gonna work," Zoey said. "Mark my words. If a woman responds to anything, it's jealousy. So, let the games begin."

Chapter Twenty-Two

Rae

Two weeks passed in a slow blur. Zeke didn't contact me, but I still dreamt about him every night. Sometimes we were going out to dinner, having a date night like we used to. But most of the time, we were making love in his bed. I woke up to my fingers pressed against my clit, touching myself in my sleep.

I had it bad.

Now that I couldn't forgive him, I expected to move on without any problem, but I hadn't made any progress at all. Everything stayed exactly the same. I went out with Jessie and Kayden for drinks after work, and we talked about my love life — like always.

"Anything happen with Ryker?" Jessie asked, her eyes on me and not her drink.

"No." Ryker hadn't made a move because I hadn't made a move first.

"Really?" Jessie asked in surprise. "You guys have been hanging out for a while. I figured something would have happened by now."

"I'm not ready," I said. "It's too soon."

"You and Zeke have been broken up for over two months," Kayden reminded me. "It's not like it just happened."

"Yeah, but I'm still not in that place." I was attracted to Ryker and remembered all the good sex we used to have, but I was still attached to Zeke. Sometimes I worried I would always be attached to Zeke.

Kayden sucked the olive off the stick in her drink. "Are you sure you don't want to take Zeke back—"

"Yes." It was hard enough for me to get over the fact he slept with one woman—but two? I couldn't look past that, especially after seeing one of them in the flesh.

Kayden backed off since she knew she couldn't change my mind. "Alright. Just wondering…"

"Are you gonna try dating in general?" Jessie said. "Or are you not ready for that either?"

Getting back into the dating scene sounded horrific. I'd been on a lot of dates, and most of them ended up badly. Very rarely did I meet a guy I really liked. I happened to get lucky with Ryker and Zeke, two incredible guys back to back. "I can't picture myself dating right now."

"Would you give Ryker a chance before that?" Jessie said.

"I don't know," I said. "A few weeks ago, Ryker asked me when he could ask me out..."

"What did you say?" Kayden asked.

"I said I wasn't ready to start something, and if I changed my mind, I'd let him know." He didn't pursue me aggressively like he had before. He respected me enough to give me time to figure out what I wanted on my own.

"He's awfully patient," Jessie noted.

"Really patient," Kayden said. "That's not the Ryker I remember."

"He's changed a lot." In fact, he'd changed so much, he wasn't the man I remembered. Now he was gentler, understanding, and open. Before, he would barely let me examine his surface. But now, he allowed me to see all the way down to his soul.

Jessie finished her drink and scooted to the edge of the table. "I'm getting a refill. Want anything?"

"I'm still working on mine." My vodka cranberry was still half full, and it was my second one for the night.

"I'm good," Kayden said. "I can't keep pounding these the way I used to."

Jessie left the table and headed to the bar, but she abruptly stopped and came back. With wide eyes and stiff shoulders, she sat back down.

Kayden and I exchanged a worried glance before I turned back to her. "Everything alright, Jess?"

"Yeah," she said with a shaky voice. "There's a long line at the bar, and I didn't feel like waiting." She immediately started biting her nails, her face turning pale despite the blush on her cheeks.

When I glanced at the bar, I hardly saw anyone. "Jess, there's no one there."

"Don't look over there." She snapped her fingers in my face. "Look at me, alright?"

Now I knew something was up. "Jess, what's your deal?" I turned back to the bar, knowing she was hiding something. I didn't notice Zeke before because of the drop-dead gorgeous woman pressed against his body like a magnet. She was short and petite, her stomach tight from intense athleticism. She had long legs that ended in five-inch heels, and her hair was long and straight, looking silky even from this far away.

When Kayden spotted them, she cursed under her breath. "Oh, shit…"

Zeke had his eyes on her the entire time, even when he took a drink of his beer. Like no one else was in the room, he only had eyes for her. She was a million times prettier than me, and her body was so fit and tight it was ridiculous.

Jessie sighed and couldn't look at me anymore.

I was crushed.

There was no way to sugarcoat it.

Seeing him with someone else was the most painful thing I'd ever felt. I wasn't mad because I had no right to be. He was single, and he'd been single for over two months now. When he gave me that ultimatum, he meant it. He really had moved on and let me go.

I wanted to cry.

"Rae…" Kayden's gentle voice broke away. "So sorry, girl."

"Yeah," Jessie whispered. "I was hoping you wouldn't see them."

"It's okay," I whispered. "It was going to happen sometime, right?" I silently excused myself from the table and walked to the exit. There was no way I could keep sitting there, watching her drool all over him. After the tab was paid, he would take her back to his place and fuck her in the bed I used to sleep in. My scent would be erased, as well as our relationship.

I'd never felt so low.

I managed to wave down a cab and get in the back seat. After I mumbled my address, I pressed my temple against the cool glass and closed my eyes, feeling the tears deep inside my chest. They didn't escape past my eyes because I'd cried enough to last a lifetime.

When I got out of the cab, I took the elevator to the top floor and hit the buzzer.

Ryker's voice came through the intercom. "Yes?"

"It's me…" I stared at the crack in the center of the door and waited for it to open.

Ryker hit the button and the doors opened, revealing him standing in his sweatpants without a shirt. The TV was on in the living room, and a cold beer sat on the coffee table from where he'd been relaxing.

He eyed me up and down, noting my bare legs in the short dress. My hair was done in curls, and he noticed that too. He stepped closer to me, his arms staying by his sides through sheer determination. He cocked his head to the side like he knew something was wrong, but he never asked the question.

"I want meaningless sex. No strings attached. Just sex." When I pictured Zeke with that beautiful woman, I suddenly felt lonely, like I'd lost more than I could afford. The love of my life had moved on to someone else, and by the looks of her, she was much better than I ever was.

Ryker came closer to me, his blue eyes smoldering in intensity. "You came to the right place, sweetheart." He gripped my ass and lifted me into the air, my legs automatically wrapping around his waist. One hand cupped my face while the other continued to hold me effortlessly as he carried me into his bedroom. His lips met mine, and he gave me a slow and tantalizing kiss, the kind that used to make me melt on the spot.

My arms circled his neck, and I kissed him back, putting all my energy into making myself feel good. With a gorgeous guy like Ryker, it wasn't hard to do. My back hit the sheets as he laid me down, still kissing me and running his hand down my thigh. When he reached my ankle, he slipped off my heel then migrated back to my waist.

My hands felt the powerful muscles of his back and arms, feeling the strength directly underneath the skin. My fingertips absorbed the searing heat, my nails slightly digging into his skin. My legs hooked around his waist, and I slipped off the other heel with my foot.

Ryker sucked my bottom lip as he reached his hand under my ass and gripped the back of my thong. He pulled it down over my legs and tossed it on the floor, his lips never breaking from mine. Then he got my dress off easily, undoing the zipper and rescuing me from the material. When I was naked underneath him, he looked down at me with worship in his eyes. "Sexy as hell, just as I remember." He kicked off his sweatpants and boxers, gloriously naked on top of me.

My legs circled his waist, and I locked my ankles together. My fingers slid into his hair, and I kissed him harder, feeling his throbbing cock against my stomach. I wanted to feel full, to be stretched until the pain turned into pleasure.

"I'm clean." He stopped kissing me, speaking into my mouth while his body gently grinded against me.

"I know." I grabbed his hips and directed him inside me, feeling his head stretch me the second he penetrated me.

Once he'd been invited, he positioned himself further over me and sank into me, every inch of his enormous cock sliding into home plate. "I forgot how good your pussy felt." He moved until he was balls deep, nine inches stored inside me.

I was already out of breath, drenched in sweat and ready to come. "Your cock feels better…"

He kissed me slowly, moaning at the same time. His hips flexed as he pushed into me, forcing my channel to acclimate to his size. He pulled out, making my body tense, and then he shoved himself inside me all over again.

My ankles remained locked together tightly, and I gripped his back to hold on, getting the kind of sex I wanted. It was hard and good, hitting me in the right spot and making me tense in every good way imaginable.

He looked into my eyes as he thrust, his chest sprinkled with sweat. His body looked sexier when it was being used to its full capability, pushing me into the mattress with his size and strength.

I was swept away by lust, using his body as an anchor to move into him, taking his cock just as hard as he was giving it to me. I didn't feel any pain because all I felt was pleasure. I wasn't thinking about anything other than this gorgeous man buried deep inside me. "Ryker, I'm gonna come..."

"You bet your ass you're gonna come."

My hands snaked to his biceps, which were bulging as he held his upper body on top of mine. I felt the muscle and the pounding blood as he hit me harder, forcing me into the mattress as he hit my G spot.

And then I came. "Oh, god..." Just like we were back in time and doing it all over his apartment, my head rolled back and I writhed underneath him, a prisoner to how wonderful he made me feel. "Yes...yes."

Ryker locked his eyes on my face, watching the O I made with my mouth and the redness flood my cheeks. His cock twitched inside me as he prepared for release, shoving himself farther and harder. "Fuck…" He inserted his entire length inside me as he came, filling me with his heavy seed. He pressed his forehead to mine as he finished, a quiet moan escaping his lips. "Sweetheart…I missed this."

"You won't be missing it anytime soon." I rolled him to his back then straddled his hips, wanting to keep going even though it was some unearthly hour. I ran my hands up his chest, feeling his come slowly slide toward my opening.

I kissed his chest then wrapped my lips around his length, tasting myself and his come on my tongue. I sucked him off until he was hard again, and then I inserted his length of steel back inside me, his cock lubricated by his own seed.

He gripped my hips and thrust underneath me. "Rae…"

***

The only time I went home that weekend was to take care of Safari. The rest of the time, I stayed at Ryker's place. We didn't talk very much. We screwed on every piece of furniture in the apartment, defiling the place and leaving my mark everywhere.

The sex was great, and not talking was even better.

By Sunday night, I knew I needed to head back home even though I was dreading it. I didn't want to sleep alone in my bed — even with Safari. When I was with Ryker, I didn't think about Zeke and the woman he'd clearly hooked up with. Life was just easier when I was distracted by my undoubtedly sexy ex-boyfriend.

"I should get going…" I pulled on my panties and dress, taking a long overdue walk of shame.

"Or you could stay here." He sat beside me on the bed, shirtless with messy hair.

"I've got to spend some time with Safari and get ready for work in the morning."

"You could always bring him here."

"Not to be rude, but he doesn't like you very much." Safari was stubborn. If he didn't like someone, he didn't usually change his mind about it.

"Then I could stay at your place..." Ryker stared me down as he waited for an invite.

My first response was no because Rex would see him. But then I realized it really didn't matter if Rex saw him or not. Zeke did exactly what I did this weekend — but with someone else. "Sure."

"Alright." He smiled before he grabbed his bag and packed his clothes. "I need to get more bones so Safari won't bite me in my sleep."

"He's harmless. He just has an attitude problem."

"Like his momma." Ryker gave me that sexy grin before he walked into the other room.

It was strange how normal our arrangement felt. We had sex all weekend, and it almost seemed like no time had passed. The only difference was the feeling in my heart. I felt the same way — just for a different man.

***

The second we walked in the door, Safari was not having it.

He growled at Ryker and tried to snatch the bag out of his hand.

"Safari." I swatted him on the nose. "I know you don't like Ryker, but you're going to have to start being polite. He's our guest, remember."

Safari folded his ears.

"Do you understand?"

He released a whine.

Ryker chuckled. "I really think he understands you."

"Of course he does. He's smarter than I am."

"I don't know about that..."

If I were smarter, I wouldn't have gotten my heart crushed twice in one year. I was done with relationships for a long time. Maybe the hit-it-and-quit-it lifestyle was for me. So far, it seemed to be working.

I walked into the bedroom and changed, getting ready to sleep in my small bed with an enormous man and a big dog.

Ryker stripped down to his boxers, the only thing he ever slept in. Before we finally fell asleep, he'd probably be naked. "Your room looks the same."

"I haven't done much remodeling." I got into bed and set the alarm. Safari jumped on the end of the bed, gave Ryker a threatening look, and then laid down.

Ryker got comfortable by spooning me from behind, his powerful arms wrapped around me. The last man I slept with in this bed was Zeke, but I tried not to think about it. "You need to upgrade your bed."

"Safari and I don't need more space than this."

"I guess if you sleep on top of me, that will fix everything." Like I was weightless, he positioned me on his hard chest, my hair cascading down his shoulder. He dug one hand into my hair then kissed my temple.

This felt too affectionate for the meaningless relationship I wanted. "We're just fucking, Ryker. That's it."

"My favorite part of fucking you is kissing you," he said quietly. "So, I'm gonna kiss you all I like." He grabbed the back of my neck and gave me a hard kiss on the mouth, just to prove his point. Then he got comfortable and closed his eyes.

I listened to his heartbeat like a lullaby and let it pull me into sleep.

***

After we both showered and got ready for work, we left the apartment at the same time. I was the unluckiest person on the planet, so of course, I walked right into Rex just as he was leaving for work.

He looked us up and down, instantly connecting the dots. "Great. I have to deal with this piece of shit again."

Ryker kept his temper in check, knowing I wouldn't appreciate him insulting my brother even if he deserved it. "Good morning to you too."

Rex ignored him, looking only at me. "You can do so much better than him, Rae. We both know it."

Ryker clenched his jaw again.

"Rex, what did we talk about a year ago?" I asked. "About how my personal life is none of your business."

"I'm not making it my business," he snapped. "I'm just telling you, as your brother, I fucking hate your boyfriend after what he did to you. And I'm always gonna hate him. So, you're gonna have to figure that out."

"He's not my boyfriend."

"For now," Rex said coldly. "I've seen this movie—I know how it ends." He gave us both a final glare before he walked off. He didn't mention Zeke, and somehow, that bothered me more than anything else.

"I'm gonna have to talk to him." Ryker started walking with me toward the elevator. "Get a beer with him or something."

"Don't bother." We were just sleeping together. I didn't see a relationship anytime soon. "Who I sleep with shouldn't bother him. It's his problem, not ours."

"Honestly, I can't blame him for being angry."

We got into the elevator and the doors shut. "We aren't seeing each other, so it doesn't matter. How I get off isn't his concern." I didn't want to mislead Ryker in what I wanted from him. Maybe we would get back together somewhere down the road. But for now, this was purely about sex.

The elevator drifted to the floor, and Ryker adjusted his watch on his wrist. "I get it, Rae. I'm just your fuck buddy. I heard you loud and clear."

I wasn't sure if he did.

Chapter Twenty-Three

Rex

The moment Zeke looked at my face, he knew. He knew what I was going to tell him.

"Don't say anything..." He grabbed his beer and took a long drink, swallowing the entire thing before he set the glass back on the table, making a noticeable thud.

I stared at the table because I didn't know what else to do. My best friend was hurting—hurting a lot. The woman he loved just screwed the man he hated—because he pretended to be interested in Monica. "On the bright side, at least the plan is working."

"On the bright side?" he asked coldly, still not looking at me.

"Kayden told me she was devastated when she saw you with Monica. She walked out because she couldn't handle it."

"I wish I could walk out right now...walk out of my heart."

"I know, man."

"So…" He shook his head like he changed his mind about what he was going to say. "Nevermind."

I had a feeling I knew what he was asking about. "She told me they aren't together—like together-together. I'm pretty sure he's just a rebound. I know it hurts, but it's not the end of the world. She just hit rock bottom, and she'll come back."

"Not the end of the world?" he asked quietly. "The woman I love is screwing her ex. Yes, Rex. It is the end of the goddamn world."

"He doesn't mean anything to her. Come on, she's still hung up on you. I'm sure she thought about you the entire time they were—"

"Not helping."

"Look, just stick with the plan. I promise it'll work."

"You can't make a promise like that, Rex."

"With Rae, I can." I knew her better than anyone else, even Kayden. "I know how her mind works. I know how she deals with grief. She's looking for a distraction right now because she's so upset. But that distraction will only last so long. Then she'll be forced with the realization that she needs to get you back before it's too late."

"But—"

"Trust me, man."

He leaned forward over the table, his elbows resting on the surface. "This is such a nightmare. These past few months have been pure hell. I just wanted it to end. I want Rae to pull her head out of her ass and just come to her senses. She's never been the type of woman to only think with her emotions. She's logical and reasonable. But she hasn't shown any of those qualities lately."

"Because she doesn't let people hurt her," I said quietly. "You snuck up on her. She always has walls up for everyone in her life—except you. She trusted you completely, so you hurt her a million times more. I'm not saying you're wrong and she's right, but that's what the problem is."

"I'm not perfect," he said coldly.

"I know. I think she just needs some time to become reasonable again."

"While fucking Ryker," he snapped.

"Hey, I'm sure you could fuck Monica if you wanted to. You wouldn't be doing anything wrong."

He rolled his eyes. "Rex, you don't get it. I don't *want* to fuck her. I want to be with Rae—only Rae."

My pity only increased.

"What do we do now?"

"We're all going to have to hang out—and you'll need to bring Monica."

"And flaunt it in her face?" he asked incredulously. "That's not classy."

"You don't need to flaunt, alright? But if any of us is seeing someone, we bring that person along. It's not like she didn't bring Ryker around. He was at her place the other night, remember?"

"Like I could forget," he said bitterly.

"So, I say we hit the courts and you bring Monica. But I won't tell Rae she's coming."

"Won't that be obvious?"

"No. She thinks I'm stupid, remember? Leave it up to me."

He shook his head and sighed.

"Make sure Monica dresses slutty. Like spandex shorts and a sports bra or something."

He rolled his eyes. "I'm not gonna tell her what to wear."

"She seems kinda easy, to be honest. So, I think she would go for it."

"Then you can tell her," Zeke said. "I'm not gonna get slapped."

"Kayden slaps me all the time, so I'm used to it." I wiggled my eyebrows.

Zeke finally chuckled, his mood picking up for the first time since our conversation began. But that would only last for two seconds. Then he would go back to being utterly miserable.

***

I walked into Rae's apartment with the basketball tucked under my arm. "Hey, you wanna play ball with us?"

"Rex, don't just walk in." She walked into the living room in a man's shirt that was three sizes too big, and sweatpants that obviously didn't belong to her either.

"Then lock the door," I countered.

"Or you could just knock. You don't live here anymore."

Ryker walked in behind her, dressed in sweats and a t-shirt.

I hate him. I hate him. Fuck, I hate him. "You wanna play ball or what?"

"Who's in?" she asked.

"So far just Zeke and me," I said. "Kayden is gonna come down and watch. You know, my own personal cheerleader."

She seemed hesitant, part of her wanting to see Zeke, and the other part wanting to avoid him.

"You wanna play?" I asked Ryker. "I'm not inviting you because I want you there, but we're down a player. Tobias is busy with Jessie." I rolled my eyes. "That guy is so pussy-whipped."

"You're one to talk," Rae countered.

"That's different," I argued. "I live with her."

"Which makes you more pussy-whipped," Ryker said.

I gripped the ball so I wouldn't throw it at his head. "You wanna die, motherfucker?"

"Whoa, Rex." Rae held up her hand and walked toward me. "Take it down a notch."

"Did you hear what that asshole just said to me?"

"He was clearly kidding," Rae said. "You need to chill out."

"I'll chill out when he's buried six feet under." Not only did he hurt my little sister, but he was the reason Zeke and Rae were so miserable right now. "So, you playing with us or not?"

"Talk about bipolar," Ryker said with that stupid, smug grin on his face. "And yes, I'll play with you."

"I'll come too," Rae said. "But you seriously need to downplay the trash talk. Ryker isn't going anywhere, so you may as well get used to him."

He better not be sticking around for the long haul. No way in hell would I ever let this guy be my brother-in-law. "Trust me, he won't be around forever. We both know Ryker will get bored and move on — like last time."

***

The four of us got to the court first with Safari in tow. Kayden sat on the bench near the hoop with Safari beside her, looking cute in denim shorts and a purple top. She had nice legs, so anytime she showed them off, I paid attention.

Ryker warmed up with the ball, making enough three-pointers to make me uncomfortable. My masculinity wasn't based on my gameplay, but I wasn't happy when a guy I hated was better at basketball than I was.

I texted Zeke beforehand to cue his entrance. I wanted to make sure he got there last. That way, Rae couldn't just slip out when she spotted Monica. All this soap opera shit had to be timed perfectly.

I spotted them coming up the block, Monica in only tight spandex and a sports bra. Her navel piercing glittered in the sunlight, and her thick hair was pulled back in a sleek ponytail. She had an hourglass figure, long legs, and a booty that caught your attention.

This plan was definitely going to work.

Rae spotted Zeke before everyone else, and the blood drained from her face instantly. She stopped trying to get the ball after Ryker made the shots because all she could do was stare. Ryker spotted them next, his eyes honing in on Monica — not Zeke.

"Hey, what's up?" I fist-pounded Zeke. "Didn't know you were bringing Monica. That's cool. Kayden can play." I gave Monica a high-five since Kayden was sitting right there, watching me. I knew I had a jealous lady, so it was best if I didn't get too close to Monica.

Zeke did a fantastic job acting like everything was completely normal. He walked over to Ryker and held up his fist, inviting him to a fist bump. Only I knew how heartbroken Zeke was when he found out Rae slept with Ryker. How he could bottle it inside and put on a show like this was beyond me. It must've been his determination to get Rae back that kept him calm.

Ryker eyed his hand before he returned the exchange.

"Ryker, this is Monica."

Monica stepped forward, smiled, and shook his hand.

Ryker stared at her, his eyes locked on to her face like he was in a trance. He held her hand longer than necessary then dropped it, clearing his throat at the same time. "Nice to meet you."

"You too." She kept staring at him the same way he was staring at her. All the girls thought Ryker was hot. Monica wasn't immune to his charms, just like everyone else.

Zeke walked up to Rae, ignoring the pained look on her face as if it wasn't there at all. "Hey. How's it going?"

She could barely talk because her voice had disappeared. She couldn't even shake off the pain because she was so caught off guard. Perhaps she thought Monica was just a one-time thing over the weekend. Now, she was realizing Monica was there to stay — and she couldn't handle it. "Good. You?"

"I'm great. Let me introduce you to Monica." He grabbed her by the hand and pulled her to his side, keeping her away from Ryker. "Mon, this is Rae."

I liked the use of a nickname — nice touch.

Perky and smiley, Monica walked forward and hugged Rae, giving her a tight squeeze. "It's so nice to meet you. Zeke has told me everything about you." When she pulled away, she was just as perky as before.

"He has?" Rae tried to smile, but it just looked like a cringe.

"Yeah. He says you're one of his closest friends even though you guys didn't work out. I think that says a lot about who both of you are. You know what your priorities are." She walked away with Zeke and introduced herself to Kayden.

My eyes were on Rae the whole time.

Ryker finally stopped staring at Monica and looked at Rae. He got close to her, pressing his lips against her ear.

I couldn't hear what he said, but I could read his lips. He asked if she was okay.

She walked away without responding, so that gave me her answer.

This plan was definitely working.

***

Monica was an awesome basketball player, almost as good as my sister. Monica kicked her ass into gear and launched down the court, throwing her elbows all over the place like any man. She stole the ball from me once, and when she blocked Ryker, she managed to snatch the ball from him and sprint down to the other side of the court.

Ryker, Rae, and I were on a team together—and we got our asses kicked.

After the game, we were all hot and sweaty. Zeke walked up to Monica and placed his arm around her waist. "You told me you were good at basketball…but I had no idea you were that good."

"I guess I wanted to surprise you." She leaned in and kissed him.

Zeke clearly hadn't been expecting it because he nearly flinched. But he kissed her back, keeping up the act because he would blow it if he didn't.

When she pulled away, a smile was on her lips, like she got exactly what she wanted.

Rae walked to her water bottle on the bench, purposely turning her back to the scene. Ryker came behind her and rested a hand on her back, silently comforting her.

Kayden glared at Monica like she might murder her.

"Let's go to your place and shower," Monica said to Zeke. "Then we can cook something. I'm starving."

"That sounds like a good idea." Zeke grabbed their water bottles from the bench where Rae was standing. "We'll see you guys later." He waved to all of us then grabbed Monica's hand, heading up the block without looking back. Monica kept moving into his side, laughing at something he just said.

I was glad this plan was working.

But damn, I felt terrible for Rae.

This must have been killing her.

When they were gone, Rae turned and walked up the street without saying a word to any of us. She didn't even say goodbye to Ryker, dismissing herself from the situation. Without seeing her face, I knew exactly how she looked.

She was crying.

***

I tried to get on her good side, so I knocked before I barged in.

"What?" Her irritated voice carried through the door.

I took that as an invitation and walked inside with two pints of Ben and Jerry's chocolate ice cream — her favorite. "It's me."

"Oh…"

I walked into the living room and spotted her sitting on the couch — in the dark. The TV wasn't even on. Safari lay on her lap on top of a blanket. She hadn't even showered since the basketball game ended three hours ago.

Now, I really felt terrible for her.

I grabbed two spoons and sat beside her. "Thought you might be hungry…"

She eyed the tub of ice cream, and against her will, the corner of her mouth rose in a small smile. "Thanks…" She took the ice cream and the spoon and slowly started to dig in.

I ate quietly beside her, giving her the opportunity to speak first. When the silence stretched on, I knew she wasn't going to say anything. "Are you okay?"

"No…" She scooped a big chunk of ice cream into her mouth. "Ryker tried to come back over, but I told him I wanted to be alone. Not even he can make me feel better right now."

"Well…what did you expect?"

"I just…" She lost her appetite and set the tub of ice cream on the table.

"Rae, Zeke is a catch. He's a good-looking doctor. The guy is a chick magnet."

"Yes, I'm aware."

"Then I don't know why you're surprised."

"I saw him with Monica at the bar last weekend. I was so depressed that I went to Ryker's place and…yeah." She didn't go into any details, thankfully. "But I thought she was a one-night stand, a piece of ass. But then I saw her again today and…she's pretty, funny, and cool…" Rae closed her eyes for a moment, and when she opened them again, tears were in her eyes. "It's just so soon, you know?"

"Not really. You've been broken up for almost three months, Rae."

"But he's actually dating her. Ryker and I…are just fooling around."

"I don't know if they're dating," I said. "So, I wouldn't jump to conclusions."

"Well, what did he tell you?"

I had to traverse this carefully. "Honestly, not much. He said she was cool and they were going to keep hanging out. Since you're my sister, I don't think he's really going to go into detail about things…"

"Yeah, true."

"But I don't think they're really serious. They just started talking a few weeks ago."

She pulled her knees to her chest, her eyes wet and reflective. "I know I have no right to be upset… I'm the one who wanted this. But I didn't expect to deal with this so soon."

"Again, it's not that soon."

"I know...but it hurts so much." She sniffed when the tears started to come. "I've never felt this bad in my entire life. Not when he told me he slept with another woman, not when he told me there were two women, not when Ryker dumped me, not when Dad left, and not even when Mom died. I just feel...so dead inside. I love him so much..." Her voice broke, and she took a moment to calm herself so she could keep talking.

I hated this. I hated hearing my sister cry. It made me want to cry.

"Just picturing him with someone else breaks my heart in ways I can't even explain. I know you don't understand what I'm saying..."

"I do." When Kayden slept around, I was so depressed I didn't know what to do with myself. All I felt was pain—nonstop. "But you still have time to fix this. If you really want him back, I think he would take you."

"Why?"

"I just do." I wasn't going to tell her the truth, that the entire thing was a setup. It would just push her away all over again. I had to keep lying to her so she would make the right decision and end this once and for all. "But you need to be certain. No going back and forth about what happened that night when had dinner with Ryker. You need to really forgive him, give him a clean slate, and move on."

She stared into the dark room, tears rolling down her face.

"And you need to make up your mind soon. If you wait too long...you never know what might happen."

She sniffed and wiped her nose.

"So...are you going to think about it?"

Her voice came out quiet and weak. "I guess...still confused."

"What is there to be confused about?"

"If I can really forgive him."

God, I wanted to strangle her. I wanted to smack her head against the wall until I knocked some sense into her. "Rae, if you don't forgive him, you'll lose him forever. I can tell you right now, Monica is a cool ass chick. And she's really into him. She's gonna sink her claws into him and never let go. So you need to just bite the bullet and do it. Because if you don't, that's it. He'll be gone."

Tears continued to streak down her cheeks. Thankfully, it was dark enough that I couldn't see the redness of her eyes. She wiped them away with her fingertips then nodded. "I know, Rex. But I still need to think about it."

***

Zeke was pacing in the living room when I walked inside. "What did she say? What happened? Did it work?"

I crossed my arms over my chest and saw the desperation on his face. Zeke had never been so antsy, so dark. "Not yet," I started. "But I think it's working."

"Rex, what does that mean?"

"She's devastated about Monica. She cried on the couch for an hour."

Zeke closed his eyes like he'd just been stabbed. "No…don't tell me that." He gripped his skull like he wanted to crush his own brain.

"I've never seen her so low. She's totally heartbroken."

"Then why the hell am I doing this? The plan wasn't to hurt her. It was to—"

"But I think it's working. She's starting to realize if she doesn't get her shit together, she's gonna miss her chance to get you back. She says she loves you and has never been in this much pain in her life. But she still needs to figure out if she can forgive you."

He rolled his eyes. "Why won't she just let it go?"

"Beats me. But I think she will. So, we need to keep waiting."

"Monica tried to get into my pants last night."

"Yeah?" I couldn't help but grin. "She's got the hots for you."

"I told her no. Then she started asking about Ryker."

"He's going to be available very soon…" If things worked out the way they should.

"I think Ryker was staring at her too. Kinda pissed me off."

"Jealous?" He wouldn't sleep with Monica, but now he was jealous?

"No," he snapped. "I'm jealous he has Rae, but he's looking at another woman."

"Oh, gotcha. In his defense, he doesn't really have Rae. They're just fooling around."

Zeke dropped onto the couch. "Please don't remind me."

"Sorry." I sat on the other couch. "So, we just need to be patient for a little longer. I think she'll come around. We need to get her in the room with you two again. I think that will really drive the nail into the coffin."

"God, I feel like an ass for screwing with her like this."

"Don't. All is fair in love and war."

Zeke massaged his knuckles like he'd just finished punching through a wall. "I hate playing games like this. But you're right, it is working."

"So, we'll stick to the plan. We'll bump into each other sometime this weekend. Rae will be so jealous she'll beg you to take her back."

"And if that does happen, do I tell her about this stunt?"

I wanted to smack him upside the head. "Dude, what is your obsession with telling the truth?"'

"I'm not obsessed. I just don't like to lie."

"If you really have to tell her, I'd wait a few weeks until the dust settles."

He nodded in agreement.

"So, I'm thinking we run into you at Scotty's Bar. Have Monica look her best, and Rae will take care of the rest. I'll make sure Ryker is there too. Maybe he can scoop up Monica once you and Rae are back together. Then you'll never have to worry about him again."

"I wish," Zeke said. "But nothing ever seems to go my way…"

Chapter Twenty-Four

Rae

A knock sounded on my door.

"Go away." I hadn't moved much for the past week. When I wasn't at work, my ass was parked on the couch. Ryker tried getting in touch with me, but I was never in the mood to do anything. Whoever was at my door was someone I didn't want to entertain.

"Rae, it's me." Ryker's voice sounded through the closed door. "Open the door or I'll break it down. Your choice."

I didn't doubt him. I walked to the front door and opened it. He was standing there in a leather jacket and jeans — and holding a vase of red roses. I stared at the flowers, immediately smelling their scent as it wafted my way. The gesture was sweet, and my eyes immediately softened. "Thanks..."

"Since you didn't get my flowers the first time, I'll make sure you get them now." He walked inside and set them on the counter.

I pressed my nose to the soft petals and inhaled. "Well, I'm sure Jenny got a lot of use out of them."

"Why?" he asked. "Did Jenny stay with you for a while?"

"No, I mean at the office."

"I didn't send them to the office. I sent them to your apartment."

"Oh...you did?"

"Yeah. I sent them on your birthday."

"That's weird because I was home." I couldn't remember much about that day other than the fact that Zeke got me the best birthday present ever. "I guess they went to the wrong address."

"The flower shop told me they were dropped off."

"Hmm...I'm not sure—" The explanation struck me like a bolt of lightning. "Rex was living with me at the time..."

"Yeah..."

"That little shithead must have thrown them away." I wouldn't put it past him to do something like that.

Ryker chuckled even though it wasn't amusing. "Maybe. He does hate me."

"I'm gonna slap him so hard..."

"Go easy on the guy. You've got the flowers now, and that's all that matters." He cupped my cheek and kissed me gently on the mouth, his cologne washing over me. He gave me an amazing kiss, the kind that made my knees go weak. He gently pressed my back against the counter and continued to kiss me, his tongue dancing with mine.

"You're being awfully nice to me after I ignored you all week..." I turned my mouth away and felt him kiss my neck.

"I like it when you play hard to get." He grabbed my ass and lifted me onto the counter, his mouth moving down my neck and to my chest. He was just about to pull my shirt over my head when Jessie walked inside.

"Hey, girl — Oh, wow." Dressed to hit the town, she stopped and tried to cover her eyes with her hands. "Sorry. Didn't know you were getting frisky."

"It's okay." I pulled my shirt down and hopped off the counter, not embarrassed that Jessie had walked in on us. She'd seen worse, unfortunately. "What's up?"

"Wanted to see if you wanted to go out tonight. But judging by those clothes and that hair...you haven't moved all day." Jessie wasn't exactly judgmental, but if I looked like shit, she would call me out on it.

"What are your plans?"

"Kayden and I are just gonna get a drink. Rex and Zeke are doing something tonight. Ryker can come too. He can be part of our girl's night."

Ryker smiled. "Thanks. Just more ways to postpone sex."

"You'll get your action later, I'm sure." She gave me a meaningful look. "Coming or what?"

"Yeah, sure." I ran my hand over my messy hair. "Just let me get dressed."

"And do your hair and makeup," Jessie added. "I can help if you need it."

"I'm not totally disabled, but thanks," I said sarcastically.

"Alright, we'll meet you down there." Jessie walked out.

Ryker followed me down the hallway. "People walk into your apartment a lot."

"Tell me about it." Just before I reached the bathroom, he grabbed me and pulled me into the bedroom. My back hit the mattress and my sweatpants were off in an instant.

"I've been thinking about these legs all week." He kissed each of my thighs then moved to my underwear. He hooked the lace in his fingertips then pulled my panties down my legs and onto the floor.

"Yeah?"

His kisses traveled up my stomach, and he undid his jeans at the same time. "I thought about them last night when I beat off."

My spine shivered, and I dug my fingers into his hair.

His bottoms were off and he shoved his hard cock inside me, taking me roughly just the way he used to. Whenever he was inside me, I didn't think about anything else because the sex was too good. He pulled me off to a faraway place, a world where nothing could hurt me.

***

Ryker ran his hand down my back as we stood at the table in the center of the room. "I like this…" He looked down at my backless dress, his warm fingers grazing the skin.

"Thanks," Jessie said. "I let her borrow it."

"Actually, I think that's mine," Kayden said. "I got it on sale last Christmas."

Jessie narrowed her eyes. "You're right. Sorry. Looks like something I have though."

"Well, you look amazing in it." He pressed a kiss to my ear, his whispers moving over my skin as warm breath.

"Thanks." His kisses were soothing, making me feel less miserable for a moment in time. The distraction was essential for me at the moment. Now I understood why people slept around to get over the person they really wanted.

Jessie moved to Kayden's side of the table and whispered something in her ear.

Kayden looked over her shoulder at the bar. "You've got to be kidding me…"

"What?" I blurted, wanting to know what they were whispering about.

"Uh..." Jessie cringed as she looked at me. "I just saw Zeke at the bar...with that stupid ho."

Stupid ho. That's what the three of us called her. I felt my heart ache at the revelation, but I kept a stoic expression on my face, not wanting to fall apart like I did at the basketball court. That afternoon, I just walked away because I'd broken down in tears. I couldn't remember the last time I had a meltdown like that.

Ryker moved closer into my side, his arm wrapped around my waist. He did what he could to make me feel better, but he knew he was helpless in this matter. All he could do was kiss me and fuck me until I stopped thinking about Zeke. "Ignore them."

"I can't ignore Zeke." He was my friend, and friends didn't ignore each other. "And he's not rude to you, so I can't be rude to that stupid ho." A part of me felt bad for calling her that because she was a nice person. She was friendly, affectionate, and if she weren't dating Zeke, I'd probably be hanging out with her.

He pressed a kiss to my temple. "Yeah, I guess so. But you look damn hot tonight, so make sure he knows what he's missing."

I smiled at the sweet words. "Thanks..."

Rex walked over with Zeke and Monica trailing behind him. "Hey, I didn't know you guys would be here."

"What are you talking about?" Kayden asked. "I told you we were coming here like three hours ago."

"Oh..." Rex shrugged. "I thought you were talking about somewhere else."

Zeke walked up to the table with his arm around Monica. Of course, she was wearing a skintight dress that fit her figure perfectly. She was rocking it, the hottest chick at our table. Her hair was perfect, and she had dark makeup around her eyes. She even made Jessie look like a troll. I saw Ryker looking at her for a second too long, but I didn't even feel jealous because I couldn't blame him. Besides, the only man whose attention I wanted wasn't Ryker.

Zeke turned to me, a smile on his face. "Hey, what's up?" He didn't hug me, but he gave me a fist bump.

I wanted to cry.

I didn't want to fist bump him.

I didn't want to be friends.

I forced myself to do it back, faking a smile. "Nothing much. You?"

"We're just bar hopping tonight." Zeke turned to Ryker and shook his hand.

Actually shook his hand.

"You remember Monica, right?" Zeke presented her like the trophy that she was.

"Of course." Ryker shook her hand and held on longer than necessary.

She stared at him like the piece of eye candy he was.

Now I was a little ticked. Not because I was possessive of Ryker, but because she was with Zeke. She had the greatest guy in the world on her arm, and she was looking at someone else. That didn't settle right with me.

"Excuse me, I need to powder my nose." Monica walked off, her hips swaying like a supermodel on the runway.

Zeke drank his beer and set it on the table. Then he asked Jessie about Tobias.

"I'm going to use the restroom too." Ryker dropped his arm from around my waist and walked away.

I was alone with Zeke. It was the first time we'd been face-to-face like this since the night we broke up. Our relationship ended on the sidewalk just outside. I remembered the defeat in his eyes when I said it wasn't going to work out. He turned around and walked away, letting me go.

Zeke finished his conversation with Jessie and turned back to me. "So, what's new?"

Could I really stand there and act like everything was normal? That it was just a regular Friday night? "Nothing much. You?"

"I got a new secretary to replace Jessica, and she's doing a good job. I'm grateful I'll be getting off work earlier from now on."

"Yeah…that must be nice."

He drank his beer again, not giving me that scorching gaze that used to pierce my skin.

I missed him so much. I hated this distance between us, this obvious gap. That connection I once lived for had disappeared, and now I would give anything to have it back. The fact that he slept with two different women didn't seem to matter anymore. All I could think about was the painful hollow in my chest. "You and Monica seem pretty serious." I didn't know what possessed me to say that, but the words came tumbling out.

He looked me in the eye, handsome as ever. "I wouldn't say we're serious. We're just hanging out right now."

"You're with her a lot." Every time I'd run into him, she was on his arm. It seemed like more than just a fling.

He shrugged. "She's pretty cool. You remember her, right?"

"Remember her from where?"

"She's Zoey's best friend. I think you guys met at a barbecue a few years ago."

She was his sister's friend? That meant if they got serious, it would be perfect for his entire family. This was worse than I thought. "No...I can't seem to place her."

"I had a crush on her when I was younger, and I ran into her the other night and we started talking... You know how it goes."

And they probably hooked up all weekend. My stomach flared at the knowledge, and I wanted to vomit all over the floor.

"So, you and Ryker seem to have fallen right back into place." There wasn't anger or bitterness in his voice. Actually, he seemed indifferent.

"We're just...not serious." I didn't want Zeke to think I was already in another relationship. I was completely lost right now, having no idea which direction to go. I was absolutely miserable, just as sad as the day we parted ways on the sidewalk. The only true happiness I felt was during that thirty minutes when we got back together.

"You know, Ryker really isn't that bad. He seems different than before. I'll try to get Rex to calm down."

I didn't know what to say to that, so I just nodded.

Monica came back and headed straight into Zeke's arms. Her arms circled his neck and she kissed him—right in front of me. "Missed you..."

He smiled as he looked down at her. "Missed you too."

I wanted to flip the table over and scream, and I also wanted to fall into a corner and sob. This was my worst nightmare playing out right in front of my eyes.

Ryker returned, but his arm around my waist didn't help this time. He looked down at me and saw the devastation written all over my face. "We really should get going if we're going to make those dinner reservations."

What dinner reservations?

Ryker circled my waist and pulled me along. "We'll catch up with you guys later." Being casual, he pulled me out of the bar until I was outside with the fresh air. The coldness entered my lungs, but it didn't comfort me much.

Ryker waved down a cab and got me into the backseat, extracting me from the horrific scene I'd just witnessed. He wrapped his arm around me and ran his fingers through my hair, doing his best to make me feel better. "I'm sorry, sweetheart."

I wouldn't let myself cry, but keeping the tears back was a constant battle. "I know you are…"

Chapter Twenty-Five

Rex

Jessie and Kayden were on the dance floor, throwing their hands into the air and moving with the music. Kayden shook her ass and looked sexy as hell, smiling and having a good time under the strobe lights. Men everywhere checked her out, but they were way too intimidated to approach her.

"Rex." Zeke snapped his fingers in my face. "Are you even listening to me?"

"Huh?" I turned back to Zeke and Monica, not hearing a word of the previous conversation.

Zeke looked like he wanted to punch me in the face. "This plan isn't working. I'm just being a complete asshole to Rae. You told me this would work, but it's only breaking her heart and pushing her away." He ran his hand through his hair, flustered.

"Dude, it is working," I said. "Just chill."

"Rex, we haven't accomplished anything except putting Rae on suicide watch. She can barely stand on two feet right now."

"Good," I snapped. "Let her suffer until she realizes she can't handle it anymore and comes crawling back."

Zeke gripped his skull and sighed. "I don't know, man. The look on her face…"

"I think it's working," Monica said, crossing her arms over her chest. "She can't stand to see me touch you. She's still possessive of you. And we need to make this work, because damn, Ryker is the hottest guy I've ever seen in my life." Her eyes moved back and forth between us. "Besides you guys, of course. And I don't want to ask him out— I *need* to ask him out."

"Nothing would make me happier…" Zeke took a long drink of his beer, needing more alcohol than was available in the entire bar. "Rex, I'm starting to worry. What if she's just clinging to Ryker more because she's upset?"

"She's not," I countered. "She didn't see him once this week because she just wanted to be alone. She's just using him."

"And he obviously doesn't mind," Zeke said bitterly.

"Just hold on a little longer, alright?" I said. "I really think she's gonna snap out of this soon."

"How soon?" Zeke asked. "I've already kissed Monica twice in front of her."

"And those were great kisses, by the way." She smiled and nudged him in the side.

Zeke was too depressed to even respond.

"Give it one more week," I said. "Be patient."

"And then what?" he demanded. "What happens if she doesn't come back to me?"

"I don't know, man. I guess you can try talking to her at that point. Or...just let her go."

Zeke drank his beer again, this time finishing it. "I can't let her go, man. You already know that."

Chapter Twenty-Six

Rae

I sat at Ryker's kitchen table and looked across the city. It was sometime in the middle of the night, and the lights were shining abnormally bright. There was a cloudless sky, but the stars couldn't be seen in the heavens.

Ryker left the bedroom and walked down the hall, in just his sweatpants. We went to bed that night without any action. I wasn't interested in sex, and he didn't seem to be either. He studied me at the table then pulled up a chair beside me.

All the lights were off in the apartment, but I preferred it that way. My face was difficult to see, so Ryker wouldn't know I'd been crying for the past hour. "You have a really nice view," I whispered.

"Yeah. Sometimes I sit here and think."

"What do you think about?"

He paused before he answered. "My father. COLLECT. You."

"I didn't realize you thought about work any longer than you had to." I knew he wasn't a fan of his job. He was there out of obligation, and his father's death would keep him there forever.

He didn't chuckle at my joke. "There are some things that are always on my mind."

I kept my eyes focused out the window, wondering what Zeke was doing. Was he asleep? Was Monica beside him? Were they in the bed that I used to sleep in every single night?

"What are you thinking about, sweetheart?"

I felt his eyes on me. "You already know."

"Do you want to talk about it?"

"There's not much to say…" The entire world knew how I felt about Zeke. I wore my feelings on my sleeve, and despite my situation with Ryker, I suspected even Zeke knew that. He must have seen the agony in my eyes earlier that night.

"Rae, I know I've said this before and I shouldn't repeat myself, but I'm going to anyway."

I closed my eyes.

"Give him another chance."

I opened my eyes again, seeing the Space Needle in the distance.

"You can't live without him, Rae. I can see it written all over your face — even in the dark."

"He's with Monica now…"

"He doesn't love Monica," he whispered. "I can tell."

"How?"

He shrugged. "I just can. If you told him you wanted to give it another try, he would take you back in a heartbeat."

I wasn't so sure.

"I know you're mad at him because of what he did. But forgive him and leave it in the past. I know you love him in a way you never loved me — and that's saying something because I know how you felt."

I finally looked at Ryker, seeing his crystal blue eyes reflect the city lights.

"Love like that doesn't happen for everyone, Rae. Whatever you guys have is unique and special. He made a mistake, but I think he should be forgiven. You know he'll never do anything like that ever again."

"But — "

"Forgive him, Rae. You're being unfair."

"Really?"

"Yes." He held my gaze as he spoke. "End this nightmare, and just take him back. Be happy."

My eyes started to water again because I knew he was right. This pain would never go away until I was with Zeke again. I loved him in a special way because he was the perfect person for me—my soul mate. I would never be happy with any other man as long as I lived. That truth was both painful and exhilarating.

But I knew what that meant for Ryker. He loved me and wanted us to have a life together. He made a mistake that he could never take back. He waited too long to do something about it.

"Don't be like me, Rae." Like always, he could read my thoughts. "I waited too long to tell you I loved you. And I missed my chance forever." His hand moved across the table until it rested on mine. "Don't let that be you."

Tears started to fall, but for a new reason entirely. "Ryker..."

He squeezed my hand. "I know you're going to go back to him, Rae. I've known this entire time. I just wanted to enjoy one last time before I had to let you go."

I placed my other hand on top of his. "I'm so sorry…"

"Don't apologize, sweetheart." He looked at me with strength in his eyes, not the heartbreak that used to be there. "I would give anything to go back in time and change what I did. I wish I told you how I felt when I had the chance. I wish we could get married and have kids…but I know that can't happen."

Both of the tears reached my chin then dropped to the surface of the table.

"You should be with Zeke. Don't feel bad for me."

"But I do. I wish things were different too…"

He pulled my chair out then patted his thigh.

I moved into his lap and straddled his hips, my face pressed close to his.

"I hope we can be friends, Rae. I don't want to come between you two, but I hope this goodbye isn't forever."

"Of course we can be friends. You've been a big part of my life, Ryker."

He gave me a weak smile.

"I know you'll find the right person someday, Ryker. She'll be a million times better than me."

When he smiled, it seemed genuine. "I hope you're right. I won't make the same mistake twice. And I hope she's smokin' hot."

I chuckled, feeling the strain leave my chest.

He held my waist and pressed a kiss to my forehead. "As much as I hate to say it, I think it's time for you to go." Ryker cupped my cheeks and brushed his thumbs across my skin, catching the moisture from my tears. His touch was warm and full of love.

"I know..."

"But I want to tell you I love you one last time. And hear you say it back." His fingers cupped my neck. "I love you, sweetheart."

My arms circled his neck, and I pressed my face close to his. "I love you too, Ryker. Forever." For the last time, I pressed my lips to his and kissed him, giving him an embrace unlike any other. It was soft and warm, full of all the love I could never give him. It wasn't about attraction or chemistry. It was simply about love — in the purest form.

***

I stood on his front porch in the middle of the night. It was past three in the morning, around the same time I came by a few weeks ago. There wasn't a car in the driveway, but that didn't mean Monica wasn't inside — sleeping in his bed.

A part of me wanted to leave because it felt wrong to try and steal him away. But another part of me refused to give him up if there was any chance of getting him back. With a steady hand and determination, I knocked.

Like before, I heard his footsteps gently tap against the hardwood floor as he approached the entryway. They stopped when he peered through the peephole, and after all the locks were undone, he opened the door.

In just his boxers, he stared me down. His blue eyes were indecipherable, his thoughts a mystery. He hid every emotion below the surface, so I had no idea what he was thinking. Like before, he refused to speak until he knew what I wanted.

"I'm sorry..." I practiced my speech a million times in my head before I got there, but now everything went out the window. My tongue was numb, and my body was shaking, but not from the cold. "I'm sorry to bother you. I'm sorry to show up like this. I just..."

"What?" he said coldly. "I'm not your fuck buddy, Rae. You want to get laid, call Ryker."

The insult stung, but I deserved it. "That's not why I'm here."

"Then tell me why you're here."

He didn't invite me inside, and I suspected I wouldn't get an invitation. "I'm sorry if I'm too late. I'm sorry if I took too long to understand how I feel. But I love you and miss you…and I forgive you for what you did. I can't stand to see you with Monica — or anyone. I want to make this work because you're the only man I want to be with." I kept my feelings in check and refused to let myself cry. I'd cried enough for the past few weeks. "Please take me back, Zeke."

He didn't welcome me with open arms — not like last time. "Rae, I'm not playing games anymore. You can't throw a tantrum next time it comes up. You can't get mad at me all over again and leave. I'm done with that."

"I'm done too."

"Then you forgive me?"

"Yes." His mistake seemed irrelevant now that I was so miserable. I knew it didn't mean anything to him, and I knew he would never hurt me like that again. He was still my best friend — no matter what.

"Are you sure?"

"Absolutely."

He continued to watch me like he didn't believe me. "Do you trust me?"

I nodded. "Of course. I know that will never happen again. Because I know you love me…"

Zeke finally dropped his hostility, his eyes softening. His shoulders were no longer tense, and his hands were bound tightly into fists. He grabbed my wrist and pulled me inside, out of the cold and into his arms. He shut the door and held me in the entryway, forcing me so hard against his chest I nearly stopped breathing.

I closed my eyes and savored the moment, finally feeling happy for the first time in forever.

He pulled away with his arms still around my waist. "I want you to do something for me."

"Okay."

"I want you to get your stuff and bring it over here. And I want you to get rid of your apartment."

My heart melted at the request. "You want me to move in with you?" After months of being apart, I thought he might want to take things slow until we returned to normal. But I was relieved he didn't.

"Yes. We have a lot of time to make up for."

This time, I did cry because I couldn't stop myself. "I would love to..."

He cupped my face and pressed a kiss to the corner of my eyes, his lips absorbing my tears.

"What about Monica?"

"Forget her. Now, there's only you."

She was beautiful and cool, and he dropped her the second I walked back into his life. I wasn't sure why Zeke loved me so much when I didn't deserve his undying devotion. "Thank you..." It was an odd thing to say, but in the moment, nothing better came to mind.

"This is it, Rae," he said firmly. "This is the end of the road for both of us. It's you and me forever. Do you understand me?"

I nodded.

"Do you understand me?"

"Yes," I whispered.

He scooped me into the air and wrapped my legs around his waist as he carried me into his bedroom. Once we were inside, he lay me down and stripped off my clothes.

I was relieved there wasn't a woman already occupying his bed.

Zeke got me naked and removed his boxers, hard for me instantly. He positioned himself on top of me and shoved himself inside me quickly, taking me with more aggression than he ever had. He claimed me, making me his forever. His mouth crushed against mine as he rocked into me, his hands pinning my wrists to the bed.

I felt his tongue move in my mouth, and I reciprocated, feeling his weight press me into the mattress. I didn't think about anyone else when we were together, especially the two women he screwed on that terrible night. I just thought about us, about our new beginning, and that's when I knew everything would be okay.

That I'd truly forgiven him.

***

When I woke up the following morning, I felt whole, like I'd received months of therapy that finally paid off. The constant pain in my stomach and heart had disappeared, and only joy remained behind. I was wrapped in Zeke's arm, his chest against my back, and I knew I could lie there all day.

Zeke kissed my neck when he knew I was awake. "Morning."

It felt too good to be true. "Morning."

He brushed his lips across the shell of my ear. "How'd you sleep?"

"Better than ever."

He trailed his lips to my shoulder where he gave me a final kiss. "Good. You're going to need your energy for the day."

"Ooh...I like the sound of that." I rubbed my ass into his lap, against his morning wood.

He chuckled. "Because you're moving."

"Today?" I asked incredulously.

"Yep. Now, let's get going." He hopped out of bed and pulled his clothes on.

"Wait...no hanky-panky first?"

He pulled on a t-shirt and running shorts. "There will be time for that later."

I got out of bed and walked to him, his eyes watching my every move. Then I fell to my knees and pulled his shorts off, his cock still hard from waking up that morning. When I grabbed the base and licked him from balls to tip, he didn't complain.

411

He closed his eyes and moaned quietly, his hand automatically moving into my hair. "Okay, maybe we do have some time…"

***

Zeke pounded on Rex's door loudly before walking into my apartment. We had boxes and plastic bags to stuff everything in. The furniture was staying behind because I was going to sell it. There was no room for it at Zeke's place.

"What?" Rex rubbed the sleep out of his eyes as he entered my apartment, in only his sweatpants. "Why are you pounding on my door on a Sunday? I'm pretty sure that's against the law."

"Because I'm moving." I shoved a box into his chest. "And you're going to help."

He looked at me blankly, not understanding what was going on because he was still half asleep. Then he looked at Zeke, still oblivious.

"Come on, Rex," Zeke said. "Keep thinking…"

Finally, it dawned on him. "Wait…are you two…?"

"Yes," I answered. "Finally."

He fist-pumped the air. "Hell yeah. Damn, I'm so glad that soap opera is finally over." He snatched the box out of my hands. "I'm getting you out of here ASAP. Just in case you change your mind again."

"I'm not gonna change my mind." I knew what life was like without Zeke, and I didn't want to experience that ever again.

Kayden walked in a moment later, drowning in Rex's clothes. "What's going on over here?"

"I'm moving in with Zeke." It felt so good to say that out loud, to know it was true.

"Really?" She covered her mouth as she gasped. "Aww, that's so great." She wrapped her arms around me and hugged me. "So happy for you..."

"Thank you. Looks like we won't be living across the hallway from each other anymore."

"Works for me," Rex said as he shoved my photo albums in a box. "I see your ugly face too much anyway."

I rolled my eyes. "Ditto."

Safari was jumping on Zeke the moment he walked in the door. Like he knew something exciting was happening, he spun in circles then licked Zeke's face.

"Whoa, boy." Zeke grabbed him and held him still. "Yes, you're coming to live with me. And I'm excited about it too."

Safari whined again and pawed at his chest.

Zeke chuckled and scratched him behind the ears. "You can poop wherever you want in the backyard. It's all yours, buddy."

Kayden lowered her voice as she stood beside me. "Sometimes I think Safari loves Zeke more than you."

"Sometimes?" I asked. "Try all the time."

Kayden chuckled. "Well, at least Safari will be happy."

"He hated Ryker, so that never would have worked," I said with a forced chuckle.

"He did?" she asked. "Then yeah, that definitely wouldn't have worked. Dogs have amazing senses. You should always listen to them." She turned back to the door. "I'm gonna get dressed then I'll be back."

"Alright. Give Jessie and Tobias a call, will ya?"

"Are you kidding me?" she asked. "It's only nine. I bet Jessie hasn't even gone to sleep yet."

I laughed because she was probably right.

***

We unloaded everything at Zeke's, putting my clothes in the hallway of the second bedroom, along with my assorted shoes. Thankfully, he had a large house, so I was able to keep all the nonessential items I couldn't part with.

I didn't feel any reluctance for giving up my apartment so quickly. Carrying my stuff into the house felt right—like I was finally coming home. Safari was in heaven the moment we got there, sitting outside in the grass and searching the trees for squirrels. Zeke's house was a little masculine in its decor, but I would leave it alone for now and slowly make my changes when he wouldn't really notice.

"You guys wanna go out tonight?" Rex asked. "You know, to celebrate."

"Sure," Zeke said.

I didn't. I wanted to stay home and have sex all night.

"But we'll need a few hours," Zeke said. "You know, to get situated."

I knew what that really meant, and all my teeth were showing.

"Alright, cool," Rex said. "So, we'll see you later." Everyone left the house, leaving us alone with the few boxes I still hadn't unpacked.

"Looks like we're officially roommates." Even in an old t-shirt and running shorts, he looked sexy. His muscular arms looked nice and his chest was powerful. His hand moved to my hips, and he looked down at me with adoration.

"Roommates?" I asked. "I'd say we're more than that. Maybe fuck buddies that live together."

He chuckled. "That works for me."

"Or maybe roommates that love each other a lot..."

"Even better." He smiled before he kissed the corner of my mouth, making my lips go numb because it felt so incredible.

We'd been together for nearly twenty-four hours, and he still hadn't contacted Monica, that I knew of. I tried not to fixate on it, but I wanted to know she was gone for good, that she wouldn't show up at the door in lingerie and a rain coat. "Zeke?"

"Hmm?"

"Did you break up with Monica yet?"

"Oh, yeah. Don't worry about her." He squeezed my waist gently before he guided me to the couch.

"But you've been with me all day. Don't you think you should let her know?"

He laid me down on the couch and pulled his shirt over his head. "I don't remember you being this talkative during sex."

"I guess I just need to know I'm not gonna see her again." I was extremely jealous when it came to that woman. She was a perfect ten. Of course, I was intimidated by her. "That she's not gonna show up at the house or something..."

"Trust me, she's not." He undid my jeans and pulled them off.

"Why won't you just call her?"

He got my panties off then positioned himself on top of me, my legs around his waist. "I'll tell you why." He pressed his forehead to mine. "I was never dating her, Rae. It was just an act."

"Just an act?"

"Rex thought it might make you jealous and you'd realize you didn't want to be without me. And it worked."

"So…you never slept with her?"

"No." He held my look as he watched my reaction. "I'm sorry if that makes you mad, but I don't feel bad for doing it. You're on this couch right now because of it."

"I'm not mad…"

"Then what are you feeling?" he asked.

"I just…" The guilt washed over me, and I felt terrible for what I'd done. "I…slept with Ryker because—"

"I know. And it's okay. You made your mistake, and I made mine. Let's just leave it in the past."

He was giving me more mercy than I deserved.

"Rae, I was miserable without you. I was willing to do anything to get you back. I couldn't picture myself ever being with anyone else, not after I found the woman I wanted to spend the rest of my life with."

"That's so sweet…"

"I've never given up on us, Rae. And I'll never give up on us." He pressed a kiss to my lips, a slow and seductive one. He guided me farther into the couch, and his cock slipped inside me, slowly stretching me as he sank in.

I dragged my nails down his back. "I love you…"

He breathed into my mouth as he moved. "I love you too."

***

Zeke ended the call and shoved his phone into the pocket of his jeans.

"What did she say?"

"She was happy for me." He pulled on his black jacket. "Said she wished we could have made it happen sooner."

That made two of us. "Well, now I don't hate her so much…"

He chuckled. "I guess I don't hate Ryker as much either."

"Really?" I did sleep with him—a lot.

"He let you go. How can I really hate a guy who stepped aside?"

I told him how Ryker convinced me to come back to him multiple times. It was the most chivalrous Ryker had ever been since I'd known him. He put me before himself, even if it made him miserable. "So, you guys are best friends now?" I teased.

"No," he said with a laugh. "But I don't despise him anymore. Monica thinks he's the hottest guy she's ever seen." He rolled his eyes. "I don't understand what chicks see in that guy. He's got trouble written all over him."

I understood far too well. "She's into him?"

"That's what she said."

An idea came to mind. It was far-fetched and may not work, but it was worth a shot. "Hmm..."

"What?"

"Let me give him a call." I fished my phone out of my purse and called Ryker.

He answered almost immediately. "Long time, no see." His confidence was back in full force. "I thought I wouldn't hear from you for a while."

"Well, Zeke just told me something interesting, and I wanted to pass it on."

"What's that?" he asked. "I hope it's not a victory speech."

"No. Actually, he told me Monica said you're the hottest guy she's ever seen."

His smile could be heard through the phone. "Really?"

"Yep. So…what do you think?"

"What do you mean?"

"We're going out tonight, and we can bring her along. You want to meet up?"

He chuckled into the phone. "Are you setting me up on a date?"

"Not really setting you up," I said. "Just saw an opportunity, and I went for it. So, are you down?"

"Well…she is pretty hot."

I thought I would be jealous at his words, but I wasn't jealous at all. "Zeke says she's really cool. Down-to-earth and fun. She's smart too."

"You know I don't care about any of those things, sweetheart."

"You did with me."

"Very different situation."

"I think you should give it a try." I didn't want to push him around, but I wanted him to get back on his feet. "See where it goes."

"I guess I can do that. Why not?"

"Great. Can you meet us in an hour?"

"Sure. I'll see you there." He hung up.

Zeke watched me, a grin on his face. "Did we just hook up our exes together?"

"I think so. I saw him looking at Monica last time we were together. I thought he might be interested..."

"He'd have to be gay not to be interested."

I glared at him.

"Not that I've ever been interested in her — only you." He wrapped his arm around my waist and pulled me in for a kiss. "So, don't worry about that."

"Good. Honestly, I'm a little interested in her... She's gorgeous."

"Not like you." He kissed me again. "She's got nothing on you, baby."

I smiled. "I like all these compliments."

"Good. Because you're going to be getting them for a long time."

***

"Aww!" Monica hugged Zeke as soon as she saw him. "So happy for you."

I finally didn't feel jealous when she touched him, knowing he was mine and was never really hers.

Monica turned to me next. "I hope there're no hard feelings."

"Not at all." I pulled her in for a hug before I moved away. "It hurt at the time, but it brought us back together — so it's okay."

"Good," she said. "Zeke was really miserable without you. He's like family to me, and I wanted to do whatever I could. And I'm so glad because you really are cute together."

"Thanks." Zeke tugged me into his side. "Imagine how our kids will look."

"Adorable, if they look like you." It was nice to talk about the future with certainty, knowing that we would get married and live in that house for the rest of our lives.

"So." Monica rubbed her hands together. "Zeke tells me you brought something for me…"

Ryker appeared at that moment, in a black t-shirt and dark jeans. He looked sexy, like always. His arms filled out the shirt, and his powerful chest led to rigid shoulders. He shaved before he came down to the bar, displaying his chiseled jaw. "It's nice to see you again." Ryker got close to her, using his sex appeal to make her tense. "I hear through the grapevine you think I'm sexy."

Monica handled his confidence a lot better than I ever did. "Sexiest guy I've ever seen, actually."

Ryker smiled, his eyes still smoldering. "Even better. Can I buy you a drink?"

"You can buy me as many as you want."

He chuckled. "In that case, we aren't leaving until you're good and drunk."

"You can get into my bed easily without it."

He brushed past her as he headed to the bar, peeking down her dress without being discreet about it. Then he moved through the crowd to the other side of the room.

Monica immediately turned and watched him walk away, her eyes fixated on his ass. "My god, that is one fine piece of man. I'm sinking my claws into him—and my teeth."

"Just be careful," Zeke warned her. "He's kind of a player."

"Oh, that's fine," Monica said. "I am too."

Rex and Kayden walked up, their hands bound together tightly.

"Aww, this is nice," Rex said. "Everything feels normal again. Zeke won't stop checking out my sister, and Rae doesn't look anorexic anymore. Now, you guys need to keep this up. Otherwise, I'm gonna kick your asses."

"No funny business," Kayden said, pointing a finger at both of us.

Zeke pressed a kiss to my temple. "I think we've got it figured out this time."

"We'll just keep our junk in our pants," I said. "Unless it's just the two of us." Now that I was happy, I could make a joke about the past. After all, it was in the past. It shouldn't be taken seriously ever again.

"And I'm not gonna be jealous again," Zeke said.

"And I won't give you a reason to be jealous," I said.

"Good," Rex said. "Maybe one day, you guys can be as solid as Kayden and I. But that takes time. Just be patient."

I rolled my eyes. "Shut up, Rex."

"What?" Rex asked. "I'm like the relationship guru. I picked up the hottest chick on the planet, convinced her to move in with me, and I love her." He flexed both of his arms, showing off his biceps. "Who's the man?"

Kayden didn't seem to care about anything he said. She just stared at him with infatuation, like usual.

"Guru, huh?" I asked. "So, when Ryker delivered flowers to me, you didn't throw them away?"

Rex dropped his arms, his face turning pale.

Zeke made a guilty face, like he knew exactly what I was talking about.

Kayden seemed clueless.

I cocked my head to the side, my gaze still drilling into him. "The guru forgot how to talk?"

"Uh…" He eyed Kayden before he turned back to me. "I gotta get my baby a drink. I'll catch up with you later…" He left the group and headed to the bar, joining Ryker at the corner.

Kayden crossed her arms over her chest, her eyes squinting. "What are you talking about?"

"For my birthday, Ryker sent me flowers. I never got them because Rex threw them away. I figured it out a few weeks ago." I could picture everything in my head. Rex probably answered the door for the deliveryman then immediately tossed them in the trash chute. He probably didn't even read the card. "And judging by the look on your face, you knew about it." I turned to Zeke next.

He shrugged. "He told me when you and I were broken up."

"Okay, you're fine." There was no reason for him to come clean to me when we weren't together. He wasn't obligated to do anything.

"I can't believe Rex did that," Kayden said. "I might have to slap him."

"No," Zeke said. "He told me he likes it when you do that."

"I'm still gonna tell him off... Excuse me." Kayden walked to the bar just as Jessie and Tobias reached our table.

"What's up with her?" Jessie asked. "We don't say hi anymore?"

"She went to yell at Rex," I explained.

"Oh, gotcha." She didn't bother asking for the scoop. "So, Kayden told me about this." She pointed at both of us. "Congratulations."

"Thanks," I said. "You better get used to it."

"We would love to be used to it," Jessie said. "Now all three of us can go out."

Tobias had a beer, but Jessie didn't have a drink, something very peculiar for her.

I narrowed my eyes and immediately jumped to a conclusion I didn't think was possible. Jessie was always so careful about stuff like that. She used two forms of birth control—the pill and the pull out method. "Jess...why aren't you drinking?"

Terror jumped into her expression instantly. "Maybe I'm not thirsty."

"Bullshit. Are you pregnant?"

Her terror only intensified.

I probably shouldn't have put her on the spot like that, but my emotions were driving me forward.

Tobias placed his arm around her shoulders. "Yeah, we're having a baby."

"Oh. My. God." I covered my mouth and screamed. "Are you serious?"

Now that the cat was out of the bag, Jessie finally relaxed. "We didn't want to say anything right now since you guys just got back together—"

"Who cares." I came around the table and hugged her. "Congratulations."

"Oh god, Rae." She squeezed me tightly. "I need some serious help. I don't know shit about babies."

"You think I do?" I asked incredulously.

"Probably more than I do," she countered.

"We'll order some baby books on Amazon," I said. "I'm gonna be the best aunt ever."

"Thank you," Jessie said. "Because we know this baby is gonna hate me."

Zeke walked to Tobias and shook his hand. "Congrats, man. How are you handling it?"

"You know, I was terrified at first," Tobias said. "But you know what? Any baby that Jessie and I make together is gonna be beautiful. Come on, look at her." He nodded in her direction. "It could be worse."

Zeke smiled. "Well said, my friend."

"We aren't going to get married, but we'll keep dating," Tobias continued. "We'll see where things go. I'm getting old anyway, so it's about time I settled down and popped out some kids."

"True," Zeke said. "I'm not sure when Rae and I are gonna start, but I hope it's soon. And if not, practice is always good."

Ryker returned with the drinks and talked quietly with Monica, both of them in their own world. She said something that made Ryker laugh, and he couldn't stop smiling, absorbed in their conversation.

Rex and Kayden returned, drinks in their hands. "What's with the commotion?" Rex asked. "Please don't tell me you guys broke up again."

I wanted to throw my drink in his face. "How are my flowers doing?"

Rex rolled his eyes.

Jessie placed her hands on her stomach even though she was flat like an ironing board. "So...Tobias and I are having a baby."

"Say what?" Rex dropped his drink on the ground. Thankfully, the cup was plastic so it didn't shatter. "No fucking way. You're having a baby? Like, a human baby?"

"What other kind of baby could she have?" Zeke countered. "An alien?"

Kayden hugged her. "Oh my god, this is huge news."

"I know," Jessie said. "I'll need help because all I know how to do is hair—that's it."

"We'll be there for you," Kayden said as she rubbed Jessie's back. "We'll be the best aunts ever."

"Good," Jessie said. "And I need to talk to Zeke about giving birth." She locked eyes with him. "Does it really hurt as much as they say?"

"I'm a dermatologist," he said. "I don't really —"

"Does it hurt as much as they say?" Jessie demanded.

Zeke shrugged then cringed. "It's not gonna be easy…"

"Oh, god." Jessie grabbed my hand. "I'm already terrified."

"You'll be fine, baby." Tobias wrapped his arm around her shoulders. "I'll be there the whole time. You can break my hand if you want."

"Good." I twisted out of her grasp. "Because she's about to break mine."

"This is so exciting," Kayden said. "You guys are back together, Ryker and Monica are perfect for each other, and now Jessie is having a baby. We're so lucky, you guys. We have everything."

Zeke gave me an affectionate look, the same expression I'd seen my entire life. It was only recently that I truly understood what that look meant. Now, I couldn't live without it, needing to see it every single day. "I know I have everything."

My eyes softened just like my heart. "Me too."

Epilogue

Rae

Jessie sat on the bench near the basketball hoop, eight months pregnant and viciously uncomfortable. "Would you guys judge me if I said I hated my baby right now?" She rubbed her hand across her stomach, obviously uncomfortable by her enormous belly and the stress on her bladder.

"No," Kayden said. "Because we know you love that baby."

"Only one more month, baby." Tobias held up a finger. "And you'll be able to sleep again."

"Ugh." Jessie grabbed the umbrella and held it over her head to stay out of the sun. She wore a loose fitting white dress, her stomach protruding out of it. "I miss sleep…"

"What are the teams?" Zeke had the ball tucked under his arm. "I don't want to be on Rae's team."

"What the hell?" I snapped. "I'm the best player."

"But I want to block you." He wiggled his eyebrows.

"How about me, Rae, and Kayden," Rex said. "Kayden doesn't count because she sucks."

"Hey." Kayden smacked his arm. "I'm trying."

"I know, baby," he said. "But I'm being honest. Rae is the best player of all of us and I'm okay. So, I think we're even."

"Alright." Zeke dribbled the ball. "Let's get this game started."

Zeke got the jump ball because he was a foot taller than me, but that didn't mean I didn't bust my ass chasing him down the court. He was stronger and thicker, but I was lean, so I could get around quickly. He made the shot but the ball bounced off the rim.

Like a tiger, I snatched it. Rex was down the court, so I threw it hard.

Rex caught it and did a lay-up. "Hell yeah. We're up by two points, bitches." He high-fived me.

"For now," Tobias said threateningly.

I stuck out my tongue at Zeke.

He narrowed his eyes aggressively, like he wanted to suck my tongue into his mouth and do nasty things with it.

It was winner's take out, so I stood behind the hoop next to Jessie and Safari. It was nearly impossible for Rex to get open, but he faked to the right and was open for just a second. I passed it.

We darted down the court and Rex passed it back to me.

But Zeke came out of nowhere and stole the ball. "Sorry, baby." He sprinted the opposite way, way faster than I could possibly run. And then he scored.

Zeke high-fived Tobias. "You're going to need to step it up, baby. I'm not going easy on you."

I rolled my eyes. "I'm not going easy on you tonight when we get home."

"Ooh..." Tobias chuckled. "That sounds like a nice threat."

Zeke smiled. "I'm gonna hold you to your promise."

"And I'm not gonna hold my vomit," Rex snapped.

We started the game back up, going back and forth and making shots. It was a close game, and most of the time, we were tied. Zeke and Tobias were both excellent players, and Rex and I were a good team. Kayden didn't do much other than run back and forth and try to snatch the ball when it bounced hard off the rim.

Zeke got the ball back and sprinted back up the court.

I wasn't gonna let him get away this time. I chased after him, close on his tail.

"NOW!" Zeke stopped and dropped the ball.

Everyone else stopped and formed a semi-circle.

What the hell was going on?

Jessie ran over with a camera and stood five feet away.

Zeke pulled something out of his pocket and dropped to one knee. It was a black box, and he popped the lid to reveal a sparkling diamond ring. "Rae, will you marry me?"

I covered my face and stood in shock, not caring about Jessie taking pictures of me and all my friends standing around and smiling. Kayden was already crying, wiping her tears away and sniffing. Rex smiled wide, all of his teeth showing and his eyes on me. Zeke looked up at me with joy in his eyes, knowing what my answer would be once the shock wore off. "Oh my god…" I finally pulled my hands away, tears in my eyes. I hadn't expected this in the least, and somehow, that surprise made it a million times better. It started off as a normal Saturday with us playing basketball in the park, and now, it was something so much bigger. "Oh my god…" The ring was beautiful, a princess cut made of white gold. I never told him what I wanted because I never really cared. Anything he gave me would be perfect. "Zeke…"

I fell to my knees in front of him, not caring about the hard concrete. I looked him in the eyes, still on the verge of sobbing. "Yes. You know my answer is yes."

He smiled and slipped the ring on my finger, fitting it perfectly on my left ring finger. The diamonds sparkled in the light, illuminous and beautiful. The second I felt the cool material against my sweaty skin, I knew I wouldn't want to ever take it off.

Zeke pulled me into his chest and hugged me, his powerful arms squeezing me tightly. His face was buried in my neck while everyone clapped around us, whistling and cheering. "I love you, Rae."

"I love you too." I pulled away and kissed him, sharing an embrace for the first time as fiancées. In my lifetime, I'd lost so much. My father abandoned us because he didn't want the responsibility of a family, and when my mom had nothing else to live for, not even Rex and I mattered and she killed herself. But I made my own family, my own group of people that I could count on for everything. And everything was truly perfect. I found the man that would always be by my side, who would love me and take care of me every single day. For the first time, I truly felt complete.

"We need to get home and pack," Zeke said.

"Pack?" I asked. "Why?"

"Because we're going on a trip."

"What? Where?"

"Hawaii. I already talked to Ryker, and he gave you the vacation time. So, let's get to the airport."

"You're serious?" Now, I was screaming, so excited that I couldn't keep my voice down.

"And you know what the best part is?" Rex asked. "Kayden and I are coming too."

"Aww!" I hugged Zeke again. "This is so amazing. Thank you so much."

"Don't thank me, baby. I'm gonna be your husband, so you should get used to this sort of thing."

"I'm so lucky." I pressed my face into his chest and resisted the urge to cry. "So goddamn lucky."

He pressed a kiss to my forehead. "No. I've always been the lucky one."

Epilogue II

Zeke

"Zeke." Rae grabbed my arm and shook me.

"Hmm?" I kept my eyes closed as I turned over, my arm moving underneath her enormous stomach. I was still half-asleep.

"Zeke, wake up."

I distantly felt the moisture underneath me, the warm liquid that soaked into the sheets.

"I think my water just broke."

My eyes finally snapped open when the realization hit me. I sat upright and felt my heart slam hard into my chest, my protective instincts kicking in. I knew exactly what happened when the water broke and what I needed to do next. "Alright, baby. Hold on." I hopped out of bed, pulled on some clothes, and grabbed the packed bag for the hospital stay. I went to her side of the bed next and helped her up. She had a petite frame so her stomach appeared to be larger than normal. Just by looking at her, I could tell our son was going to be healthy and happy.

"God, I think I'm feeling a contraction." She held her stomach as she breathed through the pain.

"In through your nose and out through your mouth," I instructed.

"Okay," she said through her deep breathing.

I pulled her up and wrapped my arm around her waist as I walked her into the garage and the Jeep. Once I pulled onto the road, I called Rex.

"Muh," he answered. "Blem car…"

"What?" I asked, not having a clue what he was saying.

"Blar blar…"

"Dude, your sister is going into labor, so get your ass up."

That made him snap out of it. "Oh, shit. For real?"

"Yes, for real. We'll meet you at the hospital. Tell the others." I hung up and drove through the empty streets to the hospital. My free hand moved to Rae's stomach, feeling my wife and son at the same time.

Rae panted through another contraction.

There wasn't much time between them, which told me she was having his baby sooner rather than later. Good for her. She wouldn't want a twenty-four-hour delivery. "You're doing great. Just keep breathing."

"Why are my contractions coming so quickly?"

"It's normal. Don't worry about it." I was just trying to keep her calm until I found a parking spot outside the hospital. Once I did, I got her out of the car and into the maternity ward. I checked her in, and they immediately whisked her off into a delivery room.

I stood beside her bed, my hand intertwined with hers.

"The baby is coming already?" she asked, breathing through another contraction.

"He's excited to meet us."

She nodded, sweat covering her face and neck. "I can't wait to meet him too. He's gonna look just like you. I know it."

"He's gonna look like both of us, Rae." I squeezed her hand.

Once she was settled in her room, I joined her in the delivery room with the doctor and nurse. Her legs were spread, and the doctor was already examining her.

"You need to start pushing, Rae," the doctor instructed. "He's coming."

I grabbed her hand and looked into her face, seeing the determination in her eyes. They had already given her the epidural but she was clearly uncomfortable. Sweat began to pour down her cheeks, and her face was blotchy and red. "The sooner you get him out of there, the sooner it's over."

"I know."

"It's gonna hurt, but you can do it."

"I'm not scared of the pain." She gritted her teeth and pushed.

My wife amazed me every single day, but her strength and determination still caught me by surprise. She was never scared of anything, taking every challenge head on without blinking.

I kept my hand in hers as I watched the doctor work. The head was crowning, and the baby was slowly coming. "Baby, you're doing great. He's coming."

"Okay." She pushed harder, closing her eyes and screaming as she pushed.

"A little more, Rae," the doctor instructed.

She held her breath and pushed again.

"Keep breathing," I reminded her.

She nodded and took a deep breath. After a few more pushes, our son was here. He cried loudly in the delivery room, the sound bouncing off the walls. The wailing was music to my ears, pure magic.

"You did it, baby." I leaned over Rae and kissed her, ignoring the sweat from her fatigue. "You did great."

"God, I'm so tired... Where is he?"

"They're just cleaning him up." I shared my last moment alone with my wife, treasuring the last minutes of our solitude. For years, it'd just been the two of us and Safari. But now our family had grown and there were three of us. While I would miss those days, I was excited to move forward.

Rae gave my hand a gentle squeeze, knowing exactly what I was thinking.

The doctor walked over with our son, the little boy with beautiful eyes and soft skin. He waved his arms in the air and continued to cry. The doctor arranged him in Rae's arms before he finally let go.

Rae took one look at our son and started to cry. "Oh my god...he's beautiful."

"He really is." My eyes started to tear up, seeing my family right before my eyes. I'd been in love with Rae since I could remember, and somehow, I was lucky enough to marry her and start a family with her.

Almost immediately, our son stopped crying. He looked up at Rae, having my blue eyes, and he seemed just as infatuated with her as I was.

"It's so nice to meet you," Rae whispered through her tears. "I'm your mommy."

I grabbed his hand and felt his small fingers, touching my son for the first time.

"And this is your daddy," she whispered. "And we love you so much."

He stared at her for a few more minutes before he closed his eyes and drifted off to sleep.

"Do we have a name?" the nurse asked.

Rae and I talked about it for the past few months until we found something we both loved. "Liam," I answered. "Liam Price."

"Very good." The nurse left the room, leaving us alone.

"Here." Rae handed him over, so I could hold him.

I took him and sat down in the nearby chair, resting my arms on my raised knee. I looked down at him in fascination, seeing myself as well as my wife in his features. He was perfect, more than I ever could have dreamed of. "I already love you so much, son."

Rae sniffed as she watched us together, falling in love with the sight.

The door opened. "There you are." Rex stopped when he spotted the baby in my arms. "Damn, you already had him?" He walked farther into the room and looked down at Liam. "Wow…he's cute."

"Thank you," I said. "But Rae is the one who made him."

Kayden walked to Rae's side and stroked her hair. "Hanging in there?"

"I'm fine," Rae said. "The meds are still strong."

Rex sat beside me, his black wedding ring contrasting against his fair skin. "So, this is my nephew, huh? Babies don't seem so scary."

"Wanna hold him?" I asked.

"Totally." Rex took him from my arms and held him like a pro. "Wow. I can't get over how cute he is. I thought babies were supposed to be ugly."

"Not ours," I said. "He's perfect."

Kayden came next and stared at our little boy. "You guys did a great job. He's perfect." She sat beside Rex and stroked Liam's head, adoring him just the way Rae and I did.

I walked back to the bed and ran my fingers through Rae's hair. "Need anything?"

"No. I feel really good." She stopped staring at Liam and looked up at me. "Childbirth wasn't as bad as they say."

"You're just stronger than everyone else."

She chuckled. "I think I was just lucky."

I sat on the stool and grabbed her hand. "Thank you."

"For what?" she asked.

"For all of this." My life wouldn't have turned out so wonderful without her. I would have married someone else, and I would have been happy, but not like this. Rae gave me something no one else ever could. There was no other woman I would have been nearly as happy with. Our difficult times were long in the past, but I was grateful things worked out the way they did.

She smiled and squeezed my hand. "You don't need to thank me. It was meant to happen anyway."

If you'd like to read my new action suspense series, check out Gladiator.

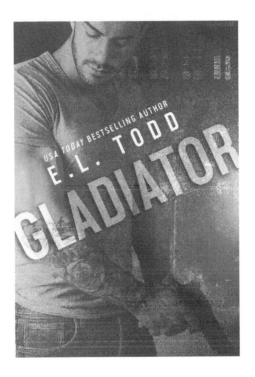

Dear Reader,

Thank you for reading Ray of Heart. I hope you enjoyed reading it as much as I enjoyed writing it. If you could leave a short review, it would help me so much! Those reviews are the best kind of support you can give an author. Thank you!

Wishing you love,

E. L. Todd

Want To Stalk Me?

Subscribe to my newsletter for updates on new releases, giveaways, and for my comical monthly newsletter. You'll get all the dirt you need to know. Sign up today.

www.eltoddbooks.com

Facebook:

https://www.facebook.com/ELTodd42

Twitter:

@E_L_Todd

Now you have no reason not to stalk me. You better get on that.

EL's Elites

I know I'm lucky enough to have super fans, you know, the kind that would dive off a cliff for you. They have my back through and through. They love my books, and they love spreading the word. Their biggest goal is to see me on the New York Times bestsellers list, and they'll stop at nothing to make it happen. While it's a lot of work, it's also a lot of fun. What better way to make friendships than to connect with people who love the same thing you do?

Are you one of these super fans?

If so, send a request to join the Facebook group. It's closed, so you'll have a hard time finding it without the link. Here it is:

https://www.facebook.com/groups/119232692 0784373

Hope to see you there, ELITE!

Made in the USA
Middletown, DE
25 May 2017